**JOHN
KELLERMANN**

OVER & OUT

THE
GOLD CONSPIRACY

Thriller

Bibliographical information
of the German National Library:
The German National Library lists this publication in
the German National Bibliography.
Detailed bibliographic information is available online
at: dnb.dnb.de abrufbar.

1. Edition 2016
John Kellermann
www.john-kellermann.de
Original German Title:
Das Gold-Komplott
Cover Design: eichfelder artworks
Translated by: Martina Lammers

© 2016
Printed and Published by:
BoD - Books on Demand, Norderstedt
ISBN: 978-3-7412-2652-6

Preface

Frankfurt am Main, 2016

The reader needs to be aware that this book is a result of my imagination, yet similarities with existing persons and circumstances cannot be completely ruled out. Statements about the future, however, will remain fiction, regardless of their plausibility. In order to protect those involved and my sources, I have altered individuals' names. Most of the locations are real.

The following events take place in the near future.

John Kellermann

Monday

Poland, Szczytno-Szymany, 0100 Hours. For a long time it had been a secret - an extremely well-guarded secret. 15 years ago, however, the barracks camp close to the small airport in the northeast of Poland had gained some notorious fame. Back then the illegal internment and torture of prisoners came to light. In the wake of the 9/11 terrorist attacks, the Polish secret service had relinquished the camp to the CIA.

But the scandals involving waterboarding, sleep deprivation, beatings and other methods to obtain questionable statements from disenfranchised detainees had already been forgotten. The Polish as well as the American governments had repeatedly confirmed that the interrogation centre with the former code name *Quarz* no longer existed.

A lie. 'Temporary non-usage until renewed demand' would have been more accurate. Like last night. After quite some considerable time, a small aircraft, a Gulfstream G550, had landed on Szczytno-Szymany airport. The airplane identification on the fuselage-mounted engines had been obscured. Evidence of a secret mission of extreme urgency which had justified reactivating the interrogation center. At least in the eyes of those in charge.

The new moon was imminent and it was correspondingly dark at one in the morning. A black Chevrolet truck with tinted windows was waiting at the edge of the runway until several people alighted from the plane. Somebody was being led across the landing strip towards the vehicle. Hands tied behind the back, a dark bag covering his head, he was flanked on both sides by guards dressed in black. It took less than a minute until everybody had climbed into the now slowly moving truck.

It was only a short drive to the camp, which was surrounded by a massive, man-high fence, additionally secured by razor-sharp wire on top. Behind the fence a passable strip, then a series of dense conifers, obscuring a closer look at the wooden barracks located behind them. It was still discernible, however, that, unlike the wooden barracks inside, the site's outer security measures were kept in good repair.

"Stopp!" shouted the heavily armed guard at the entrance gate. His camouflage fatigues had no insignia; establishing his nationality was therefore impossible. Slowly the truck approached the gate where the driver held up his ID without fully lowering the window. The guard saluted briskly and let the vehicle pass. He had evidently been instructed about the transport.

*

The interrogation had lasted five hours; usually a pure routine job for Ted Branigan, the specialist. He was in charge of such operations in Central Europe and had carried them out hundreds of times. Depending on the situation, he applied the most varied techniques to extract the desired intelligence. But today hadn't worked out the way it usually did. The problem was the time it had taken, seeing that the information was urgently needed.

"Son of a bitch!" Ted Branigan peeled of his blood-stained leather gloves and flung them onto the cement floor. Visibly pissed, he grabbed his satellite phone.

"Get Peter to ring me back on a secure line! ... Yes! Right now!"

Branigan seemed tense while he was waiting for his call to be returned. A moment later the phone rang. He held the receiver to his ear before the second ring:

"Yes?"

"What's up, Ted?" asked Peter Redman on the other end

of the line.

"Do you know where I am?"

"Yes, at a quiet place to gather intelligence," Redman replied.

"Correct. I tried to get the Huntsman to talk and at first he reacted to the treatment as expected," Branigan told his colleague without a trace of compassion in his voice. As far as he was concerned, he was simply doing his job. "He was whimpering and pleading and at the start he gave us what we wanted."

"What did you find out?"

"We now know where he's hidden the documents and the information. But we couldn't get him to reveal anything new about the subject. All he told us was precisely what we already knew." After a brief pause, Branigan continued: "We only had about two hours left, so we used stronger methods."

"And? Did it work?"

"Well... Perhaps I hit the wrong spot... Perhaps he was frail... Anyway, he collapsed right in the middle of the interrogation. And that was it."

"He's dead?"

"Yes, damn it! I couldn't..."

But before he could finish, Redman angrily hissed:

"You fucking idiot!"

The line went silent. Branigan was aware that he had messed up badly. It shouldn't have happened. But these kinds of interrogations always carried certain risks, especially when under time pressure. And the Huntsman had evidently had a weak heart, unable to survive the brutal torture.

"So you didn't get any more than we already know from the papers?" Peter Redman resumed the conversation a few seconds later.

"No."

"Did he give you any names? Who knew about the gold business besides him?"

"He mentioned some Miller guy who got in touch with him. But I guess that's an alias. He couldn't describe him because he never met him in person."

"And who gave him the dossier?"

"Apparently he didn't know that either. He said it had been left for him at the check-in desk at his hotel."

"Oh, crap! That doesn't get us anywhere!" Redman cursed.

After Branigan had described where the Huntsman had hidden the documents and the information, Redman issued new instructions: "You have to get him back to Berlin, Ted, and fast. There must be no evidence of him having been interrogated."

He hesitated for a moment. "Do you have a plan?"

"We do." Branigan knew several methods to dispose of such a badly battered body without prompting too many questions. If everything worked out according to plan, the death certificate would simply state - *Cause of Death: Suicide.* A perfunctory inspection by a doctor motivated by money greasing his palm wouldn't contradict the verdict.

"We shall discuss our future moves when you've taken care of it. And no more mistakes, you hear me?!" Peter Redman hung up without waiting for a reply.

Ted Branigan put his phone back in his pocket.

A second man, who had been sitting in a dark corner of the room from where he had silently witnessed the interrogation throughout the night, slightly tilted his head to the left, his neck vertebrae audibly creaking. He left the room together with Ted Branigan.

Now it was Ted's job to ensure that everything was properly dealt with.

*

Frankfurt International Airport, 0610 Hours. The night sky was already turning steel blue, the air cold and crystal-clear. At the end of the southern runway an orange glowing line gradually expanded. It would soon be sunrise...

The *Otto Lilienthal*, a German Air Force A310 plane just returned from New York, was landing in the military section. The time of arrival had been adhered to with military precision.

The gray, long-range, cargo aircraft belonged to the Special Air Mission Wing of the Federal Defense Ministry. It's current mission was particularly special.

"Careful, you dumbass!" the transport commander roared at the forklift driver who was in the process of transferring a Euro pallet from the plane to an armored van. "The cargo is highly sensitive!" he emphatically reminded the driver. Mistakes were out of the question. Mistakes could be very expensive. Utmost caution was called for.

A little further away, on a platform specifically constructed for the purpose, waited several journalists who were meant to record the highly guarded transfer of the valuable cargo for the public.

"The *Otto Lilienthal* is equipped with a laser-based defense system against infrared guided missiles," one of the reporters photographing the scene with his telephoto lens informed the others without having been asked. "It has a range of more than 8,000 miles, so it can cover the distance between New York and Frankfurt without layover."

"Smartass!" mumbled his shivering neighbor, rubbing his freezing hands together. He didn't like being lectured early in the morning. All he wanted was to get the job done and head straight back to his warm office.

But that time hadn't come yet. The group watched the valuable cargo being transferred to the armored van. Their assignment on this cold November morning was to get as may shots of the precious freight as possible. And real impressive ones. To ensure that everything sparkled to maximum effect, the crate of gold was even briefly opened, exposing ten layers of 24 gold bars each and each of them weighing 438.9 ounces. Perfectly stacked, like big, golden Lego bricks, alternately turned by 90 degrees to add stability. A minute later, two soldiers wearing balaclavas pulled the crate's side panels up again and placed the lid back on after securing the metal buckles. It didn't take the men long to carefully load the pallet into the van. The photoshoot was over.

The driver and co-driver briskly got into the armored vehicle and locked the doors. The van slowly started to move, escorted by a jeep carrying two soldiers.

"E.T.A. Eagle zero seven hundred!" the commander announced over his walkie-talkie. "We're moving! Over and out!"

The journalists quickly took some pictures of the departing convoy before the group started breaking up. Five of them had professional equipment with large telephoto lenses. Only Markus Manx's gear was positively antiquated by comparison; an old Canon EOS 50D and a modest 300 mm lens. The *Hessische Neueste Presse,* the *HNP,* had commissioned him to write an article about the gold being returned from New York to Frankfurt. And seeing that he would already be on-site, they'd asked him to take a few shots as well. Thus the editorial office wouldn't have to pay dearly later on for his professional colleagues' photos.

John Spencer, who was in the middle of packing away his tripod, was one of those professionals. Markus Manx knew him quite well. In the past they had collaborated on a number of assignments. John as the photographer, Markus as the writer. Meeting each other here today was pure coincidence.

"Hi, John. Need a hand? I've got one to spare," Markus offered.

"That would be great. My car's close by, but it's in a no-parking zone. You can drive back to the city with me if you like. Or did you get yourself a set of wheels by now?"

Markus wedged the folded up tripod under his armpit.

"You know how little work there is and how badly paid freelance journalists are. So, sure, I gladly accept the ride."

John Spencer nodded and the two of them walked over to his car.

*

Markus, John and the other journalists left the platform. Only one of them stayed behind and already sent the first photos back from his notebook there and then.

What can be that urgent about a routine assignment like this? Markus thought as John and he left the scene. He had no idea how urgent the assignment actually was…

The photo journalist who had remained typed on his notebook and grinned broadly when he remembered his self-important colleague's remark. *A310 with laser-based defense system? … Nearly always works, unless when deployed – like the G36 rifle.*

He was particularly delighted with a picture which didn't have any of the gold in its frame. Instead it showed the piece of paper on a clipboard the highest ranking officer was handing to the First Lieutenant. Thanks to the 800 mm lens it was easy to decipher which route the convoy's operations order specified.

"The package has been dispatched," he whispered into a

tap-proof satellite phone. "It will be delivered via Neu-Isenburg today."

"Got it. The package will arrive via Neu-Isenburg," was the response from the other end.

The mysterious photographer tucked the phone and the notebook into his equipment bag. He turned up the collar of his fur-lined jacket and vanished into the daybreak.

*

Meanwhile John and Markus had reached a brown Audi 100 Avant. *Before long, John will be able to apply for a vintage license plate. Much easier on the tax. Well, not really, I guess. That old rattletrap will never qualify, considering the condition it's in,* Markus thought, eyeing the vehicle. The Audi looked pretty rundown. As for the color – the less said, the better. He warily closed the rickety door. John removed the 'Press' sign, with which he justified parking in a no-parking zone, from the windshield and drove off.

The trip from the airport to Frankfurt's inner city didn't take long. It was too early for rush-hour traffic. Marcus and John chatted about the old days when everything had somehow been better.

"I know! With today's editing software anyone can be a photo journalist. You and your amateur camera are the living proof," John teased and shot Markus a challenging look.

"True, I agree. But it's not my fault when the guys at the top keep making cutbacks and consider every freelance journalist to be an all-rounder."

Markus tried to steer the conversation in a different direction. He was tired of the constant whining amongst his colleagues, his own included.

"Anyhow, it's pretty impressive watching three tons of gold being loaded. We're talking more than 100 million Euro."

John awkwardly extracted a cigarette from his breast pocket and lit it. He deeply, and with obvious pleasure, inhaled and blew the smoke out through the slightly open side window.

"This has already been my third time at one of these transfer operations," he commented. "Always for different clients. The Central Bank and the Federal Government are evidently hell-bent on demonstrating how they're bringing the gold back from the States."

"You're right, the whole thing is staged to reassure the general public," Markus concurred. "Ever since Greece went officially bankrupt six months ago, there's been a lot of effort to calm and stabilize the panicking financial markets."

Marcus watched John take another deep drag from his cigarette.

"I don't understand economics," John admitted after leisurely exhaling the smoke, "but I feel that our administration has been pulling the wool over our eyes for years. They must have known that the 160 billion we handed the Greeks were a write-off from day one!"

"Sure. Nobody with a sound basic knowledge of economics could have seriously believed that Greece would ever repay its debts... Next thing we know, Spain or Italy will demand we waive part of theirs as well. Then the Euro is definitely finished."

"I'm so sick of the subject," John tried to end the discussion. "Tell me where you want me to drop you off." He neatly tossed the butt onto the street through the gap in the window.

"The Taunusanlage Park near the gold pyramid would

be good. I've got to take a few more shots before I start on my article."

John drove in the direction of the station.

"Have you heard this one?" he asked.

Markus turned to face him and had to chuckle. They had never met without John presenting him with a new joke.

"Right," John started, "last night my wife jumped up in her sleep and screamed – and without thinking, I instantly took out the thrash!"

He scrutinized his passenger's reaction through the corner of his eyes.

Markus grinned politely, wisely keeping his actual opinion to himself. Shortly after, John stopped and Markus thanked him for the ride.

"See you," John said, shaking Markus's hand.

Markus got out. Almost majestically the gold pyramid towered in front of him. And he still had no idea what the day held in store.

*

Neu-Isenburg, 0630 Hours. "Everything's on schedule!" First Lieutenant Noah Schmidt radioed as the armored convoy approached Neu-Isenburg. The 28 year old Schmidt, with his well-trained body and determined manner, was the commander of the unit in charge of the transport. Beside him, on the jeep's driver's seat, sat Corporal Ali. Nobody could pronounce his last name, so he was simply known as *Cali*. Behind them, the armored van carried the seasoned First Sergeants Patrick Jakobi and Klaus Nahgold, the driver.

Yes, everything was proceeding according to plan. What could possibly go wrong? The route was constantly being changed to reduce the risk of being ambushed.

Schmidt and his unit were only briefed about it shortly before their departure.

Today the operations center had selected a secondary road through Neu-Isenburg. For good reason: roadworks on the A3 highway just before the Frankfurt South intersection temporarily restricted traffic to a single lane. The Special Forces had classified the bottleneck as *critical*, but the constriction could be safely bypassed via Neu-Isenburg the operations command had decided.

"Eagle, we clearly read your position on the monitor. Over," replied the control center at the Central Bank. The armored van had reported back from the agreed Alpha coordinate. "Alpha as in Aral gas station. Easy to remember," had been First Sergeant Nahgold's cheerful comment during the early morning briefing to discuss the route.

They had just passed the Aral station when the jeep in front suddenly stopped. A firefighter, in full uniform with fluorescent strips visible from afar, waved a signaling disc to block the way. Nahgold in the van behind Cali also stopped. Schmidt let down the window to see what was happening.

"The road is closed off. There's been an accident," the firefighter explained. "Your best bet is to take the detour through Buchenbusch. Turn right here, then left after about 100 yards."

"OK, thanks," Schmidt replied and signaled to the jeep to continue. The convoy started to move again and turned right. The GPS navigation device instantly adjusted to the alternative route. A hundred yards on was the left turn for Buchenbusch. The detour was perfectly signposted.

At the old cemetery two animatedly chatting young mothers were pushing their buggies across the street.

The convoy slowed down.

"Watch out!" shouted Nahgold in the armored van.

From the left an SUV was speeding towards the jeep ahead of him, but Cali couldn't hear the First Sergeant's warning. It would have been too late to avoid the SUV in any case.

A defeaning bang, even audible through the windows of the armored van, shattered the morning idyll. The heavy VW Touareg, which had come tearing out of a minor road, had crashed right into the jeep's left fender. Glass splintered. The impact of the collision nearly tore the steering wheel from Cali's hands. He clung to it with all his strength. In vain. The jeep was hurled against the curb and tilted onto its passenger side.

Sergeant Nahgold and his buddy Jakobi in the van stared almost paralysed at the scene in front of them. Slamming on the breaks made them stop at the last second.

The initial shock hadn't even subsided when there was another bang to the right of the van. The Mercedes driving behind them hadn't been able to brake in time and swerved onto the verge to crash into a tree.

"Was that really an accident?" The totally unnerved Nahgold was out of his depth and didn't know how to handle the situation.

"Beats me!" Jakobi replied. "But we definitely stay put."

"But those people are injured and need help!"

"You know the rules," Jakobi rebuked him. "We first inform the control center."

Just seconds later it transpired how sensible those regulations were when two masked figures with submachine guns opened fire on the jeep. It was a complete mystery to Nahgold from where they had so suddenly appeared on the scene. They must have been lying in wait close by.

One of the two mothers screamed and tried to take cover with her buggy behind the van. Lightning fast, the second woman followed with her own buggy to escape from the horror. Jakobi grabbed the mobile radio and informed the operations center.

"A vehicle ran into the jeep. Armed gunmen opened fire with submachine guns." As he was talking, it suddenly turned pitch-black inside the van. Soon after the radio connection broke down.

*

Frankfurt, Public Park Taunusanlage, 0640 Hours. "What do you want? Get lost, you jerk!" Markus snapped at the foul-smelling man in a hoodie. *If this keeps up, Frankfurt will soon be a goner. That gold pyramid attracts bums and asylum seekers like sh… attracts flies!* Despite his anger, Markus didn't even voice the 'S-word' in his thoughts. Years ago he had conditioned himself not to use it for his children's sake.

In the past there had only been a handful of junkies; everything had been under control. But now the Taunusanlage was thronged with hundreds of filthy lost causes. The city wasn't in a position or unwilling to provide adequate hygiene measures. Not surprisingly the cynics maintained that the security trench surrounding the pyramid structure was Frankfurt's biggest garbage can.

But the gold pyramid is still awesome, Markus mused. He stepped close to the glass and stainless steel barrier. The railing felt icecold and damp after the night. Only a fifteen foot trench separated him from the gold bricks displayed there in large stacks.

In the twilight of the dawn the pyramid cast a glimmering light as far as the Old Opera; its reflection dancing languidly on the bright sandstone facade of the magnificent Rennaicance building. To him it nearly conveyed the impression that the Old Opera had a two-story portal made of solid gold. The surrounding luxurious residential tower blocks, too, were bathed in some of the pyramid's glow. *What symbolism! Evidently not a neighborhood welcoming badly paid journalists,* Markus concluded. *Four figure prices per square foot attract an entirely different set of professionals.*

Malicious tongues claimed the Deutsche Bank had subsidized the building of the pyramid with millions running into three digits. The sole condition had apparently been the location at the exact bend between the Taunusanlage and the Neue Mainzer Straβe. After the last few years' numerous scandals, the Deutsche Bank wanted to bask in some of the pyramid's light, the people grumbled. The bankers didn't care. The financial institution's twin towers now shone golden every night – and in their blue corporate color during the day.

Markus was amused by the pyramid's opponents' nickname: *the Central Bank's Laxative.* Far from everyone regarded the horrendous costs incurred in the construction as reasonable. Not least of it spent on the unique security measures.

"Markus?" a voice behind him suddenly startled him out of his thoughts. Curious, he turned around.

"Gosh, Markus!" exclaimed the man. "Haven't seen you for ages. You're looking great. How are you?"

While his hand was being pretty enthusiastically pumped, Markus feverishly searched his mind for the guy's name. Just before he embarrassed himself, he remembered: Thomas! They knew each other from their student days.

"Thomas, my friend. I'm doing fine. And you?"

As hard as he tried, he couldn't recall the man's surname. What had, however, stuck in his mind was that Thomas held a well-paid position with one of Frankfurt's major banks. Their careers had taken entirely different directions and for that reason their paths only crossed every ten years or so. Like right now.

"I'm well. The jobs going great though the unstable financial markets are causing us a lot of stress. The supervisory bodies issue new directives every month," Thomas told him cheerfully.

"I hear you."

"And you, Markus. Do you get plenty of assignments? You are still a journalist, I take it?"

He jovially slapped Markus' back.

"I can't complain."

Markus didn't much fancy engaging in an in-depth discussion with Thomas, who was evidently in great form. He certainly didn't want to talk about his less than inspiring career. He had very little work at the moment and his annual income was presumably even less than Thomas earned in a month. He therefore changed the subject and pointed to the imposing structure beside them.

"If you believe Derhan, the architect from Hamburg, the gold pyramid is supposed to represent a symbiosis between the Louvre in Paris, the Great Pyramid of Giza and the dome of the Reichstag building. With a floor area of 18,000 square feet and a height of 160 feet, it's twice the size of the Louvre's glass pyramid," Markus tried to at least dazzle his old fellow student with his knowledge. He didn't mention that he'd only read up on the matter to prepare for his article.

"I know," Thomas replied unimpressed. "Without the contents, it cost twice as much as Hamburg's new concert hall, but is only half the size of the Cheops Pyramid – as far as the part above ground is concerned, that is. And at the design presentation Derhan is supposed to have ironically mentioned that one would have to roof the whole of Frankfurt to be bigger than Giza."

Thomas got more and more into his stride. Markus soon noticed that his former university buddy was far better informed than he was, and that he didn't have a hope of stopping his verbal outpourings.

"And the architectural highlight is that it's two pyramids upside down on top of each other. One above ground, its mirrored counterpart below. The whole lot covered in glass. High-security glass. Titanium steel stays. A clear view over 75 billion Euros in gold. Close to 2,500 tons, all polished and carefully stacked. Six floors, infinitely long rows of shelves, a brilliant golden-yellow sun. Fort Knox is a retirement home by comparison!"

"Absolutely," was all Markus could spontaneously think of. He had long since realized that Thomas was obviously immensely interested in the gold pyramid. And if he couldn't top the guy's knowledge, he wanted to at least tease out a few new aspects for his coverage. He promptly switched over to interviewing reporter mode.

"Tell me, Thomas, how do you as an expert actually view the Central Bank's gold retrieval plan? "

"After the USA, Germany has the second largest gold reserves in the world," Thomas started like a professor lecturing his students. "3,380 tons of pure gold. These holdings are kept at the Federal Reserve Bank of New York, the Banque de France in Paris, the Bank of England in London and the German Central Bank in Frankfurt to act as collateral to secure against the risk of non-payments."

"And why do you think the Central Bank and the government are now bringing the gold back to Germany?"

"Our Federal Court of Auditors is skeptical that the gold is in safe hands abroad," Thomas surmised.

"But they've been saying that for years."

"Exactly. But ever since the Greek economy went belly up and Italy has financing problems, the public is getting more agitated. And that's why the administration is reacting," Thomas reinforced his stance. "That's why the Parliament passed the new gold depository policy to justify bringing all our gold reserves back to Germany. With as much publicity as possible. And that's why they're actively involving the press. They want the public to see how rich our country is. The message is: No need to panic, guys, the German gold is safe!"

Markus valued Thomas' detailed information, yet his nerdy lecture style also annoyed him. He pointedly consulted his Rolex wristwatch. The Oyster model with the perpetual, self-winding clockwork was an heirloom from his grandfather.

"Sorry, Thomas, I still have to take a few photos for an article I have to deliver today. Was lovely seeing you. Take care."

Without waiting for a reply, he extracted his Canon from its bag, walked over to the left corner of the rail surrounding the pyramid, knelt down and took some shots. Thomas cast a last glance at the gold pyramid, raised his hand as a farewell gesture and left.

Markus continued taking pictures. The industrial climber, who abseiled each morning down to the trench to restore the immaculate glow, provided a welcome addition to add some action to an otherwise lifeless architectural image. Even if it abounded with gold.

It's good that we're bringing the gold back, Markus thought as he finally continued on his way.

*

Soon after, Markus Manx opened the door to his office. It was still relatively dark. With his right hand he flipped the old-fashioned toggle switch up. *Manual switches like these should have been consigned to a museum decades ago*, he thought.

He was sharing an office with other freelance journalists. His door was the first on the right after the entrance. In front of the skylight, which facilitated a halfway acceptable illumination of the room, stood a massive, old wooden desk. All the walls were lined with ceiling-high shelves overflowing with newspapers and article clips. Whatever didn't fit on the shelves and into various folders was spread over the roughly 150 square foot floor. The rent for the shared premises in the old building was affordable by Frankfurt standards, especially considering the location.

This is just what a reporter's office should look like, he thought, once again justifying the chaos to himself. *And now I need a coffee!*

The coffee maker was two doors down in the former kitchen where the plastic coating was slowly peeling off the corners of the mint-green and somewhat antiquated wall units. Last year, the landlord had decommissioned the electric cooker with its four cast-iron rings for safety reasons. A handwritten note was stuck to the vending machine, the most modern appliance in the kitchen:

1. Extract cup
2. Insert coins
3. Select preferred coffee type

Instructions for Dummies, Markus chuckled while reading the path to coffee bliss for the umpteenth time. He involuntarily scanned the instructions every time he stood in front of the machine, waiting for his eagerly anticipated beverage. *People presumably read this more often than most of my articles,* he pondered until the display at last flashed green and the machine was ready. He pulled a paper cup from the dispenser and placed it under the coffee spout. *Does the word paper cup dispenser even exist or should it be an 'individual Styrofoam cup conveyor'*? Even if there were such an elongated term, this particular one certainly didn't merit the description. As a matter of principle, it always dispensed three cups stuck together at a time. The superfluous beverage containers then piled up beside the machine as the day went on. Why nobody used them remained a mystery to Markus. Not that he did either. Perhaps the cleaners stuffed them back into the dispenser in the evening.

The 50 cent piece disappeared in the slot. A *latte* was the choice he wouldn't see materialize as the display lights went out as soon as he pressed the button. More or less at the same time the ceiling light also went out, a white circular lamp with its own peculiar 70s charm, which somehow reminded him of a UFO. *Another power cut! Sooner or later I'll sue the Government. My 50 cents are definitely gone! Once the power is back, about five minutes from now, the machine won't remember my donation, as usual. So far it owes me at least five Euros. Why do I always have to be here at the wrong time?*

Michaela, one of those with whom he shared the office space, swore she had never yet incurred any losses due to power failures. *Hardly surprising, if you only turn up at nine and others have already disarmed the trap,* was what Markus always thought then.

Ever since the administration was pushing its energy policy, power cuts had become more frequent. Whenever the pressure on the power grids fluctuated, they often collapsed. Fluctuation in wind force, widespread clouding and, and, and... Markus alleged an entirely different cause: an estimated 10,000 office workers expressing their desire for coffee by simultaneously pressing the button of their vending machines!

Be that as it may, there was no point in waiting. The last 50 cent coin he'd found in his desk drawer was gone. Coffee was therefore not an option this morning.

Slightly irritated, Markus scuffled back to his office. Four red zeros listlessly flashed on his clock radio. The power was back. *Whoops, that was quick for a change,* Marcus marveled.

His next train of thought led him to being envious of the technology in his editors' offices which were well prepared for the electricity grid taking an occasional breather. All of them were equipped with emergency generators. The technology reacted in milliseconds and a combination of buffer batteries and gas-powered generators took over the supply. No computers crashed and the coffee machines kept on bubbling as if nothing had happened.

The old building in the Ulmenstraße, however, boasted no such emergency power supply. But at least the rent was affordable. And thanks to its battery, Markus' laptop continued to work.

Not so the flashing clock radio. A black plastic casing on the outside, four large red, flashing LED numbers, a red colon in the middle that also flashed and separated the hours from the minutes. This relic from his youth Markus had 'smuggled' into his marriage, as Claudia, his ex-wife, had once humorously claimed. In line with its year of manufacture it had neither a snooze nor an alarm repeat function and just two radio wavelengths. And an ear-splittingly squeaking alarm which didn't stop for fully fifteen minutes. Sluggish as one was in the morning, it was impossible to silence the annoying pest by hand. Markus called it *Mad Max*.

Years ago Claudia had pointed out to him that the decrepit wreck of an alarm clock with its completely worn logo didn't just exude an uncomfortable atmosphere but also considerable amounts of electrosmog. Consequently the invisible electric and magnetic fields vacated the nuptial bedroom and had since found a new home in his office.

Markus took the radio clock from the shelve and adjusted the time: 06:59. Shortly past seven he took his cell phone off the charger on his desk and dialed Dorothea Mund's number. He could hear the dialing sequence, then the ringtone...

*

Frankfurt, European Central Bank, 0650 Hours. Darius Dongi had been the President of the European Central Bank for more than seven years. Tall, dark haired, tailor-made double-breasted suit, white gold cufflinks, a present from his wife at their wedding anniversary in May the previous year.

Floor-to-ceiling windows afforded a view of Frankfurt's skyline from the 650 feet high North Tower. Fantastic! Dongi adored the panorama outside his office. Sunrises were intrinsically beautiful anyway, but the sunsets behind the towers of Frankfurt's banks were spectacular from here. The architect had had to adjust the design several times to achieve this ultimate view. Now the European Central Bank's President's office sprawled across nearly half a floor of the North Tower. Thus nobody could overlook the importance of his position.

Since the ECB had relocated its seat from the skyscraper in the inner city to the new building in Frankfurt's east end in 2014, Dongi had been enjoying the privilege. The initial protests among the population about the new building soon faded into oblivion.

Dongi cultivated his contacts. Critics claimed he was too closely associated with politics. In reality the ECB was merely independent on paper. The bank had to support politics as a money manipulator, a state financiers or simply as an economic driver. The most convincing proof of the close link between commerce and the state was the continuous acquisition of government bonds. Right from the start, Dongi had been actively supporting the program, which by now had been topped up to 2,000 billion Euros. The idea itself, he claimed, had been his.

"Your visitor, Mr. Dongi," announced his PA and quietly closed the door behind Dr. Wieder who had quickly stepped into Dongi's office.

Europe's two most important central bankers, Dr. Jürgen Wieder, President of the German Central Bank, and Darius Dongi, President of the European Central Bank, met every first Monday of the month. What had originally been spontaneous and informal get-togethers in crisis situations, had over time developed into regular meetings. The follow up appointments, entered as *recurring events* in both gentlemen's digital planners, automatically updated themselves for the following year. Today's agenda only addressed routine issues.

"What do you mean, you don't know how it could have happened?" Wieder roared into the cell phone he was still holding to his ear as he entered the room.

It annoyed Dongi that his collegue was rude enough not to end the call in his presence. But Wieder's uncouth manner implied that the matter really was of utmost importance. Dongi couldn't remember ever having seen the man that angry.

"In my wildest dreams I couldn't possibly imagine how a heavily guarded, armored transport van with three tons of gold can simply disappear!"

In his rage, Wieder was involuntary spitting on Dongi's desk.

"This isn't the Bermuda Triangle! We're right in the middle of Frankfurt!" he yelled. "When was your last contact with the vehicle?"

"Six thirty at the first checkpoint," was the meek reply. "At six thirty four we received the aborted distress call."

After Wieder had listened without commenting to the investigation procedures that had been instigated, he slammed his cell phone onto the desk, his face bright red.

"I apologize for the outburst, Darius."

He went over to the window and took a few deep breaths to regain his composure.

"For the past two years we have executed countless gold transports. Glitches? None! Breakdowns? None! And today? Today an armored van simply vanishes! With the entire security team! Without a trace!"

For a moment, silence prevailed.

"Could the escort itself be involved? Or Eastern European groups?" Dongi enquired rationally.

"No idea. So far, we've got absolutely nothing. The only thing we *do* know is that the van can't be opened from the outside. Without the help of the crew, nobody can get at the gold."

Darius Dongi remained stoic.

"I always thought you monitored all the gold transports' positions via GPS, Jürgen."

"That's the next crucial point, Darius! The control room charted the GPS signal the whole time. Everything was on schedule. The signal stopped at six thirty four in Neu-Isenburg! It was abruptly gone. And so was the van."

The head of the German Central Bank had calmed down a little and now also tried to logically analyze the situation.

"Apparently we can locate the position to within about

fifteen feet. All the vehicles were not only equipped with a GPS receiver, but also with a GPS transponder that transmitted the current location to the control center. We always knew the coordinates in real-time. At least in theory."

After a pause, he added: "The emergency frequency for a short distress call was used at six thirty four. Then the contact was terminated."

"Was the frequency interrupted? Or did the escort stop the contact?"

"We don't know yet."

"Professionals," the President of the ECB observed and frowned.

"Whatever the case may be, the incident can have unpleasant consequences for us. We can't afford any further slip-ups. No matter what!"

Following a brief silence, Dongi continued: "Until we've caught the perpetrators, we should stop all gold transports. Right throughout Europe. What do you say?"

"You're right," Wieder agreed resignedly and a little preoccupied.

Ten minutes later all European capitals received an encrypted email.

SECURITY LEVEL II – TOP SECRET

ECB HEADQUARTERS

SECURITY ALERT!

TODAY A GERMAN CENTRAL BANK GOLD TRANSPORT GUARDED BY FOUR SOLDIERS WAS AMBUSHED IN FRANKFURT. ALL SECURITY ESCORTS WERE ABDUCTED.

AT PRESENT THE REASONS FOR THIS ACT ARE STILL UNCLEAR. THE WHEREABOUTS OF THE

GOLD ARE ALSO UNKNOWN. THE SEQUENCE OF THE ATTACK INDICATES UTMOST PROFESSIONALISM WHICH RENDERED THE STRINGENT SAFETY MEASURES INEFFECTIVE.

UNTIL THE SITUATION HAS BEEN RESOLVED, IT IS RECOMMENDED TO POSTPONE ALL MAJOR TRANSPORTS OF VALUABLES. SECURITY PROCEDURES FOR ROUTINE MONEY DELIVERIES TO COMMERCIAL BANKS SHOULD BE INCREASED.

THE PRESIDENT

Europe's central banks and governments had been informed. The search for the perpetrators was coordinated by the Emergency Task Force of the Federal Police with their situation center located at Frankfurt Airport. The Special Forces were assisted by the police of the Federal States of Hesse, Rhineland-Palatinate and Bavaria. Experts had calculated that the perpetrators had a head start of 40 minutes.

How quickly could a heavy vehicle of its kind disappear? Was a 25 mile radius sufficient for the manhunt? Airspace surveillance was also in progress. An activity designed to cover up the general helplessness.

*

Frankfurt, Ulmenstraße, 0730 Hours. Having kissed goodbye to his morning coffee after the power cut, Markus got to work. On his pretty much antique laptop - he disrespectfully called it 'craptop' like so many other users of outdated models - he checked his emails, caught up on the latest news and planned his schedule. His report about the gold transport for the *HNP* was due today.

Nothing important in his emails. The same applied to

the press newsletters he read for professional reasons. Now the sports news.

*** 2:1 for Frankfurt's soccer team. *Three points. About time,* thought Markus who was only marginally interested in the national soccer league. He was more into basketball, which he had played in his youth. Unfortunately he hadn't been able to make a career out of it. Although tall at 6 foot, he hadn't been quite tall enough for a basketball player.

*** 87:78. His favorite team, the Fraport Skyliners, had defeated the Bavarians. "Yes!" he cheered noisily when he read the result. *Much better than soccer. Those matches are always real one-sided. They're starting to be quite boring. But in basketball Frankfurt can even beat Bavaria.* He switched to the weather.

*** Clear skies in the morning. 44 degrees. Sunny and dry during the day with maximum temperatures of up to 60 degrees. *That's OK for this time of the year,* Markus thought and switched to the *HNP* homepage.

*** BREAKING NEWS: Central Bank's gold transport raided.

Just as he was about to click on the headline, his phone rang.

"Markus Manx," he said after being momentarily startled.

"Hi, Markus, is this a good time?"

Without the caller having revealed his name, it was obvious who it was. The deep, calm voice betrayed him: his friend Jonathan Schreiber, editor with the *HNP*.

"Can you do some research on the raid on the gold transport? I need copy for the print- and the online-editions. Put the article I commissioned yesterday on hold for the time being... A hundred lines max. for the online edition till noon at the latest and a hundred and fifty lines till this evening for the print one," he resumed after reflecting. "Can you do it?"

The question was more or less rhetorical. Jonathan assumed that freelance journalists were essentially always available and needed every assignment they could get. He was usually right.

"I don't want you to solve the case. I just need an interesting three columns." he added. "It seems to me that our own people were in cahoots with the perps. Can you deliver?"

Meanwhile Markus had clicked on the Internet link. But all it showed was that the Central Bank had lost a transport during a hold-up.

"Sure. Any more background apart from the tiny snippets on the news ticker?"

"You're on your own now, Markus."

Markus was on the list of freelance journalists for Frankfurt's newspapers. Occasionally the *Frankfurter Allgemeine Zeitung,* one of Germany's largest newspapers, hired him to cover economic issues. Some time ago the paper had published nearly a full page dedicated to the inauguration of the gold pyramid and its financial background. Markus had received a lot of praise for his research, a pretty rare event in his line of work.

Another of the city's newspapers, the *Frankfurter Rundschau,* was the most thin on the ground and hadn't commissioned him for quite some time. For precisely that reason Markus had tried to call the editor Dorothera Mund about half an hour ago.

The *Hessische Neueste Presse*, on the other hand, hired him on a regular basis to cover popular topics. The *HNP* wasn't so much interested in economic facts, but in thrilling entertainment. In this case: crime – perpetrator – motive.

The whole lot dished up with a spectacular photo. "Gold Transporter Ambushed" was a good headline. Over the past few years Markus had slowly warmed to the tabloid topics: exciting, entertaining and current, yet light-hearted and safe.

In the old days he had hated this approach. But times were changing. And sometimes a lot faster than he liked.

*

Frankfurt, Eschborn Highway Junction, 0730 Hours. Lena Eck was crossing the Eschborn junction towards the inner city in her red Fiat 500. *Like a Virgin* was blasting from the radio. Lena enthusiastically chimed in with the Madonna hit. She loved the song.

"*Touched for the very first time. Like a vir ir ir ir gin...*" Lena sang at the top of her voice. "*With your heartbeat, next to mine.*" What a great start to a promising day!

Lena, a petite young woman sporting a severely cut bob, her brown eyes nearly shrouded by her fringe, the tips of her dark hair reaching to her chin. She had inherited the German surname from her mother. She'd been living in Frankfurt since she'd moved out of the woman's place 15 years ago. Her Russian father had always been a stranger she couldn't get close to. To him raising a child meant threatening and administering punishment should his daughter not obey. So Lena had retreated into a virtual world from a very young age. Computers became her life and she turned into a proper nerd. Although, no doubt, a pretty one with distinctive Slavic features. After completing a degree in computer studies, she accepted a job in the IT division of a major bank, yet terminated it pretty fast. Surprisingly fast, actually. But she didn't like to talk about it. Her department head at the time had sexually harassed her, more than once, also during working hours. Lena had reported him to his superiors, but the bank hadn't believed her. Had even defended the man and urged her to resign.

For the past eight years she'd been working as a self-employed IT specialist, analyzing security systems. Today, she was delivering a speech about IT security in SMEs at the Frankfurt Fair Congress Center. Start 9 a.m. She was happy with her fee of 1,200 Euros for a 60 minute talk. Everything she needed was on the passenger seat beside her: the laptop and her mascot, a small, white cuddly toy with black, drooping ears.

"When you hold me, and your heart beats, and you love me," Madonna belted out when suddenly a profusion of brake lights mushroomed up in front of her. Stepping onto the brake pedal curbed Lena's speed as well as her euphoria.

Gridlock. Lena silenced Madonna and consulted her cell phone to find out more about the congestion from her traffic app. *Just as well I left early enough to have plenty of time to spare,* she thought.

*

Frankfurt, Ulmenstraße, 0810 Hours. Slightly irritated, Markus hefted his feet onto the desk and dialed the same number for the fourth time. "… We're sorry we can't take your call right now…," jeered the voice at the other end of the line.

Markus glanced at his mismatched socks. Ever since his divorce, more and more individual socks had disappeared. By now he couldn't have cared less if they were one of his washing machine's favorite snacks or if extraterrestrials snitched them to convert them into fuel. He had long since given up on trying to determine the cause of the mystery.

The socks never resurfaced and he now always wore two different ones as a matter of principle.

"... We're sorry we can't take your call right now...." He finally got through at the fifth attempt.

"Hello, you are talking to the press office of the German Central Bank. My name is Rose de Jong. How can I be of assistance?" a friendly voice enquired.

Such a pleasant, personal response surprised Markus after all that frustrating time spent in the queue. He needed a moment to organize his thoughts, take his feet off the desk and sit up straight.

"Markus Manx here. I'm a freelance journalist. Let me get right to the point. Can you give me some background information on today's raid on the bank's gold transport?"

"Certainly. What exactly would you like to know?"

Markus had roughly outlined his questions on a piece of paper.

"Well, quite a bit, actually. Let me start at the top of my list. What was the specific reason for this particular transport? And from where to where was the gold being taken?"

He was pretty sure he knew the answers, but had to make sure that it was really the same operation he had witnessed earlier.

"It was a routine transport from our depot in New York to Frankfurt, Mr. Manx. There was no specific reason. It was just part of the Federal Government's decision to return all our gold reserves to Germany."

The press office lady with the pleasant voice had remembered his name. *Of course, it's part of her job. But would she be just as friendly if she knew that I'm one of the accredited journalists who documented the loading process at the airport this morning?* Never mind. Markus felt uncomfortable not being able to address the woman just as professionally by her name as well.

"Can you tell me if special security measures were in place?"

"All our transports are executed and guarded by units of our armed forces. Starting with the landing at the airport, the logistics and security surveillance are coordinated by our operations management in Frankfurt," the press officer explained. "The standard security measures apply."

"OK. My next question is: Are there any indications who might be behind the heist?"

"I currently don't have any information on that, Mr. Manx. But, let me assure you, police investigations are well underway."

"Was there anything special or conspicuous prior to today's transport?" Markus continued.

"I do not have any information on that."

"Have you already issued a press release with official details?"

"Our press release will be online within the next few minutes. You can access it on our homepage: *www*-dot-*germancentralbank*-dot-*de*-forward slash-*de*-forward slash-*press*-forward slash-*gold*. Don't forget the second *de*. It directs you to our German page. We will keep updating the page as soon as we have more news."

Pleasantly efficient and very professional, this lady. And always friendly and obliging, Markus summed up. But he hadn't learned anything new.

He still wanted to somehow make up for his earlier abruptness.

"Sorry, the connection wasn't very good when I got through to you and I didn't quite catch your name."

"Don't worry, Mr. Manx. My name is de Jong, Rose de Jong."

Markus thanked her profusely for her help and put the

cell phone back on its charger. *Phew! Thank God the call didn't last much longer or I would have been embarrassed again,* he thought, relieved. The available call duration of fifteen hours specified by his cell phone's manufacturer had been reduced to just about thirty minutes over the years. The battery was worn out, he guessed. Until he could afford a new one, his silver phone, he privately called it *Silverback,* would have to mostly live on its charger.

Markus opened the specified link. Already quite a lot of information was available for downloading. Information about the amount of gold reserves, the storage concept, transport updates and technical details of the vehicles' security systems. The Central Bank's security specialists were convinced, so it said, that the van would be impossible to open from the outside. At least not without totally destroying it.

So what did the robbers do? They were hardly standing there with a can opener trying to get in. Where were their accomplices? It was still too early for speculations. First Markus had to do his homework. This also entailed consulting the police. He found the number of their press office in Frankfurt and dialed.

"This is Marie Meier, Frankfurt Police Press Office. What can I do for you?" Markus heard another extremely polite voice. *How much training does it take to sound that friendly yet detached in a crisis situation?*

"Markus Manx here. I'm doing some research for the *Hessische Neueste Presse* regarding today's heist of the Central Bank's gold transport. Can you tell me who could answer some questions for me?"

"You'll have to contact the public relations department of the specially set up gold crisis unit. I can give you the number if you have something to write."

"Please do," Markus said, took down the number and

dialed it right after finishing the call.

"Good Morning, Manfred Krüger, Federal Police," was the prompt reply after only the second ring.

"Markus Manx. I'm researching on behalf of the *Hessische Neueste Presse* regarding the armed robbery of the Central Bank's gold transport," he repeated his, by now, standard introduction. How many more times would he be using those words today? "Can you update me on the status of the investigations?"

"There isn't much to say, unfortunately. We're doing all we can. We are running an extensive dragnet operation and large-scale checks in the area around Frankfurt. We're also appealing to the public for information that may assist in solving the case."

"Have you any idea at this stage what might have happened?"

"No. Forensics are still at the crime scene. My colleagues are also interviewing the local residents. The usual."

"Anyone dead or injured?"

"The two soldiers who drove the armored van and the two soldiers in the escort jeep are missing. Unfortunately I can't tell you anything about their condition."

It was no use continuing with his questions, Markus knew. Either it was really still too early to say more or the press officer was not prepared to give anything else away.

"OK. One last question. Where exactly did the heist take place?"

"In Buchenbusch in Neu-Isenburg."

"Many thanks. May I contact you again later for more updates?" Markus asked.

"Certainly, anytime," Manfred Krüger ended the conversation.

Even though his enquiries hadn't produced much news,

Markus was quite content. At least he had the location of the crime scene and was now in a position to start some on-site research. But did the police really not have any suspects? *Perhaps a Mafia gang or a similarly structured organization,* Markus wondered. If his hunch was correct, the abducted soldiers were already as good as dead. Unless they were accomplices.

*

Frankfurt, Trade Fair Exhibition Grounds, Congress Center, 0900 Hours. "Ladies and Gentlemen, I welcome you all to this year's IT symposium," the MC opened the proceedings. An audience of about 400 people had assembled in the auditorium to listen to Lena Eck's presentation on the subject of IT security in small and medium sized German enterprises. Everyone had a perfect view of the stage – the hall's seating was arranged in a semi-circle with ascending rows.

Following the usual organizational instructions, the MC introduced Lena Eck as the opening speaker.

"Please join me in giving a big welcome to Lena Eck. She may still look very young, but when it comes to IT security concerns, she's an old hand. One could nearly say she's a young old hand," he tried to break the ice. With moderate success. The audience was still a little tired. Some of them had traveled a considerable distance.

"Since Edward Snowden publicized to what extent the NSA and other intelligence services are spying on us, nobody among us isn't concerned with IT security. How can we protect ourselves? Where are the biggest risks? These are all questions Lena Eck will now address."

He invited Lena onto the stage.

"Lena has already advised many well-known companies

on the subject. She's a regular contributor to the *IT Security News*, which, no doubt, counts many of you among its readership. She's also widely known for her hacker attacks, which constantly prove the vulnerability of our IT systems. Perhaps she will target your company next to try and infiltrate your sensitive information. But better her than a real hacker. I don't want to give too much away about her talk, but one company in particular, which is represented here today, should listen carefully. She will present you with yet another of her successful hack attacks. Ladies and Gentlemen, I give you Leeena Eeeeck!"

*

Frankfurt / Neu-Isenburg, 0900 Hours. For the trip to Neu-Isenburg Markus had treated himself to a car2go. He neither had the time nor the inclination to walk over a mile from the train station at Neu-Isenburg to Buchenbusch. Besides, he would charge the expenses to the *HNP*. During the drive he pondered what to write for the online edition. *It's too soon to speculate about possible accomplices. But how did the robbers manage to get inside the armored van? Were the convoy's soldiers involved in the heist? A hundred million would have been more than enough to tempt anyone.*

His Sat Nav indicated that he should take the next left turn to Buchenbusch. On the Herzogstraße a police roadblock impeded his progress. He drove on regardless and flashed his press card.

"OK, you can pass. But you have to park your car on the right behind the barrier. Some of my colleagues will assist you from there," the female officer told him with a pleasant smile. Markus did just that. Every woman he had so far been talking to had been extremely friendly. *Must be my charisma. It's all pretty promising.*

Having arrived at the crime scene, cordoned off by red and white tape, the less pleasant reality caught up with him. A grim-looking officer was visibly unimpressed by his credentials. Why didn't he talk to the press office and leave the police alone to do their work in peace, the man wanted to know. But Markus wasn't that easily deterred. A small group of onlookers was standing a little apart beside the old cemetery, hoping to catch a glimpse of the crime scene. Markus walked right over.

"Good morning, all. My name is Markus Manx. I'm a reporter. Can anyone tell me more about the robbery?"

An elderly woman pushed herself forward.

"I can," she exclaimed excitedly. I live in number fifty seven and this morning I heard shots. Sounded like a machine gun. Just like those gangster movies on the TV, you know. I couldn't see an awful lot from my window. But I called the cops anyway."

"And then?" Markus probed her. He had instantly noticed how enthusiastically the old lady had reacted to the word 'reporter'. It was rare to find such a keen eyewitness.

"What happened next?" he reiterated.

"The cops advised me strongly to stay inside. I only dared to leave the house when the first patrol car arrived, you know, about ten minutes later."

"I understand." Markus nodded at her encouragingly. "And what did you see when you left the house?"

"At first I saw nobody apart from the two cops. But in the Merc over there, you know, there was still a driver and a passenger inside. I've no idea what was wrong with them. An ambulance took them away eventually."

"Did you still see the armored van?" Markus probed.

"No. No, it was already gone. Everything happened so fast."

"Thank you. Here's my card. If you remember anything else, please give me a call, will you? May I also take a note of your name and your phone number?"

The flattered old lady smiled as she accepted his card. *An armed robbery! Right on my doorstep! And a real-life reporter is asking me questions! How exciting. The center of attention, at last...*

Markus carefully unpacked his Canon to shoot a few photos of the crime scene. He first used the wide-angle lens to capture as much of the scene as possible, then switched to the telephoto lens. It was easy to take a few impressive shots of the details – the overturned military jeep, the buggy, so out of place amongst the general destruction, and the Mercedes crashed into the tree. He zoomed into the sticker attached to the back of the car – *Pet Cemetery Frankfurt.* He even got a photo of the cartridge cases amidst a sea of glass splinters once a corpulent forensics guy had finally stepped aside.

After Markus had packed away his camera equipment, he wondered if he should also shoot a short video. The editors would be grateful to bolster their online coverage that way. But somehow it looked all a bit too stilted. *I won't get any usable footage here in a hurry,* he decided.

Before he left, however, he wanted to calmly deduce how the heist could have happened. Just like the detectives on TV, his legs wide apart, he planted himself in front of the barrier tape and memorized his overall impression. Then he closed his eyes. On his mental monitor he saw the dented Merc on the right with its doors open, diagonally in front of it the overturned, totally demolished jeep. And behind the house at the corner the back of a forklift.

Forklift? He opened his eyes. And there it was. *What's a forklift doing here? The police doesn't use forklifts to remove a military jeep.* Just in case, he made a note of the type and the company who owned it. *HOLLMANN* was printed in big letters on the vehicle. The smaller letters underneath read *SVETRUCK 25120.*

Markus sensed that this detail might turn out to be very important.

*

Frankfurt, Trade Fair Exhibition Grounds, Congress Center, 0945 Hours. The audience's enthusiastic applause impressively confirmed that Lena Eck had more than fulfilled its expectations. Once it gradually ebbed away, the MC joined the speaker on the stage.

"Thank you for your fascinating talk, Mrs. Eck. Personally, I'm scared by the vision you presented. That although we can store, process and monitor everything, it is far too easy to attack today's IT systems from the outside. The idea alone that our industrial secrets could end up in the wrong hands is alarming. Ladies and Gentleman," he smoothly continued, "you now have the chance to ask Mrs. Eck any questions you might have."

"Great lecture, Mrs. Eck. My name is Kurt Gieseke, security manager with an engineering company. I'd like to know if you can envisage possible approaches to protect fully automated production chains against external hacker attacks."

Another member of the audience, whose name she didn't catch, asked what kind of IT standards were needed for manufacturing-, control- and security systems to safely work together?

Lena Eck answered everyone's questions concisely and clearly. The audience used the opportunity to also ask about partitioning of operational processes from the Internet, robust IT systems, sabotage prevention and the potential and risks of cloud storage.

Apparently Lena's talk had hit the mark, as the MC's comments confirmed.

"Mrs. Eck, on behalf of the organizers I sincerely thank you for your topical and highly interesting lecture about IT security. The many questions and lively debate show that you have used the right approach to the subject. Let me thank you again!"

More applause. The MC warmly shook her hand and she left the stage.

After saying her goodbyes, Lena walked buoyantly through the congress center's brightly lit lobby towards the Ludwig Erhard Park. As always, her inner tension had vanished just a few minutes into her presentation. The Q&A session had been fun and today's audience had been extremely interested in what she'd had to say. Perhaps the shock over the past few months' data breaches and the latest news of the NSA spying out German industrial corporations would be good advertising for further presentations...

The IT symposium was her only appointment today, the rest of the day was hers. Lena decided to walk the twenty minutes to the inner city to have a coffee. She could collect her car later.

Ten minutes after, she crossed the Taunusanlage right beside the gold pyramid. *Pretty crazy what they've put up here. Is that really all gold that glitters?* She was thinking *of the jewelry stores that replaced the real stuff with cheap imitations in the evenings. Bad luck for potential thieves,* she grinned to herself...

Soon she had reached her destination at the Kornmarkt. *Full up, as usual,* she thought and joined the queue outside the Café Wacker.

*

Neu-Isenburg, 0950 Hours. Before heading home, Markus checked out a few websites on his smartphone and found two numbers. Ignoring the hands-free option, he dialed the first one and drove in the direction of downtown Frankfurt.

"Hollmann Haulage, my name is Angelika Spinnrad. How may I be of assistance?"

"Good morning. This is Markus Manx. I live in Neu-Isenburg and have a question for you. Earlier on I noticed one of your forklifts just a few yards from my house. Would it be possible to hire it on short notice for a small job? I need to lift a heavy water trough into my garden. Shouldn't take more than five minutes. Seeing that your machine is already just around the corner, I was wondering if you could just quickly do it."

"Which forklift do you mean? Did you write down the plate number?" the receptionist wanted to know. She sounded a little irritated to Markus.

"I didn't, but beside your company's name it said Svetruck 25120."

"Where exactly is the forklift?" she asked, now evidently excited.

"On the Birkenweg in Neu-Isenburg. Real close to where I live."

"I'm afraid we won't be able to help you," the woman said, "but you've helped *us* a lot. I will immediately pass this on to the police. The forklift was stolen last night, you see. We've already reported the theft, but we never thought it would be found that fast."

"Too bad," Markus lied. "That's it then. Good luck getting it back. Have a nice day. Bye."

This is my lucky day! The forklift was stolen and surely isn't parked at the crime scene by coincidence. He entered the second number he had found into his cell phone and raced back to the city.

"University Hospital Frankfurt, good morning," a friendly female voice announced.

"Hello, my name is Markus Manx. My aunt Elisabeth and my uncle Franz were admitted to your hospital today. They were brought in by ambulance. Can you tell me how they're doing?"

"Alright. What's their surname, please?" the woman enquired.

"Elisabeth and Franz Altmeier. Meier as in M-E-I-E-R."

"One moment, please."

Markus could hear her typing on the keyboard.

"I'm sorry. I don't have anybody by that name. When were they admitted?"

"Must have been around half seven. They were in a car crash."

"They won't be in my system yet. I'd say they're still in the ER. I'll put you through."

While he was on hold, Markus listened to the background music before another female voice came on the line.

"Nurse Hildegard, ER," the voice said curtly.

"Good morning, nurse. My name is Markus Manx and I'm anxious to know how my aunt and uncle are doing. Elisabeth and Franz Altmeier. They were brought to your hospital by ambulance around half seven after they'd been in an accident."

"I'm sorry, Mr. Mank," the nurse stopped him. Markus was used to people getting his name wrong and he didn't correct her. At least she hadn't called him *Marx*, as happened quite frequently.

"We cannot disclose patient information over the phone. I hope you understand."

"Of course, nurse. I know you have your regulations.

But can you at least tell me if they're OK? I'm real worried about them," Markus tried playing the pity card. But she wouldn't budge.

"Again, I'm sorry, but I can't."

"Please, just tell me if they're fine."

"I suggest you drop by this afternoon to visit your relatives."

"Thank you, I will. Have a nice day," Markus ended the conversation.

Hit the jackpot twice! Man, I'm good. I now know that the forklift was stolen and that the two witnesses are in the University Hospital. And just because of that little sticker at the back of the Merc. 'Pet Cemetery Frankfurt', complete with photo and name of the Altmeiers.

Twenty five minutes by car and two phone calls later Markus reached Frankfurt's inner city, extremely pleased with himself. He turned into the Sandgasse to park the car2go. He was lucky again. The free parking space was just around the corner from the Café Wacker.

And he really needed his caffeine fix by now.

*

Frankfurt, Federal Police Situation Center, 1000 Hours. A crisis team, embracing several agencies and authorities, had immediately been established. Hardly surprising considering one hundred million Euros had been stolen. Never mind what would happen when the press got hold of the explosive news.

"Gentlemen," Hans-Joachim Hartmann, Chief of the Federal Police Force, opened the first meeting. His voice sounded grave. "We are dealing with extremely violent criminals."

The men had assembled in the conference room at the

Federal Police Headquarters at Frankfurt Airport: six rectangular tables with gray laminate tops pushed together in the middle of the room, surrounded by twelve chairs of the cantilever variety with chrome-plated, tubular frames and worn fabric covers. Garish, fluorescent neon lights on the ceiling illuminating the room. In stark contrast, the latest technology: three large screens on the wall – the connection cables still dangling down, each with a sticker with the numbers one to three. In the middle of the table state-of-the-art computers, speakers, cameras and projectors.

"Continue," a commanding voice sounded from one of the speakers. The voice of Sven Stahl, Minister for Special Affairs. He was in charge of coordinating all line ministries and intelligence services. Stahl was the Chancellor's right-hand man and the second most powerful person in the State.

Hartmann took a deep breath: "So far we have reconstructed the sequence of the attack as follows. At approximately six thirty a.m. the perpetrators stopped the convoy, rammed the lead vehicle with a passenger car and opened fire with submachine guns. Forensics found lots of blood at the crime scene. The driver and co-driver are missing. The armored van behind, manned by two more soldiers, vanished with its cargo. We suspect that a forklift found at the site was used to load the armored van onto another vehicle. All in all it shouldn't have taken more than a few minutes. Our colleagues are still gathering evidence and questioning the local residents," Hartmann ended his summary. "Mr. Brandner will now update us on the Central Bank's findings."

"Thank you, Mr. Hartmann," Brandner, Personal Assistant to the President of the Central Bank, started. "We monitored the transport from the time it left the airport. At six thirty it reported from Neu-Isenburg as per schedule. The line was permanently open and we therefore know that the convoy took a small detour via Buchenbusch after being redirected by the fire department. The robbers had obviously staged an accident. At six thirty four we received a distress call from the armored van stating that the lead vehicle had been rammed by a black passenger car. Shortly after, the distress call was aborted in mid-sentence. We lost the GPS signal at the same time."

"Do we know how the connection could have been terminated so abruptly?" Stahl interjected.

Silence. The men glanced at each other. Central Bank representative Brandner helplessly shrugged his shoulders.

Several seconds passed without any of them saying anything. Everyone was at a complete loss. Finally Army General Alfred Steiner took the floor.

"The military police is currently questioning the comrades of the four soldiers involved in the transport to establish if any of them noticed any unusual behavior. Even though we consider it unlikely, we are checking if one or more of our men could be possible accomplices. We are talking about a hundred million Euros, after all. I have frequently pointed out that we should pay our soldiers a more decent wage."

"Mr. Steiner," was the irritated response through the loudspeakers. "Please stay on track."

"Yes, Minister. We also sent the military police to the four soldiers' apartments where they are interviewing their relatives as we speak," General Steiner hastened to wrap up his report.

Hans-Joachim Hartmann crossed his arms over his chest and stared at Steiner in amazement. "Isn't that the task of our regular police?" he strongly criticized the army's transgression of competences.

"Mr. Hartmann, the Minister for Special Affairs replied

instead of the General, "let's not explore competences in this matter. If General Steiner is prepared to take full responsibility, we shall not discuss minor transgressions of boundaries. We are concerned with results. And fast. I expect everyone involved to contribute."

"Certainly," Hartmann conceded sheepishly. "Next is the Federal Intelligence Service. Mr. Gmeiner, if you would be so good."

Friedrich Gmeiner first emphasized his agency's importance in solving the case. Everyone present was aware, however, that armed robberies like these were clearly beneath him. At every opportunity he stressed that it was the police's job to solve crimes of this nature and to leave the intelligence service alone. But today he elaborately outlined the measures he had implemented: analysis of telephone networks, searching for keywords, assisted by the NSA, evaluation of satellite images. In other words: Gmeiner knew nothing. Apparently the perpetrators had left no evidence.

"OK," Hartmann took charge again. Focusing on solutions and self-control were his typical traits. But he was quite sensitive when it came to Gmeiner's arrogance. Hartmann had used the last few minutes of the man's deliberations to carefully arrange his documents and stack them. He knew very well that this would provoke Gmeiner. "If that's everything, I thank you all for your contributions. If nobody objects, I schedule the next update for three p.m."

"Agreed," sounded from the loudspeaker. Everyone physically present in the room nodded and left to press ahead with the investigations in their respective departments.

*

Frankfurt, Café Wacker, 1020 Hours. Lena Eck eyed the queue in front of her. Students, bankers, two street sweepers in their municipal uniforms. *An eclectic mix, as always,* she thought.

A man joined the queue. Lena surveyed him unobtrusively in the mirrored glass of the counter. Jeans, white, slightly creased shirt, old-fashioned sports coat, sneakers. Nearly six foot tall, not the usual career type, but somehow likeable. He smiled when he noticed her looking at him.

"Hello," he said a little hesitantly. "You're also waiting for coffee?"

What a stupid question. What else would she be waiting for? he thought. But never mind. Perhaps his dumb remark would be enough to start a conversation.

"Yeah, I like their Honduran Marcala dark roast.

"I agree. I love it, too. Not so bitter and distributed by Fairtrade. Good choice."

"What can I get you," the waitress interrupted them.

"Two Honduras Marcala to go, please," Lena said while turning to face the man behind her.

"One's for you."

"Oh, thank you!" Markus said surprised. "But I only accept if you join me." He smiled gallantly.

Lena paid, took the two cups and handed one of them to Markus. They stepped outside.

"The stone wall over there is one of my favorite spots."

"Another excellent choice. I'm Markus, by the way… Is it OK to call you by your first name?"

"Sure. I'm Lena."

They sat beside each other on the wall, enjoying the last bit of sunshine the season had to offer.

"Yum, this coffee never ceases to surprise me… Do you come here often? I've never seen you before."

"Only occasionally. Today I fancied a really good coffee. Particularly since I couldn't get one in the office this morning."

"What happened?" Lena grabbed the chance to keep their chat going.

"The machine tricked me. We have a coffee maker that promises decent coffee for fifty cents. But no, just as I inserted the money in the slot and pressed the button, the power went. Only for a few seconds, but the money was gone and the machine wouldn't part with my beverage."

"Didn't it deliver once the power came back?" Lena probed.

"I didn't wait. But how would the dumb machine remember my fifty cents once it was back in action?"

"That's easy," Lena started to explain. "Vending machines like that have storage batteries which secure certain basic settings. Like how much water has to run through at the selection of a specific button. That way it remembers that you inserted fifty cents even during a power cut."

"Are you a coffee maker sales rep?" he wisecracked.

Lena laughed.

"No, I'm just quite into the whole technology thing."

"What a shame. I could do with someone who knows how to lay their hands on a good coffee maker." Markus smiled and quickly added: "But as a journalist I could also use an IT specialist."

Lena had to laugh again. She liked Markus' humor.

Markus also liked Lena and her carefree manner. Why did he have to be under so much time pressure right now!?

"I'm so sorry, Lena, but I have to be rude and interrupt our pleasant chat. Damn it, I still have to write an article." Lena gave Markus a puzzled look, so he elaborated. "This morning a Central Bank gold transport was ambushed, you know. And the *Hessische Neueste Presse* hired me to write about it."

"Sounds exciting."

"It is. I'll tell you more about it later, if you like. What do you say about dinner tonight? I also still owe you an invitation."

"Don't' worry," Lena waved him off, "No need. But I gladly have dinner with you."

"Great." Markus racked his brains where he could take her. "Seven thirty at Hamsilos & Schenk?" he finally proposed. "It's a fish restaurant close to the central station."

"I'd like that. Just give me your cell phone number in case anything else crops up."

Markus gave Lena his business card and she handed him hers in turn.

"May I ask you a quick technical question?" he asked.

"Sure."

"Is it possible to block the transponder inside an armored van to such an extent that it can no longer transmit signals?"

"Absolutely. There are various methods to shield a transponder in a way that the signal won't ever reach a satellite. One of them would be adequately dense lead sheathing. That way nobody knows from where the transponder transmits. But why are you asking?" Lena wanted to know.

"I'll explain tonight. But thank you for now."

He turned around and waved goodbye to her.

Cheerfully, he went back to his office. His high spirits were much inspired by his research. And just as much by Lena.

*

Berlin, American Embassy, 1030 Hours. Peter Redman, CIA Coordinator for Europe, was still pissed at his colleague Ted Branigan who had let the Huntsman die too soon by acting like a complete rookie. Now their most promising source had been lost forever. It should never have happened to a pro.

Of course, Redman was aware of the risks. Twenty years earlier he had also killed a man prematurely. Back then he'd still been young and green and his target had been a foreign agent familiar with the methods. Those people were always harder to crack. But this Huntsman had been just one of those civilians who usually spilled the beans at the slightest threat of violence. At least he had still revealed where the information was hidden before he had died. Perhaps that might provide them with some crucial hints regarding the leak. Nobody must endanger the operation.

Peter Redman had sent Aaron straight away. Now Aaron was standing outside the door of the old building in Berlin, smoking a cigarette. He needed to get to the third floor, the dead victim's office. He waited for somebody to leave the building, so he could enter without ringing the bell. But nobody did.

Ok, it'll be the old trick so! Aaron rang the bell of the top floor apartment. From the intercom he heard a creaky "Who is it?"

"Mail delivery," Aaron shouted and the door opener buzzed promptly. The trick nearly always worked. Already halfway through the door, Aaron took a last, deep drag, flicked the butt aside and sprinted up to the third story.

Once he'd reached the door, he rang the bell again to ensure that there was really nobody inside. Since the man operated on his own - or had operated, to be more precise – Aaron didn't anticipate a reaction. He was right. The door opened easily and now he was standing right in the middle of the two-room apartment which had been the Huntsman's office.

Aaron knew where to look. First he checked the desk, pulled out the storage container underneath and tipped it over. He actually found a brown envelope with packaging tape glued to the back. The man had told the truth.

Aaron tore the envelope open to reveal a stack of copies. He quickly scanned through them and immediately recognized their significance. The copies clearly limited the range of potential suspects. With a satisfied smile, Aaron put the documents back into the envelope and stuffed it into his jacket pocket.

Then he turned on the computer. The Huntsman had also revealed the password: *Melinda*. Aaron soon found the files he was looking for. He quickly deliberated if he should take the whole PC with him, but that would indicate a burglary and invite unnecessary questions. He decided to copy the files onto his USB and delete them from the computer. So he started the Eraser program on his USB stick to permanently delete the data from the hard drive. While the computer was busy deleting the files, he looked around the office to ensure he hadn't left any evidence that he'd been here. Even if it was unlikely that anyone would notice tiny changes, he didn't want to take the risk. Nothing must imply a break-in.

Half an hour later, the Eraser program had done its job. Aaron was now convinced that the involuntarily terminated interrogation had revealed the truth. Apparently the Huntsman had really not known any more than he had told. Aaron shut down the computer and left the office as undetected as he had entered it.

He had everything he needed.

*

Frankfurt, Ulmenstraße, 1200 Hours. Markus was pleased with himself. He was standing in his office mentally organizing the information he had collected. For once, he decided to clear his desk so he could document everything properly and fully focus. First he stacked all his research papers and looked for a suitable place on the shelf for them. It was hopeless. All his shelves were already overflowing. He spontaneously started a new pile on the floor.

Mission accomplished, he sat down at his unusually tidy desk and got the latest official statements from the police and the Central Bank. Then he wrote the online version for the *HNP*. Before sending it, he critically proofread it one last time.

BIGGEST HEIST IN GERMANY'S HISTORY
100 MILLION IN GOLD STOLEN

THIS MORNING AS YET UNIDENTIFIED PERPETRATORS AMBUSHED A THREE TON GOLD TRANSPORT. THE GOLD WAS ON ITS WAY BACK FROM NEW YORK TO BE ADDED TO THE EXISTING GOLD RESERVES IN FRANKFURT'S TAUNUSANLAGE. BUT IT NEVER ARRIVED. "WE HAVE NEVER HAD ANY INCIDENTS WHILE RETRIEVING THE GOLD FROM THE US," THE CENTRAL BANK'S PRESS OFFICER STATED WHEN QUESTIONED.

ALLEGEDLY THE ARMORED VAN TRANSPORTING THE CAREFULLY STACKED GOLD BARS IS IMPOSSIBLE TO OPEN FROM THE OUTSIDE. YET THE PERPETRATORS STILL MANAGED TO MAKE THE GOLD TOGETHER WITH THE VAN AND ITS CREW VANISH WITHOUT A TRACE THIS MORNING FROM BUCHENBUSCH IN NEU-ISENBURG.

ALL THAT REMAINED WAS AN OVERTURNED MILITARY JEEP WHICH HAD ESCORTED THE TRANSPORT AND A

CONSIDERABLE AMOUNT OF CARTRIDGE CASES, A BUGGY AND A MERCEDES WHICH HAD EVIDENTLY JUST HAPPENED TO BE AT THE CRIME SCENE.

WELL INFORMED SOURCES BELIEVE IT IS POSSIBLE THAT ONE OF THE SOLDIERS IN THE ARMORED VAN WAS AN ACCOMPLICE. A HEAVY DUTY FORKLIFT FOUND AT THE SITE, STOLEN FROM THE HAULAGE FIRM HOLLMANN DURING THE NIGHT, HOWEVER, CRONTRADICS THE THEORY. THE PERPETRATORS COULD HAVE USED IT TO LOAD THE VAN AND CREW ONTO A GETAWAY TRUCK. IT IS ALSO LIKELY THAT THE GETAWAY TRUCK WAS EQUIPPED WITH DENSE LEAD SHEATHING TO OBSCURE THE TRANSPONDER SIGNAL WHICH OTHERWISE REVEALS THE EXACT POSITION OF THE ARMORED VAN. MANFRED KRÜGER, FEDERAL POLICE PRESS OFFICER, REFUSED TO COMMENT ON THE GROUNDS THAT THE INVESTIGATIONS HAT NOT YET REVEALED ANYTHING CONCRETE. THE PUBLIC IS BEING ASKED TO CONTACT ANY POLICE DEPARTMENT WITH RELEVANT INFORMATION.

OK, that's ready to go. Plus two photos of the loading operation at the airport this morning and several of the crime scene. That should do it.

Was the escort in cahoots with the perps? Markus pondered. Anyway, until some concrete evidence solved the puzzle, he had to rely on speculation.

He was looking forward to his date with Lena that evening.

*

Frankfurt, Federal Police Situation Center, 1200 Hours.
"This is Manfred Krüger from the Public Relations Department, Chief."

"What is it?" Hartmann asked. For the duration of the investigations his office was located adjacent to the conference room. The furniture had evidently been procured from the same storage that had also furnished the room beside his: a table with a gray, plastic coated top, in front of it a swivel chair on casters with a half-height backrest whose frayed, anthracite upholstery on the seat and the armrests indicated numerous previous occupants. On the table, between phone and monitor, a self-supporting picture frame with a slightly faded photograph of Hartmann, his wife and their two children. *Two years to retirement,* he thought. The children were grown up by now, as indirectly evidenced by the photo's yellow tint. The room smelled musty.

"A journalist just called me to ask for a statement about a forklift. Apparently it was stolen from some haulage firm last night and is now at the scene of the armed robbery," Manfred Krüger came straight to the point.

"So? We already knew that," Hartmann replied gruffly. He turned his chair around to face the wall and got up. He had pinned a road map of Neu-Isenburg, a sketch of the crime scene and various pictures and photos of the vehicles involved onto the plasterboard wall with red thumbtacks. Hartmann took the picture of a forklift and repositioned it on the top left beside the map. The collage was the only thing adding a bit of color to the bleak room.

"I just wanted to inform you that he's about to publish it in the *Hessische Neueste Presse*. In his article he will also speculate about the forklift having been used to load the armored van onto a truck with lead sheathing. He reckons that's how the robbers immobilized the transponder signal."

"They boy's good," was Hartmann's now slightly more

amiable reply. "So far that's exactly our reconstruction as well. Did he ask anything else?"

"Yes he enquired about the two passengers in the Merc. He knew their names and was wondering if they were doing alright at the University Hospital."

"I hope you didn't comment on that and indirectly confirm his findings!"

"Of course not. But I guess he was just trying to test how I'd react."

"What's the guy's name?"

"Markus Manx. I'd never heard of him before."

"Thank you. Please inform me if he calls you again for another update." The Chief of Police hung up.

Hartmann scribbled *Markus Manx!* on his notepad and gathered his documents. He remembered the crisis committee's next meeting at three o'clock, knowing that he urgently needed some results by then. Minister for Special Affairs Stahl was an extremely impatient man.

*

Frankfurt, Taunusanlage Subway Station, 1239 Hours. Markus took the city train to the University Hospital. The trip only took ten minutes.

At lunchtime the train was quite empty. Markus sat on a window seat and let his thoughts run free. Some real investigative journalism again, at last. Something completely different from those trivial tabloid articles. It felt great! As a young reporter he had loved the snooping. The digging into things other people would rather forget. Sensitive investigations were right up his alley. But one could also get badly burned in the process, as he had learned the hard way. In the past, his research had taken him to the red-light district in the city of Offenbach. The deeper he had looked into the backgrounds and connections within the pimp milieu, the more exciting it had been. But also the more risky. That the pimps had sometimes threatened to beat him up had been a downright thrill, kind of the icing on the cake. Until everything went badly wrong one day.

"Can you get that, honey?" Markus had shouted over to his then wife Claudia because he had been busy descaling the coffee maker. Their two children, Lisa, eight at the time, and the six-year-old Max, were at school.

"Mrs. Manx?" the caller had said without revealing his name.

"Yes. Who is this?"

"Doesn't matter!" was the rough reply. "Don't stick your nose into other people's business and look after your family! We know what school Lisa and Max go to."

That was it.

The caller knew the children's names and their school! The blatant threat was devastating. Claudia, who usually reacted quite calmly to unexpected events, was inconsolable. It took days until they let the kids cycle to school on their own again.

A few weeks later they had suppressed the incident, at least for the time being.

But the next warning wasn't long coming. Fortunately Claudia had been out shopping.

"Stop your fucking snooping, Manx! By the way... where are Lisa and Max right now?" asked a sly voice. That was all, but it was enough. Several zillion alarm bells started ringing in Markus's head.

It was half past eleven. School would be over in half an hour! Markus rang the secretary just in case.

"Classes have been dismissed early on account of the heat. The children went home about an hour ago," the friendly secretary told him. She knew more or less every child in the small place and was happy to oblige. "Lisa and Max, too," she said.

"But...," before Markus could voice his indignation over the school administration's irresponsible behavior, she added: "All the children had a note for their parents two days ago."

That idiotic note listing potential days and times of the kids being let off early because of the heat had escaped Claudia's and his attention because their children had never shown it to them.

Damn it! Markus felt his pulse racing after ending the call. He grabbed his leather jacket. *Where are the kids? I'll never forgive myself if something happened to them!* He snatched the car keys and ran to the door.

At that moment the bell rang. Lisa and Max stood beaming outside the door.

"They let us go early, dad, because of the heat!"

He trivialized what had happened to Claudia. But he was visibly shaken by the repeated threats. At times he would wake up remembering it all.

They now completely emptied the kids' bags every day to ensure nothing like it would ever happen again. They also quickly decided that the children would no longer cycle to school. Either Claudia or Markus would bring them and the other would collect them.

They drew up a timetable.

A few weeks later another situation proved to be the final straw. It subsequently made Markus stop his investigative research into the Offenbach red-light district.

I happened on a Tuesday. Claudia had taken the children to school that morning. Markus was scheduled to collect them at half past twelve. He had put in a brief appearance at the office and been slightly delayed by a traffic accident. But at thirty five minutes past twelve he was waiting outside the school gates. A few children were still leaving the building; others were waiting for their parents outside. There was no sign of Lisa and Max though. And the two of them were always on time... Markus waited for another few minutes. Still no sign of his kids.

His heart nearly skipped at beat. He sprinted across the schoolyard – his children's classroom was empty. On to the secretary's office.

"Lisa and Max have been collected by a young woman. I only saw her briefly from the back."

Markus heaved a sigh of relief. *I must have forgotten that it was Claudia's turn to collect them.*

"Thank you," he muttered as he left. *Those threats are slowly driving me insane,* he thought.

"Mid thirties, about five foot six, brunette," the secretary shouted after him. There was little she missed. The windows in her office, one facing the front door, the other the schoolyard, guaranteed a next to perfect view. Her inbred curiosity took care of the rest.

Her description hit Marcus like a knife in the back. *Claudia is a blonde not a brunette. This time it really happened. All my fault. Damned holdup. Why didn't I leave ten minutes earlier. I have to warn Claudia straight away!*

But Claudia didn't answer her phone. Instead her voicemail said: "Please leave a message after the tone… beep."

"This is Markus. Ring me back right away, Claudia. Something terrible has happened."

Should I call the police or find Claudia first. Markus decided on the latter option. He searched the stores Claudia was going to visit that day. NOTHING! A panicky phone call to two of her closest girlfriends. STILL NOTHING! Then back home. Desperate and soaked in sweat Markus climbed out of his car. *How can I possibly explain the ab-*

duction to the cops? They'll declare me insane if I request a manhunt after the kids have been just five minutes late. How could they possibly understand how urgent this is? His thoughts were all over the place.

Or would the investigating officers just try to play down the issue: "Calm down, Mr. Manx. Tell us again what happened from the start and slowly, please. Most children's disappearances can be easily explained..."

Markus' head was spinning. He still tried to keep it together and get his thoughts in order. *What should be the first, decisive step?* Incredibly agitated, he unlocked the door to his house.

To be greeted by the smell of freshly brewed coffee and cake. Claudia and her best friend Susanne had set the table for afternoon refreshments. They were busy chatting while Lisa and Max were playing softball in the garden!

A glance at the weekly timetable showed that it had been Claudia's turn to pick up the children. She had stopped the car outside the school in a no parking zone, the engine running. Susanne had got out to collect the children, he learned. *Thank God, nothing happened!* Markus thought and took a deep breath. The relief was incredible.

And still both Claudia's and Markus' nerves were more and more on edge. The tension between them kept growing in the weeks to come. Only a few short months later they had parted ways.

The kids didn't suffer from our separation. We're both taking good care of them, Markus tried to justify what had happened eight years earlier in his mind. Ever since he had written a lot for the tabloids. *There's also life before death*, he liked telling his baffled colleagues whenever they asked awkward questions.

"Next stop, Stresemannallee," the announcement over the speakers catapulted him back to reality. He picked up his backpack and started walking towards the University Hospital. Since his divorce he hadn't been able to afford a car.

*

Berlin, American Embassy, 1300 Hours. Peter Redman, CIA Coordinator for Europe, glanced across the Stelenfeld Holocaust Memorial. His office on the fifth floor of the American Embassy had a striking view over thousands of up to 16 feet high cement blocks. An oppressive feeling... In the background the redeveloped Potsdamer Platz. Two doors to the right of his office were the rooms of the U.S. Ambassador to Germany.

A moment later, Aaron entered. After a short greeting, they sat down opposite each other at the conference table. Aaron briefed Redman on the second half of the investigations. The *Huntsman* was actually called Felix Armbrüster. They often used code names during an operation to avoid a person's real name. Aaron handed Redman the documents he had found in Armbrüster's apartment and the USB flash drive with all the electronic data. Before he left, he advanced some suggestions about how to proceed from here on.

Peter Redman sat back down at his desk and pushed the computer mouse to the side to make room for the documents Aaron had given him. A little yellowed, standard US format, the pages slightly wider and shorter than the German A4 size. The top one contained an American goldmine's production figures for the past few years.

Then Redman clicked his way through some of the data on the USB before leaning back in his comfortable executive chair. Bullseye! That Armbrüster guy had done a great job and tapped into a good source. The data had never been published in its present form, hence the leak must be inside the mining company itself. This considerably narrowed down the group of suspects – only one of the employees with access to the secret production data could be the potential traitor. Unfortunately nobody within that group could be definitely pinpointed. The copied computer data didn't solve the problem either.

Redman dialed a phone number in the States. He didn't care that it was now six o'clock in the morning in the USA.

The informer had to be found as soon as possible before he could do more damage.

*

Frankfurt, University Hospital, 1305 Hours. "Hello, can you direct me to Elisabeth and Franz Altmeier's room?"

"They're in this building, room 246 on the third floor. Up the stairs and then the first left," was the metallic sounding response through the intercom.

Wonderful, Markus thought. *They've already been moved from the ER, so they must be doing fine. That will make it much easier.*

Soon after he stood outside their room. Only two names on the sign beside the door. The right names. He knocked, somebody said "come in", he opened the door and entered the room.

"Hello, Mrs. Altmeier, Mr. Altmeier," he cautiously started the conversation. "My name is Markus Manx. This morning I saw your Mercedes in Buchenbusch in Neu-Isenburg and I noticed the *Pet Cemetery* sticker. I also love animals and I'd like to ask you some questions. Can you spare a few minutes?"

Elisabeth and Franz Altmeier were sitting in their beds over a late lunch. A band-aid was stuck to the woman's forehead; her husband had no visible external injuries. They had obviously both been very lucky.

"Do you want to discuss a pet funeral with us?" Elisabeth Altmeier asked skeptically.

"No, absolutely not," Markus replied with a smile. "I'm here to ask you about the armed robbery this morning. I'm a journalist and I'm writing an article about it for the *Hessische Neueste Presse*."

Markus could feel himself tensing up. Statements like that could lead to the critical moment for a reporter. Either they'd throw him out right away and he'd have to leave with his tail between his legs or they would be positively disposed towards the press and readily volunteer some information.

Franz Altmeier put down his forkful of potato salad.

"Do you intend to publish our names in your article?"

"Don't worry, Mr. Altmeier. I'll do whatever you prefer. I'd gladly print your names, but if you don't want me to, I won't reveal my source to anybody."

"We won't be able to tell you a lot, anyway," his wife said. "Everything happened so fast. We were driving down Buchenbusch when the van suddenly braked in front of us. My Franzy couldn't stop in time. But he still had his wits about him and avoided the van at the very last second. Otherwise we would have crashed right into it."

Franz Altmeier grinned at his wife's praise. "Unfortunately there was a tree in the way," she continued. "And when we hit it, those balloon things exploded."

"Airbags, darling," her husband gently corrected her.

"Airbags so. They're great, really. I only slightly hurt my forehead. Without them we wouldn't have gotten away so lightly. I don't dare thinking about it…"

"And what happened next?" Markus stirred the conversation back to the heist.

"Two masked men with submachine guns were standing in front of the military jeep and fired shots," Franz Altmeier took over. "One of them ran over to us and tore open the driver's door. Nearly at the same time somebody else ran to my wife's door. We both held up our hands so they wouldn't shoot. But they apparently didn't want to harm us and just sedated us."

"They sedated you?" Markus probed incredulously.

"Yes. They held a cloth to our mouths and noses and suddenly everything went black. The doctors here told us it was probably chloroform. It smelled kind of sweet as they said it would. They won't know anything more definite until they've analyzed our blood samples."

"Incredible," Markus sympathized. But he still needed more.

"Did you notice anything else before you were sedated? Did anyone get out of the armored van for instance?"

"No. I was so terribly scared of that man with the rifle, I didn't see anything else."

"Submachine gun, darling..."

Turning to Markus, Franz Altmeier confirmed: "It happened exactly as my wife said."

"Right. Thank you. By the way, do you want me to mention your names or not?"

A moment of silence. "I think it's better if you leave us out of it," Franz Altmeier decided and his wife nodded. "We don't want any hassle and just forget about the whole thing."

"No problem. I won't mention your names, I promise. And now I shall leave you in peace. Oh... may I give you my phone number in case you remember anything else?" He put his card on the nightstand.

"I hope you get well soon and thank you very much for your help."

Markus left the room and walked out of the hospital. *I didn't learn an awful lot, but it could have been worse. They could have refused to talk to me.*

On the train back to his office he thought about the possible detailed sequence of the robbery. At least his theory about the forklift and the getaway truck hadn't been contradicted. And it had again been confirmed that the perps were absolute pros who had evidently not wanted to harm the Altmeiers.

The couple had presumably just been at the wrong place at the wrong time. But he still had no concrete indications as to where the other four people involved had disappeared.

*

Frankfurt, Federal Police Situation Center, 1500 Hours. "Gentlemen," Hans-Joachim Hartmann opened the second gold crisis meeting. He looked visibly depressed. "Unfortunately, despite enormous efforts and the involvement of numerous police departments, we still can't report any progress in our investigations regarding the missing vehicles. It's unbelievable. The gold robbers have vanished without a trace. We've searched several factory buildings without success. Umpteen road blocks and hundreds of vehicle inspections were also fruitless. The perpetrators are still at large."

His summary evoked a nervous mumbling amongst those present. Everyone knew only too well that the first few hours after a crime were crucial. If there were no arrests during that time, the investigations could drag on for weeks or even months. Perhaps they would never catch the robbers who had made no mistakes whatsoever so far.

"Before I go into the details, I have some positive news: About an hour ago three of the four soldiers involved in the gold transport were found alive and mainly unharmed. The robbers abandoned them in Offenbach. One of my colleagues will update you in the next few minutes about the results of their interviews."

"That's positive," General Steiner conceded. "But what about the fourth soldier?"

Hartmann hesitated: "We have to assume that he's dead." Silence in the room. One could have heard a pin drop onto the floor.

"And how do you figure that?" Steiner interrupted the tense silence.

"As I said this morning, we found a lot of blood in the escort jeep. It's from a person with blood type A. The co-driver has blood group O and is uninjured, as we now know. It is therefore unlikely that the driver survived considering the amount of blood in the jeep."

"Then it was cold-blooded murder," commented Stahl, the Minister for Special Affairs, who attended the meeting via video link. Larger than life, he was presently looking at them from screen 1. Today the men weren't sitting around the table, but had arranged their chairs on one side of the room, facing the monitor and the video camera.

"Sadly that's what we have to assume. But let us address forensics' other findings at the crime scene," Hartmann continued. "The seventy nine cartridge cases come from two different submachine guns of the Israeli brand Uzi. Evidently magazines with forty rounds of ammunition each were used. One of the magazines must have been completely emptied. In the other case, one cartridge is missing."

"What can we conclude from the weapons?" Bernd Brandner asked.

"Not much, unfortunately. The Uzi is the most widely sold and used submachine gun. Armies and police forces all over the world deploy them. The magazine size of forty rounds is unusual. More normal are twenty five or thirty two rounds. As far as I know, our army uses magazines with thirty two."

"You're right. We currently still mostly deploy the old MP2 models although we are gradually replacing them with the more up-to-date MP7," said General Steiner, leaning slightly over the table, his upper body directed at the microphone in the middle.

Hartmann had often noticed that people at a video conference no longer spoke to each other but addressed the monitor. The worse the video link, the louder they talked although, in this instance, everyone in the room except one person sat only twenty inches apart. For that reason Hartmann hated video conferences. He didn't agree that modern forms of communication were better than the old ways. *Never mind. Only two more years to my retirement. After that people can beam each other back and forth, for all I care, in 3D or whatever they like.*

"Thank you, General. We are currently feeding the ballistic data of the cartridges we found into our database. But we're not very hopeful. The perpetrators won't have used registered weapons. Interviewing the local residents unfortunately didn't yield much either. Nobody witnessed the raid from the beginning. Only after she heard shots, one woman looked out the window. But her statement just confirmed what we already know. The same applies to the two people in the Mercedes who nearly crashed into the armored van."

"Did I hear you correctly? They drove behind the van, saw everything and are still alive?" Friedrich Gmeiner interrupted in disbelief.

"Not quite. After the driver couldn't brake in time, he swerved to the right. Their airbags opened, so the couple wasn't badly injured. Then they were sedated and left in their car. They subsequently only witnessed part of the ambush."

"And to what extent were you able to reconstruct the robbery?" Brandner probed.

"We're still missing pieces of the puzzle," Hartmann started when there was a knock on the door. It was Nils Schuhmacher, an experienced colleague of Hartmann's, who was in charge of the investigations.

"We have the first results from the interviews with two of the soldiers, Chief."

"Come in, Schuhmacher."

"Gentlemen," Hartmann interrupted the meeting, "let's have a look at the latest findings." And turning to Schuhmacher, "Tell us, please."

"The situation assessment or the interview recordings first?"

"The recordings, so we can form our own view. Use monitor 2," Hartmann replied.

"It's just a voice file. No image."

Nils Schumacher inserted the USB drive into the port marked '2'.

Monitor 2 remained blank, but they heard a crackling noise from the speakers, then Schuhmacher's voice introducing himself and stating the time and date.

"First Interview with First Lieutenant Schmidt, commander in charge of the held up transport." Somebody cleared his throat. "Lieutenant Schmidt, please describe what happened from the beginning."

Schmidt: "I can't remember the attack itself. The last thing I recall is a black vehicle racing towards us from the left. Probably a VW SUV. From the time it crashed into us, I draw a blank. I must have passed out."

Schuhmacher: "When did your memory come back?"

Schmidt: "When I regained consciousness, I was sitting on the floor in a dark room. My hands were tied behind my back. I could feel what I guess were cable ties cutting into my wrists."

Schuhmacher: "Were you alone in that room?" Or with your comrades?"

Schmidt: "I couldn't hear any sounds or breathing close to me. Only voices from the next room. Suddenly the light went on and two men entered. Their faces were masked with balaclavas."

Schuhmacher: "Did they wear uniforms?"

Schmidt: "No, they were all wearing the same jeans and sweaters. Also gloves, military boots and the balaclavas I mentioned. All their clothes were black and looked the same."

Schuhmacher: "What did the men do after they came into the room?"

Schmidt: "The taller one, at least 6 foot 2, yanked me up from the floor and started interrogating me. He wanted to know the names of the soldiers in the convoy. Then he asked me how the transport was armed and protected."

Schuhmacher: "And?"

Schmidt: "I told him. Then he wanted me to order Sergeants Nahgold and Jakobi in the armored van to open the vehicle from the inside. I informed them that they both had clear instructions not to open it and that they would refuse the order."

Schuhmacher: "And then?"

Schmidt: "The taller one pushed me to ground and they both left. I was in a changing room with metal lockers. Then the lights went off."

Up to this point, the First Lieutenant had been in control of himself; now his voice sounded shaky. "The voices in the next room got louder. Somebody was roaring at someone. I couldn't hear what was said. Then there was a muffled shot."

Schuhmacher: "Relax, Lieutenant Schmidt. Take a deep breath."

Schmidt: "The door was pushed open. The tall guy pulled me up and out of the room. We were standing in a large warehouse. The armored van was there and Corporal Ali was lying in front of it, covered in blood. He was definitely dead."

They could all hear Schmidt taking deep breaths in and out. His voice faltered. "They had shot Ali in the head. The van's windshield was splattered with blood and…" Schmidt didn't finish the sentence. His voice sounded as if he was trembling all over.

Schuhmacher. "Slowly… take your time."

Schmidt: "The tall guy pulled me real close to the van and pushed my face against the windshield. Everything happened very fast. I recognized Nahgold and Jakobi inside the driver's cab. They looked terrified, white as ghosts. The tall guy held a gun with a silencer to my temple. I didn't understand what he was saying, I was that scared. I guess I pleaded with him a few times. I didn't want to die… Suddenly the driver's cab was opened from the inside and Nahgold got out."

Schuhmacher: "Go on."

Schmidt: "That's all I remember. Somebody hit me on the head and I passed out again. My memories only start again from when we were found."

Schuhmacher: "How many perpetrators could you indentify?"

Schmidt: "At least three inside the warehouse. All of them dressed the same and wearing balaclavas."

Schuhmacher: "Thank you, Lieutenant!... End of the first interview with First Lieutenant Schmidt, Commander of the transport."

A crackling noise from the loudspeaker, then silence until Nils Schuhmacher formally announced the second interview, again with time and date.

"First interview with First Sergeant Nahgold, driver of the armored van. Please describe what happened, Sergeant Nahgold. Start with the accident in Neu-Isenburg."

Nahgold: "This car appeared out of the blue and rammed our lead vehicle from the left. The jeep overturned. By slamming hard on the brakes I just about managed to stop the van before it would have crashed into the jeep."

Schuhmacher: "Who else was at the scene of the accident?"

Nahgold: "Two mothers with their buggies and a vehicle behind us that couldn't brake in time."

Schuhmacher: "Were the women injured?"

Nahgold: "No, the jeep had already passed them by a couple of yards. At first I assumed it was a traffic accident. The jeep was lying on its passenger side. Suddenly several persons opened fire on the jeep."

Schuhmacher: "How many?"

Nahgold: "I can't remember."

Schuhmacher: "You stayed in the cab?"

Nahgold: "Yes."

Schuhmacher: "Did you send a distress message?"

Nahgold: "I did, but suddenly the cabin went dark. We could not longer see what was happening outside. Just like somebody had thrown a black blanket over the van. Then the vehicle started shaking and moving. I belief we were lifted onto something and driven away. It was all very quick. Just took a minute or two perhaps."

Schuhmacher: "Did you maintain radio contact with the command center?"

Nahgold: "Jakobi tried the whole time, but there was no

more contact. Even after the jerking stopped a little later. Suddenly it got real bright inside the cabin. Somebody had pulled off the blanket or whatever it was."

Schuhmacher: "Could you see Schmidt and Ali?"

Nahgold: "I'd no idea where they were and if they were still alive. One of the masked kidnappers came over and demanded we open the doors. They told us we'd be fine. We refused as per our orders. He started yelling at us that they'd be able to open the vehicle anyway. That we'd pay dearly for every minute we wasted." Nahgold's voice was fading.

Schuhmacher: "Here, have some water."

Nahgold: "He went into a side room. When he came back, he was dragging Ali behind him. He jerked him up and pressed his back against our windshield. Then he asked us again to open the van. When we didn't react, he shot Ali right before our eyes. Jakobi screamed. I was paralysed with the horror of it all."

Schuhmacher: "What happened next?"

Nahgold: "He just dropped Ali and went back into the side room. This time he returned with Lieutenant Schmidt and pushed him against the bloody windshield. I could see Schmidt's face. He was downright whimpering. I think he kept saying "please, please." Then the masked guy repeated his demand and we opened the door. When I got out of the van, somebody pressed a cloth in my face. I lost consciousness."

Schuhmacher: "How many men did you count?"

Nahgold: "Five in the hall. Three of them standing in front of the van and I could see two more in the rearview mirror."

Schuhmacher: "What's the next thing you remember?"

Nahgold: "Somebody threw us out of a mini bus. I was still very drowsy and can't recall any details."

Thus ended the interview with First Sergeant Nahgold, the driver of the transport. The loudspeakers fell silent. Deathly quiet in the room. Schuhmacher hadn't sat down the whole time. Instead he was standing in front of monitor 2, his hands behind his back. With the speakers to his left and right it seemed like the words came out of his mouth and not the USB drive.

"And now your assessment of the situation," Hartmann interrupted the awkward silence.

"The third soldier isn't yet fit for questioning," Schuhmacher started. "One: we take it as a certainty that Corporal Ali, the driver of the jeep, was shot dead by the perpetrators. Two: neither of the soldiers reported that any of the perpetrators spoke a dialect or a foreign language. This indicates a German background. Three: the precise execution and the elaborate planning of the attack show certain military characteristics. To spare the prisoners also points to an army code of conduct. We estimate that between ten and twenty people were involved."

"How does the murder of the driver fit into the picture?"

"We can't yet say for definite. But we suspect that he already died during the attack or soon after due to heavy blood loss. But since First Lieutenant Schmidt fainted as a result of the collision, he can't tell us anything. And he would have been the only direct witness. The two sergeants in the armored van couldn't see how Corporal Ali reacted in the escort jeep. Perhaps he drew his weapon and that's why the robbers shot him. But that's only conjecture."

"Thank you very much, Mr. Schuhmacher. You may leave," Hartmann dismissed his colleague. The authentic audio recordings of the interviews had shocked everyone. Nobody spoke. Finally they agreed to meet again at 9 a.m. the following morning.

The air in the conference room smelled stale now.

Hartmann opened the windows before he was the last to leave the room and disappear into his office. Just like the other members of the crisis committee, he still had to digest the latest news. One thought kept preying on his mind: *if the driver of the jeep had already died at the scene of the robbery, and in view of the blood found there, the gold robbers had shot a dead man to get the drivers to open the armored van.*

*

Frankfurt, Ulmenstraße, 1500 Hours. Back in his office Markus first checked the Central Bank and Federal Police homepages for updates. Nothing. *At least it's clear that they didn't get the perps yet,* he thought. *They'd publish an arrest as soon as they've slapped the handcuffs on.*

While he considered how to structure his article, the clock radio in the background announced the news.

THE POLICE IN OFFENBACH APPREHENDED THREE EVIDENTLY CONFUSED MEN…

He jumped up to stand beside the radio.

… ASSUMED TO HAVE BEEN UNDER THE INFLUENCE OF NARCOTICS. EARLY INDICATIONS POINT TO THE MEN BEING THE SOLDIERS GUARDING THE CENTRAL BANK'S GOLD TRANSPORT WHICH WAS ROBBED IN NEU-ISENBURG THIS MORNING.

That disproves the theory about Eastern European criminals who brutally kill all potential witnesses, Markus thought. *Releasing unarmed prisoners instead of shooting them may indicate some code of honor. But why did they only talk of three people?*

He sat down and avidly searched through the Central Bank's press releases he had only skimmed over in the morning. There it was. "Typical security arrangements for a gold transport," was the headline. "… always two people in the transport vehicle and two more people in an escort. All of them armed…"

I was right. There's one person missing. Considering the robbers' methods, there's no reason not to release the fourth man as well. Unless… he is dead! Or…he was an accomplice. But why all that forklift business? And why were there so many cartridge cases at the crime scene?

*

"Federal Police, Manfred Krüger," was the curt response from the other end of the line.

"Hello, Mr. Krüger, it's me again, Markus Manx."

"Hello, Mr. Manx. Are you trying to be my new best friend? This is your third call today already," jeered Krüger.

"True," Markus admitted, "but all good things come in threes. Besides, I have a few more questions that have only just come up."

Krüger took a deep breath: "Alright, let's get it over with."

"Is it true that one of the soldiers is dead?"

"How would *you* know that?" the officer finally asked.

A moment of silence.

"It's true then, I take it…"

"Please don't print that." Krüger exclaimed. "We aren't sure ourselves yet. We're still questioning the two passengers of the armored van and the escort's co-driver. But yes, we have to expect that one of the soldiers was killed during the raid."

"Great. Sorry, of course I don't mean great," Markus corrected himself. "Is it alright to write about it as a supposition in tomorrow's print edition of the *Hessischen Neuesten Presse*?"

"That's OK. But on no account publish it before let's say six o'clock this evening."

"If you promise not to release it either before that…"

"Agreed. What else do you want to know?"

"Is it correct that the soldiers were sedated with chloroform, just like the two civilians in the Mercedes?"

"You're obviously well informed! But you didn't get that officially from me either. We still don't have the results of the blood tests. Let me make you an offer: if you don't publish the information until after six, I promise to call you if it turns out it wasn't chloroform after all."

"Deal!" Markus agreed.

"I need your phone number… just in case."

Markus gave him the numbers of his office landline and his cell phone.

"Many thanks, Mr. Krüger. Talk to you soon, I guess," he ended the call.

Manfred Krüger didn't put the phone down, but immediately pressed a speed-dial key to put his boss in the picture.

*

Berlin, Office of the District Attorney, 1730 Hours. "The windshield of my driver's cabin was hit hard by something. It's a miracle it didn't shatter into a thousand pieces. There was no chance I could have stopped in time. You have to believe me! I couldn't see that there was someone standing on the bridge about to jump. It was already getting dark."

Herbert Mahler was still in a state of shock. It was his first accident involving a person. A suicide. At a yearly average of 700 to 900 deaths on railroad tracks, Mahler was aware that he would sooner or later be involved in one of them. Statistically two to three suicides would happen to him over the course of his career. One of the drivers, who covered a route particularly favored by suicide victims, had already experienced twelve of them. After a two week vacation, he'd always return to his job. Among his colleagues he was idolized, even though he was in no way proud of the record himself.

"Mr. Mahler, I'm aware that you're in no way to blame. But I still have to ask you some questions for the record."

D.A. Heinrichs knew the procedure inside out. This was his seventh suicide case of the kind.

"How fast were you driving before the man hurled himself in front of the train?"

"45 miles an hour, the stipulated speed limit."

"How exactly did the accident happen?"

"He must have jumped from the pedestrian bridge. He was still in midair when he hit my train. I only saw him when it was too late."

"I know this is very difficult for you, but can you describe if the man fell head or feet first?"

"It all happened so fast... As far as I remember he was nearly horizontal in the air... His head was slightly lower and was the first... to hit just below the windshield... His feet were a bit higher and bashed right into it."

Herbert Mahler kept holding back the tears while he was making his statement. The incident was clearly getting to him. He hadn't been able to look at the scattered remains of the corpse. The people who had to collect the bloody body parts were to be pitied. What a nightmare. How could they possibly cope with all that horror?

"Would you like to take a break, Mr. Mahler?" D.A. Heinrichs offered.

"No, no… I just want to get it over and done with."

"OK. …Did you see anyone else on the bridge or notice anything conspicuous?"

"I didn't. It was pretty dark already and I didn't pay a lot of attention to the bridge. I was looking at the tracks, you know…"

Heinrichs tried to find the right words to convince the man that this wasn't about holding him in any way responsible.

"Mr. Mahler, even if you had noticed the victim on the bridge, you would never have been able to brake in time. Don't blame yourself! I'm only trying to establish if the man jumped of his own accord or not."

"I have no idea."

"Let me stress again: it was absolutely not your fault. You didn't make any mistakes."

"I know. We've been trained to handle situations like this. But to be confronted with them in reality is still a shock," Herbert Mahler replied, consumed by self-doubt.

"Thank you, Mr. Mahler, I think that's enough for now! I'll be in touch over the next few days. Then we can calmly take another look at your statement. Feel free to call me should you remember anything else. Here's my card."

The train driver left the room. Heinrichs opened one of his desk's drawers and extracted the dead man's ID, credit cards and last belongings. Everything pointed at suicide.

But let's wait for the autopsy report, he thought. He neatly arranged everything on his desk and contemplated the victim's photo.

Why would anyone in the prime of his life like this Felix Armbrüster kill himself?

*

Frankfurt, Restaurant Hamsilos & Schenk, 1920 Hours.
Markus was ten minutes early and as nervous as he had been on his first ever date. When they'd bumped into each other at the café Wacker, Lena Eck had impressed him. He liked the type and not just her physical appearance. It was also her confident manner, he guessed... She'd spontaneously treated him to coffee... Then there was her smile. She'd downright bewitched him in those few minutes they'd shared.

I wonder what she'll be wearing, he thought while he was sitting at the table, waiting for her. *I hope she won't mind that I didn't change. Should I tell her that I didn't have time to drive home because of that gold business? Or should I just not mention the subject?*

He was as excited as a little boy waiting for Santa. *Christ, Markus, get a grip! Your clothes will do fine for this joint... But what if she doesn't like the Turkish décor. Or the plain furniture? Besides, this isn't exactly the most exclusive part of town.*

"Hi, Markus! Have you been waiting long?" Lena's voice brought him back to reality. He hadn't seen her come in. *Wow!* he thought. She was wearing a blue, white and red patterned mini dress under a dark brown leather jacket and knee high brown boots. *Casual, sexy and fashionable. Full marks,* was his mental verdict.

"No, I just got here," he lied. "May I take your jacket?"

What a gentleman, Lena thought. *Seems promising.*

"You picked an interesting place."

Interesting! Does that mean she finds it cheesy?

"I enjoy coming here. The fish is sensational. I hope you like fish?"

"I love fish," Lena said animatedly.

They both studied their menus. "What would you recommend?"

"I like the Loup de Mer or the Dorade Royale. They're both excellent."

"Oh, yes, sea bass or gilthead sea bream. Both very tasty."

Sea bass! Gildhead sea bream! Impressive.

They both put down their menus. And now? A little flirting? Some small talk? … None of it. Far from romantic, Lena started quizzing him.

"Tell me, Markus, why did you ask me about shielding a transponder earlier today?"

Markus felt a bit cheated. *Is she less interested in me than in my line of work. Is she just curious?*

"Because of the gold heist I mentioned this morning," he enlightened her.

Lena nodded, "Yes, I also heard about it on the radio earlier."

He continued: "I wondered how the robbers managed to abduct the armored van and its crew without the cops being able to locate the transponder signal."

"How do you think they did it?"

"I thought about that. When I was at the crime scene this morning, I found a heavy-duty forklift and called the company who owned it. Their name was on the driver's door. Turns out the forklift had been stolen during the night. Well, then I started suspecting that the transponder had been interfered with."

"Thumbs up, Detective!" Lena quipped. "You think they used the forklift to hoist the armored van onto another vehicle, let's say a big truck, covered in lead sheathing, so the transponder signal could no longer be located?"

She considered this for a moment while slightly biting the left side of her lower lip with her perfect, white teeth.

How cute, Marcus thought before Lena commented on his investigations.

"But the control center would have noticed right away when they couldn't pick up the signal. They would have instantly activated the alarm."

"True," Markus confirmed. "They presumably received a distress call even earlier over the radio. The perps must have known that, too. They just had to act fast, so they'd be gone before the police arrived."

"Risky, but not impossible. It's not far to the freeway from Neu-Isenburg. Or they hid in some warehouse. A normal truck wouldn't be conspicuous in those surroundings."

"Are you ready to order?" the waiter interrupted them, looking at Markus.

"What will you have?" Markus passed the buck to Lena.

"I'll have the bream. And an apple spritzer."

"Same for me, please, but a wheat beer instead of the spritzer."

"Good choice," the waiter nodded, taking down the order. Once he had left, Lena returned to their discussion. "Let's try and mentally reconstructed the sequence of events."

"Good idea, Deputy Eck," Markus said. "According to my theory somebody rammed the lead vehicle and disabled the armed escort. Then someone loaded the armored van onto a truck with the forklift. It should have only taken two minutes if everything was well planned. And now they had to make sure that the van could no longer be located."

"Not difficult," Lena contributed her technical knowledge. "All you have to do is clad the inside walls of the truck with various layers of materials that absorb high and low frequency signals, so nothing can get out."

"Sounds complicated."

"Well, I'm no expert. The perps presumably didn't know how well the armored van was equipped. They therefore had to include all possible bandwidths."

"Expert or not, at least we've made some more progress. How everything worked in detail isn't that important. But it is actually possible, isn't it?" Markus needed confirmation.

"I don't investigate gold heists in my precinct. Data theft is my area."

"I read that online. I googled you, you know," Markus smiled. "You've hacked into several company networks. I'll bet that requires a lot of systematic and logical thinking."

"Damn right, it does. But I hope you also read that I always announce my hacking activities beforehand. When I'm successful, I point out the system's flaws to the company concerned. I'm interested in exposing weaknesses so they can be addressed."

"Sounds a bit like journalism. We also research shortcomings, so something can be done about them after we've exposed them," Markus attempted a comparison. With less than moderate success."

"Not really. What could the tabloids possibly change? I googled you, too, of course." Now Lena also smiled. "If I may be so frank after we've only just met: I preferred your investigative journalism. Why did you switch to the trivial stuff?"

Markus flinched.

"That's a dark chapter from my past. Let's talk about it some other time, OK?"

This put a stop to the conversation and suddenly silence prevailed. Fortunately, a few seconds later, an invisible movie director sent over the waiter who relieved them from their temporary embarrassment when he served the fish. They switched to a more easily digestible subject.

Markus hadn't exaggerated. The fish was a dream and Lena evidently couldn't care less that this restaurant wasn't one of the more upmarket ones. He was glad. But he was even more delighted that his emotional faux pas had apparently not done any damage.

"What's for dessert, Detective?" Lena teased him from under her bangs. "Perhaps a tasty little robbery?"

Markus laughed. "OK, what would you do with three tons of gold?"

"If you're talking about the gold that was stolen, I doubt it would be easy to get rid of."

"That's for sure. It has a market value of one hundred million Euros. But we should deduct ten to twenty percent for money laundering. That would still leave enough to see the world and have some fun."

They became increasingly more relaxed as the evening progressed, discussing foreign travel, their professional visions and private dreams. They laughed a lot.

When Lena visited the restroom, Markus pulled a black, felt-tip pen from his jacket pocket. He took a cream-colored paper napkin from the next table and started to draw. The first few lines confirmed that the paper quality was suitable when the color didn't run. A few lines later revealed two large, almond-shaped eyes, followed by a perfect nose and a mouth with luscious lips. The lips were a little overemphasized, chin and high cheekbones nearly elfish. He quickly added ears, hair and neck.

Markus scrutinized the caricature. After a few more additions he signed it with his two Ms superimposed over each other in the bottom right corner. He was happy with his masterpiece, put the pen back in his pocket and placed the drawing on Lena's side of the table. Not a moment too soon; he could already see her at the other end of the room.

Once she had sat down again, she looked startled.

"Did you draw that?"

She picked up the napkin.

"Do you like it?"

"I sure do. A pretty good likeness. Don't tell me you just did that in the couple of minutes I was gone?" Lena asked, visibly impressed and flattered by the overstated beauty.

"May I?"

She didn't wait for his answer and quickly stowed the napkin away in her purse.

Markus told her about the pictures he occasionally drew for the newspapers. They appreciated his humorous portrayal of current topics. The payment was, however, just as meager as that for his articles.

Around 11 o'clock, after coffee, they finally left. Markus helped Lena into her leather jacket.

"Have you anything planned for tomorrow evening?" he wanted to know. Lena had made it very clear that she wouldn't 'invite him for coffee yet' in her apartment on only their second date.

Markus inwardly rejoiced at the 'yet'. Outwardly he remained offhand.

"Nothing in particular. What do you suggest?" she asked.

"I really enjoyed having dinner with you. I wouldn't mind a repeat."

"OK. Will we meet at the same time at the Gallo Nero?"

"Great. I'd like that," Markus replied, noticeably stunned by her forthright answer.

Lena kissed his cheek and disappeared nimbly in the direction of the parking garage.

Tuesday

Luxembourg, Banque Privée de Luxembourg, 0730 Hours. Frank Semeyer briskly turned into the Avenue Amélie and parked his BMW fifty yards further on with a spirited swerve in the bank's customer parking lot. The slightly dull, black metallic paintwork indicated that his car had seen better days. It had been a present to himself when his company, Semeyer Auto Parts, SEFAKO KG, had still been extremely profitable.

Semeyer was late and sprinted up the stairs to the entrance. The receptionist recognized him instantly and buzzed him through the door which automatically closed behind him. Semeyer and his firm had been with the BPL, the Banque Privée de Luxembourg, for what seemed like forever.

"Good morning, Mr. Semeyer. Mr. Bellini is expecting you," the woman at the front desk greeted him with a smile. She got up and escorted him through the foyer.

How kind, Semeyer thought, who knew very well how to find Mauro Bellini's office. Ever since he had started banking with the BPL, Mauro had looked after his accounts. He knew everything about Semeyer's business and hadn't changed office in the meantime.

The receptionist opened the door for the visitor. "Mr. Semeyer is here, Mr. Bellini."

"Lovely to see you, Frank!" Mauro Bellini welcomed him.

"Good morning, Mauro."

"How are you?"

"Well, I'm not exactly looking forward to today's transaction," Semeyer replied. "And how are *you*?"

"I'm fine, thank you."

Without it having been mentioned, Mauro Bellini was

well aware of the purpose of his client's visit today. SEFAKO had suffered badly through the China crisis. The company's costly expansion had led to more and more financial difficulties over the past two years.

"How was the freeway? Real busy?"

"Pretty much so," was Semeyer's short reply.

Heavy traffic had easily added an extra thirty minutes to the ride from his office in Saarbrücken to Luxembourg. His BMW M5 Touring's five liter engine and 507 horsepower hadn't made the least bit of difference.

"Can I get you some coffee or water?"

Mauro didn't bother offering tea. In all those years his client had never asked for it.

"No, thank you."

"Have a seat." Mauro gestured towards a comfortable armchair in front of an elegant Louis XVI style table.

"No, thanks," Semeyer said again. "Can we go straight to the vault? I'm in a bit of a rush today."

"Sure, Frank, certainly," Mauro Bellini replied and got up. He put on his suit jacket and led the way. At the elevator, he typed in a number combination and placed his right hand on the scanner beside it. The door opened and they rode down to the strongroom. They swiftly walked along the corridor. Whitewashed concrete walls; rooms with heavily protected doors lined the left and right. Bellini stopped outside one of them. A number combination and scanner also opened this one.

"I'll wait outside, Frank," Bellini explained the usual procedure.

Without answering, Frank Semeyer stepped into the vault, the heavy door closing behind him. He walked straight over to the data terminal in the middle of the room, entered the number of his deposit box and then a secret PIN before placing his hand on the scanner. The vault door locked itself with a dull, metallic thud. Nobody could enter from the outside now. Semeyer had complete privacy.

All the walls were lined with safe deposit boxes from top to bottom. Each box the same size, the same design, brushed stainless steel, all of them with an invisible 12 point bolt locking system, interior hinges. The only difference was the numbers engraved on them.

A few seconds later Frank Semeyer's box opened automatically. He extracted the steel container and lifted the lid to reveal a single gold bar besides various documents. After the turn of the millennium, when the economy was booming, SEFAKO had been able to build up a lot of reserves. Now only one gold bar remained. Semeyer had been forced to sell the others over the last couple of years to pump the proceeds back into the company and pay the wages.

At least the gold was a good investment, he thought. He had bought the 400 ounce bars for roughly 150,000 Euros apiece. Now they were worth nearly three times as much. Mauro Bellini had given him the tip back then.

Semeyer took out the last bar, pushed the container back and locked the deposit box again. His PIN and biometric recognition opened the vault from the inside.

"That didn't take long," was Bellini's comment as Semeyer re-emerged.

"Yeah, I'm done."

They went back to the office where Bellini had everything ready.

"Sign the sales order on the bottom right as always," he said and spread the documents he'd prepared on the table. "We'll lodge the exchange value to your personal account."

He handed the gold bar to an usher who had miraculously appeared out of nowhere. *Mauro probably has a button under his desk to summon people*, Semeyer thought, who was handling the transaction without displaying any visible emotions. *The Lord giveth and the Lord taketh away…*

Soon after the two gentlemen took their leave and Frank Semeyer hit the freeway back to Saarbrücken.

*

Luxembourg, Banque Privée de Luxembourg, 0750 Hours. The phone was ringing in Mauro Bellini's office.

"Would you come up to the trading floor, Mauro!" ordered the head of the BPL's Precious Metals Sales and Trading Department.

Less than five minutes later, Mauro Bellini faced the caller in person.

"Good morning, Etienne."

"Hello" replied Etienne Peeters, a highly attractive, middle aged Belgian lady. Wearing high heels, an extremely short skirt and far too much jewelry, to those who didn't know her she hardly looked like the woman in charge of Precious Metals Trading at a reputable private bank. But those who did also knew that she was perfectly informed about every movement on the market, about every rumor concerning the production, depositing or sales of precious metals. Allegedly she could spot forgeries blindfolded.

"What's so urgent, Etienne?"

She was holding a gold bar in her hand.

"What's this supposed to be, Mauro?"

"I don't understand, Etienne…"

She handed him the bar.

"This thing is anything but gold!"

"What?"

Bellini's face turned pale. "In my view, the thing, as you call it, is a 438 ounce Heraeus pure gold bar with an estimated market value of about four hundred thousand Euros."

"Far from it, sunshine! I've hardly ever handled such an amateurish fake. It looks alright at a first glance, but the density, the weight… it's all wrong. This is nothing but gold plated lead."

Bellini's face turned even paler.

"You're sure?"

"Absolutely!"

"I don't get it."

"Anyone who tries to flog fake gold on the market uses tungsten at least as the base metal because it has a similar density to gold. But nobody sells forgeries like that to a bank equipped with ultrasound and x-ray equipment," Etienne Peeters hissed.

"Right."

"Was your client on drugs today?" she added.

Mauro's world was shattered. *Semeyer a forger? Inconceivable!* "What do we do now?"

"You're not going to do anything for the time being."

"Shouldn't I inform my client?"

"No! You stay out of it, get it!? And whatever you do, don't tell your customer. I shall inform the authorities and the IRS. They'll do whatever it takes and grill your client," Etienne ended the conversation and picked up the phone. She knew exactly how to take it from here.

*

Frankfurt, Ulmenstraße, 0815 Hours. The clock radio's four red, flashing LED digits informed him that it was a quarter past eight. Markus Manx was sitting at his old wooden desk where he had been checking the news portals for the last half an hour.

The phone rang. Markus picked up to hear the sonorous, calm voice of Jonathan Schreiber, the *HNP's* editor.

"Good job, Markus, your online and print copy was excellent. The readers like the subject. The online article got plenty of clicks, so I need an update. As soon as possible and roughly the same amount of words as yesterday. OK?"

Schreiber had already hung up as Markus said: "Sure, no problem." He stretched his legs, rubbed his aching back – he tended to slouch in his chair – got up and coaxed another coffee from the usually reluctant machine in the kitchen. Although the paper cup dispenser presented him with three cups stuck together once more, at least the coffee maker worked without a hitch for once.

A positive omen? Let's see if the press guy from the police is available…

"Good morning, Mr. Manx," was the friendly greeting.

"Hello, Mr. Krüger. You already recognize my number?" Markus started pointedly casual.

"You may not believe it, but even the cops have modern phones. And since I entered your details in my contacts, your name appears on the display. But I suspect you didn't call to discuss the Federal Police's telephone system," Krüger jibed.

"You're right. I just wondered if you have any more news about the armed robbery."

"Well, nothing the public is yet supposed to hear."

"Does that mean you have a trail on the perps?" Markus probed. He wasn't going to be fobbed off that easily.

"We're working on it, Mr. Manx. We're working on it."

"Really, Mr. Krüger," Markus reproached him wryly, "yesterday I accommodated you and stuck to our agreement… Go on, tell me what you discovered by interviewing the soldiers. How did the heist actually happen?"

The press officer liked talking to someone who didn't take himself so seriously for a change. But he still wasn't prepared to part with classified information.

"I can't give you any details that may jeopardize the investigation. All I can tell you is that the guys operated pretty damn fast. It appears they threw some kind of cover over the armored van so the passengers couldn't see what was happening. Then they used the forklift to hoist the van onto a large truck and two minutes later they were gone. The truck must have been well screened to obscure any radio and tracking signals, just as you suspected yesterday. I'm afraid that's all I can tell you right now. I really am sorry, Mr. Manx."

"OK, that will have to do for the time being. Many thanks and have a nice day," Markus ended the call. To be on the safe side, he checked the Central Bank's homepage for news and, of course, read a number of articles his colleagues had written about the robbery. Perhaps he would find some information or ideas he could use for his update.

But he didn't come upon anything useful. Most of the coverage simply padded the report about the raid with background information about depositories and changing gold prices. One paper had asked 20 people across Germany what they would do with 100 million Euros in gold, nearly creating the impression that the robbers' audacity and ingenuity was commendable. That the Central Bank was an evil institution which had rightly been robbed. *How mad is that?*

Markus wanted to quickly publish his new information before somebody else got there before him. He started to write.

100 MILLION EURO IN 2 MINUTES
THE BIGGEST AND FASTEST ARMED ROBBERY OF ALL TIMES

POLICE INVESTIGATIONS INTO YESTERDAY'S SPECTACULAR HEIST OF A GOLD TRANSPORT ARE GOING. SO FAR WITH LITTLE SUCCESS.

THE RAID HAD EVIDENTLY BEEN PLANNED AND EXECUTED WITH MILITARY PRECISION. WHILE A CAR BRUTALLY RAMMED THE LEAD VEHICLE AND IMMOBILIZED IT, SOME OF THE GANG IMMEDIATELY THREW A COVER OVER THE ARMORED VAN BEHIND IT WHICH HAD COME TO A HALT. THE VEHICLE'S CREW THEREFORE COULDN'T WITNESS WHAT TOOK PLACE OUTSIDE.

THE ROBBERS USED THE SITUATION TO LOAD THE VAN ONTO A TRUCK, USING A FORKLIFT. LESS THAN TWO MINUTES LATER THEY HAD LEFT THE SCENE.

THE TRUCK WAS EQUIPPED IN A WAY THAT NO RADIO SIGNALS COULD BE DETECTED TO LOCATE THE ARMORED VAN, FACILITATING THE MOST SUCCESSFUL ESCAPE IN THE BIGGEST AND FASTEST HEIST OF ALL TIMES.

Markus wrote his report in one go. Then he read through it and added one or two style corrections.

An incoming email flashed on his monitor. As a response to an alert he had posted yesterday, Google automatically sent him any gold related news. The subject heading 'Luxembourg' aroused his curiosity. He quickly changed to his inbox.

+++ Police Grand-Ducale Luxembourg – Press Release – Caution: Counterfeit Gold Bullion +++

The guys in Luxembourg cumbersomely forge gold bars while the Germans just steal three tons of the real stuff,

Markus thought. *The latter option should be far more lucrative, no doubt.*

He opened the attached PDF with the actual press release.

A PRIVATE BANK INFORMED THE AUTHORITIES THAT AN UNNAMED INDIVIDUAL TRIED TO SELL A COUNTERFEIT GOLD BAR WEIGHING 440 OUNCES. THE POLICE ISSUED A WARNING THAT PRIVATE BUYERS SHOULD NOT PURCHASE PRECIOUS METALS FROM UNKNOWN SOURCES. WELL FORGED BARS ARE NOT OPTICALLY DISTINGUISHABLE FROM AUTHENTIC ONES.

The image underneath the newsflash showed the counterfeit bar; the inscription clearly legible: Heraeus – 997,4 – 13023,7 - 20863. Markus was fascinated. By now he was familiar with the inscription: Manufacturer – Pure Gold Content – Weight – Serial Number. He googled the name *Heraeus* and found a link to their press releases on their homepage. Another click revealed the firm's contact person for precious metals. Markus dialed the number.

"This is the Heraeus public relations department. What can I do for you?" announced a somewhat throaty but congenial woman's voice.

"Hello, my name is Markus Manx. I'm a freelance journalist based in Frankfurt. May I ask you a few questions about your products?"

"Sure, as long as you don't ask who bought how much from us and when," she replied pertly.

"I'm enquiring about a counterfeit 440 ounce gold bar that turned up in Luxembourg today. Do you produce bars of that seize?"

"We do, yes."

"But your homepage only lists bars weighing between

one gram to one kilogram…"

"Our homepage is tailored towards private investors who most often buy minted bars up to a kilo. That's why our product overview on the internet stops there."

"And who buys the big bars from you?"

"Sorry, but that is confidential."

"I'm not looking for names, just the type of investors."

"The so-called 12.5 kilo bars are purchased by central banks, gold funds and ultra-high-net-worth-individuals."

"OK. And the figure 997.4 on the bars is the fine gold content?"

"Exactly."

"I thought the bars always had a pure gold content of 999.9?" Markus checked.

"That's also correct. Minted bars for private investors always have a fine gold content of 999.9 and a precise weight like 100 grams embossed on it. But the older, cast gold bars may vary in fine gold content and weight."

"Is a fine gold content of 997.4 unusual?"

"Not at all. It's within the normal range of variation."

"You mentioned so-called 12.5 kilo bars. The forged one weighed more than 13 kilos. Can there be deviations of over 500 grams?"

"That's also not unusual."

"So the buyer got a real bargain seeing that he got an extra pound of gold for his money."

"That would have been a piece of luck, but an investor is always charged the exact fine gold weight, which means the gold purity multiplied by the actual weight."

"That's all extremely interesting. Thank you so much. I have one last question."

"Go ahead."

"Did you ever use the serial number 20863 for one of your bars?"

There was a slight delay while the PR woman was obviously looking this up.

"Yes," she said eventually, "we have used that number."

After a brief pause she added: "But every manufacturer can use any random number. So it could be one of ours, but isn't necessarily."

"But if it also has the Heraeus logo?"

"Then it's definitely ours. In that case, however, the number doesn't refer to a specific bar, but an entire melt."

"And what exactly is that?" Markus enquired.

"In the past roughly twenty bars were cast at the same time for the bigger investors. These bars are of the same purity, slightly differing weights and have the same serial number. The number you gave me applies to all twenty bars that were cast."

"So you produced twenty bars with the same number?"

"In this case yes."

"Can the individual ones still be sold separately?" Markus asked.

"Certainly, but it is unusual. And somebody trying to make a forgery would rather choose small, minted bars weighing considerably less than a kilo."

"Have you any idea who may counterfeit large bars?"

"We have never come across a forgery of cast 12.5 kilo bars or of a complete melt. I personally find it all very unusual, Mr. Manx."

Markus thanked her and hung up. *Why would a private individual forge one bar out of a melt and then offer it for sale to his own bank of all places? As soon as it was authenticated, he'd be busted.* Something didn't add up…

*

Frankfurt, Federal Police Situation Center, 0855 Hours.
Hartmann's field office smelled fresh; the window to the inner courtyard was wide open. The collection of images on the wall had grown overnight. Several arrows in blue marker connected the new additions to a coordinate on the street map. This red-circled point was very close to Rödermark near Neu-Isenburg.

In a foul temper, Hartmann viewed the various pieces of the puzzle. The results so far were meager, to say the least. But even if he had hardly anything to show himself, he hoped that the arrogant Gmeiner from the Federal Intelligence Service hadn't unearthed something of importance either. He could just picture the man's patronizing grin if he had.

Hartmann glanced at his wristwatch. The crisis committee meeting was due to start in five minutes. He shut down his computer, closed the window and went over to the still empty conference room where he arrived more or less at the same time as Gmeiner. *You look pretty exhausted,* Hartmann thought while shaking his rival's hand.

Normally a sure sign of not much success. He felt downright relieved. They both sat down at the middle of the table, facing the monitors.

Shortly after they were joined by Bernd Brandner from the Central Bank and General Alfred Steiner. Today the Minister of Special Affairs, Sven Stahl's angular face appeared on the middle, wall-mounted screen.

"Good morning, gentlemen," Hartmann opened the third meeting of the gold crisis committee. "Let me start with a brief summary of the intelligence my colleagues gathered yesterday evening and last night to reconstruct the raid."

Hartmann didn't omit even the smallest detail of their findings. If he couldn't announce any definite arrests, he wanted to at least create the impression that they had already achieved quite a lot.

"Respect! That sounds like precision planning," General Steiner commented once Hartmann had finished. "Avoiding unnecessary violence also indicates a military background."

"Have you been able to reconstruct the escape route? Or did you find any evidence pointing to the perpetrators," Stahl quizzed Hartmann.

"Well, we more or less know the route they took. The truck as well as several other vehicles involved in the heist drove to a warehouse in Rödermark, roughly ten miles further on. We suspect they arrived there as early as twenty five minutes after the robbery. That means at a time when the large-scale manhunt had only started. The police found the armored van, which had been opened, and a dented VW Touareg the perps used to ram the escort jeep. The VW had been reported missing two days previously. The license plates had been stolen the night before. We found numerous fingerprints and other DNA traces in both vehicles as well as in the warehouse. But we're apprehensive that none of them are the robbers'. So far the transport truck and other vehicles haven't been located."

"Not a lot," Stahl noted. The grim sound of his voice showed he wasn't exactly pleased with the weak results of the investigations. "Anything else that may be constructive? I'm in a rush to meet the Chancellor and I'd like to have some positive news for her."

Brandner and General Steiner shook their heads. Gmeiner stoically stared straight ahead as if he hadn't heard the question.

"We have some new evidence from Luxembourg," Hartmann continued his report. "This morning a German industrialist took a 12.5 kilo gold bar from his safe deposit box in Luxembourg and offered it for sale to his bank."

Hartmann leaned over the table and pressed some buttons on a keyboard. A large-sized image of the gold bar appeared on monitor 3.

"It turned out the bar was a forgery. That's unusual enough in itself. Nobody in their right mind would offer a counterfeit gold bar to his own bank, you'd think. But in this case the serial number led to the Central Bank's gold reserves."

Brandner winced, but nobody noticed. All eyes were on the monitor.

"My colleagues are in the process of establishing if the bar could be connected to the gold heist. I would appreciate if you could facilitate them as much as possible, Mr. Brandner."

"Certainly," Brandner agreed, outwardly confident. Inwardly he was scared of the results.

"OK. I can't really see what good it will do, but keep at it, Hartmann. I've got to see the Chancellor now. Can we meet again at half past four this afternoon?"

Everybody nodded. They wouldn't have dared to deny the Minister for Special Affairs' wishes anyway. Hartmann confirmed the time for all those present and terminated the connection. The other remaining members of the crisis committee stayed to exchange even the most insignificant information.

Hartmann leaned back. General Steiner reported on the fruitless questioning of the soldiers involved in the transport and their relatives by the military police. No suspicion of possibly being accomplices in the robbery had been revealed. Friedrich Gmeiner reluctantly admitted that the National Security Agency's wiretap operation of phone calls and emails hadn't yielded any clues although the range of keywords had been specifically expanded to include anything pertaining to the raid.

Hartmann was careful to conceal his glee over the agency's failure to produce results.

Finally the crisis committee disbanded with the horrible suspicion that the gold robbers had possibly committed the perfect crime.

*

Frankfurt, Ulmenstraße, 1105 Hours. The phone was ringing. The number seemed familiar to Markus, but he had no idea whose it was.

"Markus Manx," he answered the call grumpily.

"Hi, Markus, Lena here!" Her voice sounded as if she was pleased to have reached him.

"Hi, Lena, how lovely to hear from you. How are you?"

"I wanted to thank you for a lovely evening. And…"

Markus suddenly felt apprehensive. He was looking forward to their date. *Please, let her not cancel.*

"Can we meet half an hour later than arranged? At eight? I won't be able to make it otherwise."

Markus heaved a heartfelt sigh of relief.

"No problem, I'm still busy with that gold heist story as well."

"Anything new on the gold thriller front?" Lena asked.

"There are some developments that could be connected," Markus started.

"Put me out of my misery, go on," she teased.

"This morning some guy in Luxembourg tried to sell a counterfeit gold bar to his bank. But the forgery was so bad that he got busted right away."

"And?"

"The bank reported the incident to the police. This is where it gets interesting. I know somebody on the force in Luxembourg, so I called him. He told me there were four things he'd never seen before. One: the police in Luxembourg started their investigations straight away, not weeks later. Two: his colleagues didn't protect their country's reputation as a financial center, but instantly requested the German authorities' cooperation."

"How are the Germans involved in the forgery?" Lena interrupted.

"The client selling the fake comes from Germany. And now the third weird thing: the German authorities didn't take several days to check the request for cross-border cooperation, but just a few minutes."

"Um... that's interesting..."

"Exactly. Only an hour after the request the German police issued a search warrant. My source told me this usually takes a week. Apparently there's a special counterfeit money department."

"What did they find?"

"I don't know yet."

"OK. And the fourth thing?"

"The Luxembourg police had the bank's premises searched just as fast as the Germans issued the search warrant for the seller's apartment."

"They believe that the client was the victim rather than the perp..."

"You've got it. That's also the police's theory."

"Exciting as all this is, where is the connection to the raid on the gold transport?"

"Sorry, I forgot to fill you in on something else. The guys in Luxembourg published a photo of the faked gold bar on the net. Earlier I talked to Heraeus, the bar's manufacturers..."

"And?"

"Its serial number traces it back to being one of a batch of twenty. Only central banks or the super-rich buy those."

"Do you see a connection?"

"It's possible," Markus told her. "I'm about to call the Central Bank. Let's see what they have to say about the matter."

"You can tell me all about it over dinner this evening. See you then."

"See you, Lena." Markus was looking forward to their date. Incredibly so…

*

Berlin, American Embassy, 1115 Hours. Peter Redman was sitting at his desk, several classified documents listing America's annual gold production and data concerning individual US companies spread out in front of him.

Redman was deeply absorbed in his thoughts. How the hell had Felix Armbrüster noticed that the production had been accounted for by hundreds of tons too much? And how could anyone establish the origin of the gold smuggled into circulation? There was nothing to indicate that the gold was the same the Allies had deposited in the States. Besides, nobody could check if this was the case anyway. America didn't permit inspections of its gold holdings, not even random checks. And the CIA ensured this wouldn't change in the future either. Otherwise one of their biggest funding sources for covert activities would be jeopardized. Redman was well aware of the many expensive operations being financed without Congress knowing about them.

At least his phone call to the States this morning had taken him a small step further. His colleagues had checked up on the former directors of the government-owned goldmine. The documents he had just received via email concentrated on five suspects who could provide the link between the mine's production and gold sales. One of them must have passed the top secret files to the German journalist Felix Armbrüster.

It was enough to drive you mad. The timing couldn't have been more inconvenient. If the information was made public, not just some people important to him would end up behind bars. The current operation was also endangered. And that simply mustn't happen.

The CIA had already compiled a dossier on one of the five suspects. Jeremy Glenmore was the CFO of the Rocky Mines Corporation; a post he had held for more than fifteen years. Those in the know understood why Glenmore was likely to keep his job until he retired and could look forward to spending his twilight years in the kind of luxury other company executives at his level could only dream of.

Why should Glenmore of all people betray the trust placed in him to such an extent? Redmore pondered. But he felt the same about the other four suspects. He knew every one of those five personally. It made him biased and also explained why he found it so difficult to identify one of them as the traitor.

Glenmore's phone calls over the past month didn't reveal anything out of the ordinary. The NSA recorded all his calls from his office phone, his private line and his cell phone. And, of course, also screened his emails. Nothing.

His business trips didn't reveal anything either about a connection to Armbrüster. Each time the German had been in the USA, Glenmore had always been more than a thousand miles away at another location. Nothing pointed to Glenmore having a contact person in Germany.

Glenmore has a perfect alibi, thought Redman.

He put down the dossier. If Glenmore wasn't the leak, that left four suspects. He now had to check one after the other. Whoever had provided information to Armbrüster had to be stopped. Drastically and forever.

*

Frankfurt, Ulmenstraße, 1125 Hours. Markus dialed the number of the Central Bank's press center. Yesterday he had forgotten to directly take down the name of the woman he had talked to. Quite an embarrassing slip seeing that he may have to prove where he had obtained his information. On top of the piece of paper outlining the questions he meant to ask he had written in capital letters: GET NAME!

This time, instead of being put on hold forever, he had gotten straight through.

"Good morning, this is the press office of the German Central Bank, Rose de Jong speaking. How may I help you?"

"Hello, Markus Manx here. I'm a freelance journalist from Frankfurt," he introduced himself while jotting down the name *Rose de Jong*.

"Hello, Mr. Manx, I remember talking to you yesterday."

That was lucky! The same person as the day before. Besides, she was the official media spokesperson, as he knew from the Central Bank's website.

"Mrs. de Jong, I'm so glad to talk to you again."

"What can I do for you today?"

"I have some more questions about the raid on the gold transport."

"Go ahead, Mr. Manx!"

"What size bars do you transport?"

"More or less exclusively 12.5 kilo bars used for possible collateralization. Smaller bars would be rather awkward in that respect."

Perhaps there really is a connection between the incident in Luxembourg and the raid in Frankfurt, Markus reflected.

"Do you have bars with the serial number 20863?" he asked frankly.

He could hear her typing on her keyboard.

"We do. But you know that the numbers aren't standardized and can be used by different refineries at the same time?"

"And are your bars with that number from Heraeus?"

"I don't have that information."

"Does your depository in New York also have bars with that number?" Markus quickly added.

"Absolutely. In New York we have a melt with 20 bars of that number, another with 21 bars and one single bar," Rose de Jong admitted openly.

"So there are 42 bars with the same serial number in New York?"

"Exactly," she confirmed.

"Were any of these bars included in the raided transport?"

"That I don't know. But we publish a list of all our gold depositories, including the bar numbers, on the internet. It's updated every year. The address is: www.bundesbank.de. Then type 'gold bar listing' into the search field."

"OK. Do you know any more about yesterday's heist?"

"I have no information on that, but the police are doing everything they can, Mr. Manx. We immediately publish any updates on our homepage."

Markus thanked her politely and hung up.

"Let me recap," he thought out loud. "Assuming there are bars with the number 20863 in New York, and also assuming those actual bars were transported yesterday... why then does a counterfeit with that number turn up in Luxembourg today?"

*

Frankfurt, Central Bank, 1135 Hours. After a discreet knock on the door, Rose de Jong entered the office of her boss, Dr. Jürgen Wieder, President of the German Central Bank.

"What it is, Rose?"

Wieder usually addressed his staff by their surnames. He considered them subordinates. Rose was an exception. A few years ago, at the World Bank Conference in Washington, they had become quite intimate. Back in Frankfurt they had terminated their relationship by mutual agreement so they wouldn't risk losing their families. But they were still on first name terms.

"I just had a call from Markus Manx, the reporter. I only told him what he can easily find on the net, but it looks as if he's already established a connection between us and the forgery in Luxembourg. He asked me for the melt number and the depositories."

"Are the forgeries ours, Rose?"

"No Jürgen, definitely not. They've always delivered genuine bars to us from New York."

"Under no circumstances must they link the forgeries to us, Rose, or those conspiracy theorists will again claim our holdings aren't authentic."

"How do you intend to prevent that from happening?"

"No idea. We have to come up with something!"

Silence. They were both thinking hard.

"Do we even know if any of the bars delivered had the number 20863?" Rose asked.

"I'll get someone on it straight away. As far as I know, we didn't receive a list with the numbers before the transport. But we have to request one right now!"

"OK, I'll tell that Manx guy the truth when he calls again. That we don't know the numbers of the bars involved in the transport. Besides New York stores over a hundred thousand of them. It would be some coincidence if that particular number had been included in the delivery."

"But if it was, we'll have a problem by next year at the latest when we publish our updated depository list... Also: if that number actually was part of the delivery, we have to find out why a counterfeit bar with the number randomly turns up a day after the gold robbery."

"Did you have any news from the police?" Rose enquired.

"No, unfortunately. They're still clueless. They've no idea where our stolen gold is."

Shortly after Rose de Jong had left the room, Bernd Brandner, Wieder's right-hand man entered. He reported on today's crisis committee meeting and the forged 12.5 kilo bar that had shown up in Luxembourg. That the Central Bank was increasingly being associated with the fake made him nervous.

Wieder filled him in on what Rose the Jong had told him in the meantime and then continued: "Ask the Americans for the list of numbers of the transported bars. I want it as soon as they're at their desks over there!"

"I don't like it that they're linking us to the forgeries," Brandner growled.

"Neither do I. But there's nothing we can do about it at the moment."

"There's an increasing risk that the Federal Court of Auditors will order a spot check of our holdings in the gold pyramid at short notice."

"How big is the hole?" Wieder asked.

Brandner knew exactly what his boss was referring to without explicitly mentioning it. "Twenty tons. Just about one percent of the reserves held here."

"But nobody else knows about this business except

those initiated?"

"That's correct," Brandner stated firmly. He hoped that all those in on the secret would keep their mouths shut.

"OK, but I still want you to prepare for a possible inspection. We have to be ready for the auditors."

Thus Dr. Wieder concluded the unpleasant subject and got up. Brandner took the hint and left.

*

Frankfurt, Ulmenstraße, 1135 Hours. Markus Manx forced himself to stay calm. He sensed that he was onto a groundbreaking story. *The Central Bank's press officer must have been besieged with calls after the heist, yet she actually remembered me phoning her yesterday! That's real strange. As a freelance reporter researching an article for the HNP, I'm basically of no interest to her. Normally she'd forget all about me ten minutes later.*

Markus got up from his chair and paced around his office. *It must have been the questions I asked her. Maybe I hit the jackpot yesterday. And today she was pretty cool at the start, but once I mentioned the bar numbers, she seemed to get nervous. As if she wasn't sure how much she was allowed to divulge. Does the Central Bank not know what bar numbers were in the transport either?*

Markus walked over to the meeting room he shared with the other journalists. Perhaps it would be empty and he could use the flipchart. *It might be useful to have a clear overview of the key data...*

He was in luck. The room was empty. He went up to the flipchart and quickly sketched a pyramid in the middle of a blank page, shading the inside of it with a yellow marker. Underneath it he wrote the keywords:
- *GOLD PYRAMID TO CALM PUBLIC*

- *240 BARS TRANSPORTED TO FRANKFURT*
- *MELT #20863 IN NEW YORK DEPOSITORY*
- *MELT #20863 STOLEN???*
- *WHAT'S THE CENTRAL BANK HIDING???*

On the right side of the pyramid he drew a truck.
- *GOLD HEIST, MONDAY, CA. 6:30 AM*
- *DURATION 2 MINUTES: PROS!*
- *WINDOWS BLACKED OUT WITH COVER*
- *FORKLIFT, SHIELDED ESCAPE TRUCK*
- *WHAT HAPPENED TO THE GOLD???*

He finally outlined a three-dimensional little box on the left side and labeled it LUX - the safety deposit box.
- *GERMAN INDUSTRIALIST SELLS COUNTERFEIT GOLD BAR*
- *BAR HAS SERIAL NO. 20863*
- *POLICE INVESTIGATES UNUSUALLY FAST*
- *HOW DID THE FORGED BAR GET INTO THE DEPOSIT BOX???*
- *IS BAR NUMBER A COINCIDENCE???*

What is the connection? Markus pondered while drawing a circle around all the parties involved.

He tore the sheet from the flipchart and took it back to his office. He had to ring Jonathan Schreiber to get the go-ahead for a follow-up article. This was a huge chance for the *HNP*. Being a small paper way ahead in a big scoop could enormously enhance its reputation.

*

Twenty minutes later Jonathan had okayed the story and given Markus free reign to write an article including his own take. Surrounded by all the shots he had snapped on Monday, Markus racked his brain how far he could go. No way could his coverage sound like pure speculation; he would have to at least include some evidence.

The photos of the crime scene didn't get him any further; they revealed nothing conspicuous. But what about the pictures of the gold transport he intended to use in the article about the gold being returned? He saw the masked soldiers with the machine guns. He saw the armored van with its doors open. He saw the pile of neatly stacked gold bars. One of the shots was a close-up of the stack.

Not bad at all, he mentally slapped himself on the back. Then he noticed that the inscription was nearly legible. He enlarged the relevant section, but the lettering remained blurred.

Damn, if only I'd had a better lens, he thought disappointedly... Suddenly he had a flash of inspiration. *Perhaps John took a photo that shows the inscription. His gear is far more sophisticated and he's a more experienced photographer. His 800 mm lens would have got a clear shot.*

Excitedly he looked for John Spencer's number.

The phone in John's office rang three times before the answering machine kicked in. *Shame, he isn't in.* Markus didn't leave a message. Instead he dialed John's cell phone. *He's out with his camera, I guess...*

"Spencer."

Markus was delighted.

"Hi, John. Markus here. Have you got a minute?"

"Go ahead. But I'm driving and don't have a hands-free kit."

"OK, I'll be brief, so. Will you be back in your office any time today?"

"Yeah, but not before late afternoon. I have to do a photo shoot first."

Markus got right to the point.

"Tell me, how did your pictures of the gold transport turn out?"

"Not bad. It wasn't exactly a challenge to get a few usable shots from up on that platform. Why do you ask? Did yours not work out?" He sounded slightly gleeful.

"They're alright actually, but not quite good enough," Markus tried to preserve some of his professional pride. "Can I quickly drop by later and have a look at your photos to see if there's anything I can use?"

"No problem. I'll be back by five at the latest. You know how to find me."

"Perfect. See you at five then!"

Markus hoped that seeing the inscription might help to reveal the secret...

*

He published another online article to keep the story going. He had checked with Manfred Krüger from the Federal Police again, just in case. But Krüger didn't have anything new to tell him. He evidently hadn't yet heard about the counterfeit bar in Luxembourg with the serial number that indicated a connection with the Central Bank.

CENTRAL BANK MAINTAINS STOIC SILENCE
COUNTERFEIT GOLD BAR WITH SERIAL NUMBER FROM CENTRAL BANK'S RESERVES

POLICE INVESTIGATIONS INTO YESTERDAY'S RAID ON A CENTRAL BANK GOLD TRANSPORT, IN WHICH THE ROBBERS ESCAPED WITH THREE TONS OF GOLD, ARE ONGOING. SO FAR WITHOUT DEFINITE RESULTS.

THIS MORNING A COUNTERFEIT BAR WEIGHING 13 KILOS TURNED UP IN THE DUCHY OF LUXEMBOURG, ACCORDING TO LOCAL POLICE REPORTS. THIS MAY PROVE TO BE MORE THAN A COINCIDENCE. EXPERTS STATED THAT THE QUALITY OF THE

FORGERY IS RELATIVELY POOR. THE SERIAL NUMBER OF THE BAR INDICATES A LINK TO THE GERMAN CENTRAL BANK, WHO CONFIRMED THAT GOLD WITH THE SAME SERIAL NUMBER AS THAT OF THE LUXEMBOURG FORGERY (20863) IS ALSO HELD IN THEIR NEW YORK DEPOSITORY. THE BANK WAS UNABLE TO STATE IF BARS WITH THIS NUMBER WERE INCLUDED IN YESTERDAY'S HEIST.

WHY DID THE US FEDERAL RESERVE, WHO STILL HOLDS MORE THAN 800 TONS OF GERMAN GOLD, NOT RELEASE THE SERIAL NUMBERS TO THE CENTRAL BANK? FOR YEARS THE GERMAN FEDERAL AUDIT OFFICE HAS POINTED OUT THAT THE PRINCIPLE OF TRUST DOESN'T APPLY TO GOLD DEPOSITS. IT BELIEVES THAT THE GERMAN GOLD IS NOT SAFE ABROAD AND DEMANDS ITS RETURN TO GERMANY.

IS THE FEDERAL AUDIT OFFICE RIGHT? IS THERE A LINK BETWEEN THE LUXEMBOURG FORGERY AND THE GERMAN GOLD RESERVES? IT IS HIGH TIME THAT THE CENTRAL BANK BECOMES MORE TRANSPARENT. SILENCE IS NOT ALWAYS GOLDEN.

Markus was aware how speculative his questions were. But faced with the authorities' stonewalling, sometimes the only choice was to publicly pose legitimate questions so that as many citizens as possible got involved and demanded an answer. After all, the gold belonged to the entire German nation.

*

Frankfurt, Federal Police Situation Center, 1630 Hours. One of Swen Stahl's, the Minister for Special Affairs, colleagues had established the video link to the four permanent members of the gold crisis committee. He now informed them that Stahl would join them in a few minutes.

"Good afternoon, gentlemen, I apologize for the slight delay," Stahl addressed the men as he sat down in front of the camera. "Let's start. Any new developments?"

"We still don't have a breakthrough in the manhunt for the gold robbers," Hartmann began to summarize the police investigations. "But the trail to the counterfeit bar in Luxembourg proved to be promising. We were able to match the serial number of the forgery to the bars included in the gold transport. It is unlikely that the German industrialist who tried to sell the fake was involved in the robbery. Apparently it was purely accidental that he tried to sell it today. Our colleagues in Luxembourg informed us that a search of the bank's premises revealed that more 12.5 kilo bars were stored in its vaults. All the serial numbers matched those of the bars we have brought back. This means we can rule out a coincidence."

"What does that mean?" Stahl asked impatiently. "How can stolen bars, which should be genuine, turn up the following day in a vault in Luxembourg?"

"More than likely the bars were laundered there. We have no proof as yet because the manager in charge of the strongroom has absconded. He must have been an accomplice and exchanged authentic gold bars with those from the transport."

"I don't get it," General Steiner demanded an explanation.

"The bars from the transport were numbered and therefore the robbers couldn't sell them anywhere without arousing suspicion. They had to swap the Central Bank's bars with clean ones so they could get rid of them. The strongroom manager presumably thought the bars stolen from the Central Bank transport were genuine and would lie dormant in his vaults for the next few years," Hartmann expounded.

"How much gold did that bank launder?"

"Our colleagues in Luxembourg seized thirty seven more bars. All the serial numbers were part of the transport, so it's out of the question that it happened by chance. And nobody knew in advance which numbers would be on the bars that would be sent back from the States. Consequently the counterfeit bars must have been bars included in the gold transport," Hartmann said.

"What are you implying?" Brandner challenged him.

"Once it is 100 percent certain that the numbers of all the bars in Luxembourg correspond to those from the transport, and if nobody could make counterfeit bars overnight with those numbers and deposit them there, the bars in the vault actually have to be the stolen ones from the transport. And seeing that thirty eight bars in the vaults were fakes, we can assume that all those in the gold transport were forgeries."

"Are you telling us that the Americans tried to plant fake gold on us?" Gmeiner interjected, visibly horrified at the allegation made against the American colleagues he was constantly in touch with.

"It definitely looks like it," Hartmann confirmed.

"But that's impossible," Brandner contradicted him.

"Why?"

"We have already conducted numerous transports returning our gold from the States. Authenticating it is part of the standard procedure. We would have noticed if there had been counterfeits before."

"I can't comment on that," Hartmann griped. "But we can't ignore the fact that this delivery consisted of forged bars."

"OK," Stahl interrupted. "You need to urgently find out how this could have happened. The situation is extremely delicate and could have grave implications for the financial markets. Confidentiality is of the utmost priority, understood?!"

"It's too late for that," Gmeiner said. "My colleagues sent me an article from the *Hessische Neuste Presse* just a while ago. It already talks about a possible connection between the counterfeit bar in Luxembourg and the gold transport."

"How can that be?" Stahl asked, indignantly.

"A reporter called... Just a second..." Gmeiner consulted a printout of the article, "...called Markus Manx compared the bar number on a photo of the Luxembourg police to the numbers of the Central Bank's inventory."

"Christ Almighty!" Stahl exclaimed angrily. "Why did they even publish a photo?"

"It's the usual routine. The police also need to impress the public after all," Hartmann explained. He felt a growing resentment that the conceited Gmeiner of all people had won some respect from the Minister. Of course, he, Hartmann himself, had also known about the article.

"You make sure that the press doesn't discover the numbers of the stolen bars, Brandner. Or we might have an international incident on our hands. And that's the last thing we need right now."

"Yes, Minister."

"Anything else I should know?" Stahl asked, "Or did those criminals really commit the perfect crime?"

"Not quite," Hartmann said. "Accidentally finding the counterfeit bar in Luxembourg gives us a huge advantage the robbers don't anticipate."

"Spit it out, I don't have much time," Stahl pressed him.

"With the help of our colleagues in Luxembourg we've already been able to establish quite a few of the serial numbers of the original bars kept in the vaults. Seeing that the robbers worked to a tight schedule, we can assume that they'll sell the clean bars as soon as possible. And we're trying to catch them in the act by using the serial numbers we now know."

"Sounds promising. We could do with reporting some positive news," Stahl commented. "I've got to go. We'll meet again at nine in the morning. Goodbye."

He had barely uttered those words when monitor 2 flickered and the screen went blank. The connection had been terminated.

"You heard him," Hartmann took the lead again. "At least we have a first, small breakthrough," he indirectly praised himself. He made his excuses and went back to his office, clenched fist in his pocket, leaned back in his old-fashioned chair and briefly closed his eyes. *Let me just solve this one last case in charge of a crisis committee! Then the younger generation can take over... Two more years to retirement.*

Even though things had progressed quite well today, Hartmann had had enough...

*

Frankfurt, Egestraße, 1700 Hours. Markus walked the 300 yards to the station at the Old Opera from where he took the subway to the last stop. John Spencer's studio was in a small apartment in the Egestraße.

"Hi, Markus," John greeted him, a cigarette dangling from the corner of his mouth.

"Hi John, thanks for seeing me."

Markus cautiously shook his hand because the ash from John's smoke threatened to fall off.

"Come in. I've got the photos ready for you. We can sit at the computer. Perhaps you'll find something you can use... What do you need them for anyway?"

"I'll make a long story short. No doubt you know about

the raid on the transport we photographed yesterday."

"Sure I do. I had several enquiries. Some papers and magazines still needed some shots for their articles. For once one of my jobs paid off handsomely."

John contentedly glanced at Markus who had sat down beside him.

"I'm not interested in photos for publication. I'm looking for information for my research."

"Interesting. What do you think I might have snapped that you haven't?"

"Can you show me the shots with the stack of gold bars? You zoomed in on some of them."

"If you only need them as background information, I can show you all the shots, even the ones I've already sold exclusively."

"Great. I'm interested in the serial numbers on the bars. Can you open the files that only show individual ones?"

John lit another cigarette, pulled out an overflowing ashtray from under some old photographs and pulled it close to his keyboard.

"I've got a whole series of them."

He clicked on the first one and enlarged it to fill the screen.

"It has several numbers on it. Which one is the bar number?"

"The one at the bottom," Markus told him, delighted with the legibility. "The other figures are the weight and the fine gold content."

"Right, I've got 4633, 4603, 8741 and 7299," John read out. "On the last one I can only see the first three digits, 730. The last one could be a 0 or an 8."

"Damn! Can you go to the next shot? It might be more detailed..."

The next three photos were virtually copies of the first

one with minimal adjustments to the lens. But the fifth one had been taken from a different perspective. Other bars were also recognizable in this one.

"There are more numbers on this. I see a 11266 and another 11266 and..."

Markus jumped up.

"That's it," he shouted triumphantly. "Here is 20863. And here it is again." He pointed to the numbers on the screen.

"So you found what you were looking for?"

"Absolutely, John. I could kiss you!"

"Christ, Markus, don't you dare! Just tell me what it all means. And why do some numbers occur more than once?"

"That's because in the past they frequently cast whole batches of bars. They used the same casting mold several times. There are 20 copies of the number 20863 for instance. Perhaps even more if another refinery coincidentally used the same bar number."

"And why is that particular number so important to you?"

"Fair question. Let's make a deal. I need the photo with the number to support a theory. If it turns out to be correct, there could be quite a good fee in it for you. Because then that photo could become pretty valuable."

John hesitated for a moment. "I'm in," he eventually agreed. "I'll make you a color print and also send it to you by email. I haven't sold this one yet, anyway, so there are no problems with the publication rights. And you tell me when your story gets hot. But you can't publish the picture without my permission." John extinguished his cigarette butt in the ashtray.

"Have you heard this one?" he asked while leaning over the printer.

Markus knew what was coming.

"A Frankfurt United fan tells his friend: 'My wife's threatening to divorce me if I keep going to the stadium every weekend.' 'That's terrible,' his friend replies. 'It sure is, I'm going to miss her.'"

With those words he extracted the copy from the printer and handed it to Markus with a grin.

"Funny, eh...?"

"You've had better ones," Markus commented with an exasperated chuckle. Soon after he left the small studio feeling pretty much on top of the world.

On his way home he phoned Rose de Jong from his cell to get an official statement why a counterfeit gold bar could have the same serial number as one of the bars of the hijacked gold transport.

She promised to email him by half past eight the next morning at the latest. Allegedly there was nobody still available after five in the evening to clarify the matter.

Another lie, Markus thought. Just one day after the biggest gold robbery in the history of Germany no doubt everybody at the Central Bank was putting in the extra hours. Even if it was just for the sake of their careers.

*

Frankfurt, Gallo Nero Restaurant, 1955 Hours. Lena was already sitting at one of the tables when Markus entered the restaurant. They hugged and kissed each other on the cheek.

"How are you, Markus Manx, the gold hunter?"

She looked stunning. All in classical black - mini dress, tights and knee-high leather boots - she could have applied to any modeling agency. Her eyes sparkled as much as the pearls around her neck. Markus nearly felt shabby beside her. He had donned his best, anthracite colored jacket and a dark blue shirt, but perhaps he shouldn't have opted for jeans. A tie wouldn't have gone amiss either...

"Hi, Lena, you look great!"

"Thank you. Sit down and tell me about your research. How did the Central Bank react? I really want to know what's happening."

Markus felt a little taken by surprise. Had he jumped to the wrong conclusions? Was this meeting perhaps not a date after all? *Well, let's make the best of it...* He sat down and told her about the evasive answers he had received, about his feeling that he'd been lied to and then about his lucky discovery of the photo with the right bar number. While they were chatting, they ordered an antipasti platter for two and ravioli filled with porcini and sage butter. A Castello Banfi Chianti Classico Riserva to wash it all down.

"I'm really impressed. But why would the robbers steal counterfeit gold bars? And what's more, how does a bar that was stolen on a Monday get to a deposit box in Luxembourg by the following Tuesday morning? "

"Well, I guess the perps didn't know that the bars weren't genuine. But I have to pass on your second question."

"Please don't take this personal, but could it be that you are getting a bit too carried away?"

"I don't think so. I'm not ruling out that it's all just a coincidence, you see. But one thing is for sure: the Central Bank is hiding something. Yet it may be something entirely different," Markus explained confidently. Do you know what a stratagem is?"

"Isn't that some kind of a war strategy?"

"Precisely. Stratagems were military directives developed by a Chinese General in the fifth century. There are thirty six of them altogether. One of them is called *Beat the grass to startle the snake.* You may have heard of it before."

"I have. So you basically want to put the Central Bank to the test. Sounds a bit like David taking on Goliath," Lena remarked.

"I've got nothing to lose. If it doesn't work, so what?" Markus shrugged his shoulders.

"Good thinking."

"Let's see what tomorrow will bring. I can't wait what they have to say about the identical bar numbers... But that's enough about me. Tell me what you did today."

"I had a debriefing session with a company whose IT system was as full of holes as a Swiss cheese. Two months ago I was able to download their confidential documents and information about their production processes. I disclosed this to them today and then deleted all my relevant files."

"But you don't do this for nothing, I take it?"

"Of course not. More than every second firm reacts like professionals and thanks me for my tips. They usually then ask me what they can do to effectively protect themselves. That's when I help gladly. In the other cases, I delete everything and write it down to experience."

"What an interesting profession you picked," Markus applauded. "But how did you actually become a hacker? Did you ever do anything illegal?"

"Well, when I was younger. I've always been skeptical how airtight these so highly praised new technologies really are. Spent a lot of time at my computer trying to figure how to hack into confidential confirmation."

She paused for a moment. "Once you're in the community, you're under pressure to compete."

"How?"

"Everything is transparent. Everybody knows who has hacked into what homepage. Not under your real name, of course, but under a pseudonym."

"What was yours?"

"Snoopy."

Markus grinned. "Charlie Brown's cute little dog. But in your case, I guess, being called a beagle must have been a big compliment."

"I wasn't bad, I admit. I cracked a few tough nuts others couldn't."

"So how did you get back on the straight and narrow?"

"Through the cops, really. They could never prove anything, but I featured regularly on their list of suspects. I realized it was only a matter of time until I would slip up."

"And then?"

"I ended up working for a large bank's IT department. I attached some confidential documents I had hacked into from their servers to my application form. I guess that convinced them to hire me."

"Wow!" Markus was impressed. "But why did you quit? You had a guaranteed steady income."

"In those days I enjoyed flaunting my looks. I loved teasing my male colleagues with my skimpy dresses. Unfortunately one of them couldn't keep his hands off me. He molested me. Reporting him didn't do any good. Nobody believed me. So I cut my losses and left."

"Bad luck for the bank," Markus laughed.

"Should we order some coffee here?" he asked after the Mousse au Chocolat und Panna Cotta with an unmistakably suggestive look.

Lena chuckled. "You remembered that. Why doesn't that surprise me?"

"Il conto, per favore," Markus signaled to the waiter who was clearing the table beside them.

"It's my turn tonight," Lena declared, leaving no room for discussion. "I billed that company tonight after the final meeting. The whole deal was quite profitable."

"OK so. I won't argue." Markus put his arm around her with a proprietary smile. She didn't object and looked at him invitingly.

"Right," she said, "I'll pay and then I'll show you where my car is parked."

*

Twenty minutes later they left her car in the underground garage and stepped into the elevator to take them to the fifth floor of Lena's apartment building. He gently stroked her hair and ran his fingers down her throat.

"Do you know that you have a beautiful profile?"

Lena didn't reply. Instead she took his hand with an enchanting smile and pulled him into the apartment where she closed the door and leaned against him. A passionate kiss while she took off his coat.

"Now I'll make you some coffee!"

"But..." Markus protested.

"No buts. We have all the time in the world."

She invited him to sit down on the couch and walked towards the kitchen, evidently getting a kick out of prolonging the situation.

Markus glanced after her as she floated through the den into the open room next to it. He couldn't take his eyes off her. She was toying with him as she emphatically slow and gracefully put one foot in front of the other.

My goodness, that's pretty provocative! responded the part of his brain in charge of all things erotic. *Catwalk*, his cerebrum cheekily piped up.

"Would you prefer ordinary coffee or an espresso?"

"I don't care as long as it's quick."

"Well, well, well. We are a little impatient, aren't we?"

Lena filled the coffee maker with water. Then she took a dishtowel from its hook to wipe away a few drops of water that had splattered onto the countertop. With noticeable intention she dropped it on the floor. Ever so slowly, she bent down to pick it up. Markus felt the tension growing inside him. Lena retrieved the towel with one hand while caressing her posterior down to the upper thighs with the other.

The girl's driving me crazy! Markus thought with appreciation and pleasant anticipation. *She looks divine in that dress. I can't wait to...*

Lena's strategy was far more subtle.

"I made us espressos. Is that OK?"

She sat down beside him and deposited the cups on the coffee table.

"Will I get you some sugar?"

"No, thanks. I'll have mine black," Markus declined.

Lena smiled, pushed him back and sat on his lap. Her mini dress slid up seductively. Underneath Markus spotted the ornamental seam of her stockings; temptingly emphasizing the flawless white skin. Lena enjoyed the way he was looking at her. She turned a little to the side, dipped her finger in the espresso and licked it off.

"Would you like some?" Without seriously expecting an answer, she dipped her finger in the espresso again and this time spread the liquid over his lips. Markus instinctively used his tongue to lick the coffee from her finger.

He remembered an old Elvis song. *You look like an angel. Walk like an angel. Talk like an angel. But I got wise – You're the devil in disguise...*

Seems like there really is a little devil inside you, Lena Eck, he thought.

After Lena had repeated the tantalizing ritual three times, she finished the rest of her espresso in one gulp, took the full cup and held it to Markus' lips.

It was the best espresso of his life. And a creative overture...

*

Iphofen, Hotel Zehntkeller, 2110 Hours. Two black Audis A8 had reached Iphofen in quick succession and turned into the inner courtyard of the hotel Zehntkeller. Now they were parked side by side, pointing towards the exit gate. The chauffeurs leaned against their hoods in the darkness and smoked.

The hotel owner had welcomed the passengers in person and led them to the private booth beside the entrance.

"We have a problem, Sven," Dr. Jürgen Wieder immediately started. He had come here right after the Central Bank's meeting in Frankfurt and, unusual for him, appeared to be stressed.

Iphofen, a village with barely three thousand souls, was easily accessible from Frankfurt. More importantly, it was close to the direct route from Berlin to Munich. The small wine-growing community of Iphofen's anonimity had been in its favor. Today they had chosen the hotel Zehntkeller, a historical estate resembling a monastery in the heart of the village.

"Let's order first, Jürgen. I haven't eaten anything since breakfast apart from those disgusting conference cookies," said Sven Stahl. Mid-fifties, athletic, muscular build, slightly receding hairline, perfectly dressed in a white shirt and gray suit. Wearing shades, some of his friends claimed, he resembled agent Smith from *The Matrix*. But every time that proposition was made Stahl would stress that he sided with the goodies.

"Sure," Wieder agreed.

A press of the button summoned the waitress. "Are you ready to order, Sir?"

"I'll have the venison with rosemary potatoes and half a bottle of your best white – the Silvaner Iphöfer Julius-Echter-Berg, please." Stahl ordered. "One of my favorite regional wines," he explained, turning to Wieder.

"I'll have the same." Today Wieder was too restless to make his own choice. The last few hours had thoroughly spoiled his appetite.

Stahl enjoyed his saddle of venison while Wieder just picked at his meal.

"We are in trouble Sven, in real big trouble!"

"Be more specific!"

"We can no longer keep the lid on the whole gold business."

"Where's the problem?" the Minister for Special Affairs probed.

"Some reporter has connected the counterfeits to the Central Bank."

"But there'll always be forgeries. You Central Bank guys can't be held responsible for all of them," Stahl tried to calm him down.

"This time it's more serious."

"Why?"

"This afternoon the online portal of the *Hessische Neueste Presse* published an article by some Markus Manx which neatly established a link between the gold heist and the forgeries in Luxembourg."

"You sent me a copy. I don't get why you're so worried. It's all just speculation."

"True, but that Manx guy is persistent. This evening he demanded another statement. He can prove that the counterfeit bars were from the hijacked gold transport."

"How?"

"He has a high definition photo that reveals the serial number, the fine gold contents and the weight. All the details correspond to the ones on the forgery. Nobody will buy that's a coincidence anymore."

"Have you established how one of the bars from the transport ended up in a deposit box in Luxembourg?"

"A search of the bank revealed that there were more bars from the transport in its safe deposit boxes. All of them forgeries!"

"And should those boxes have contained corresponding genuine ones instead?"

"So far our colleagues have only been able to check this in two cases. In one of them the owner was able to prove that he bought his bar five years ago, so it must have been real. The second was a case of tax evasion. At the start the guy who owned the deposit box denied having stored a 12.5 kilo bar in it. Due to a lack of initial suspicion it would be difficult to use the information, so we guaranteed him impunity if he makes a retrospective declaration to the IRS. He gladly accepted, otherwise he wouldn't have been able to claim on his insurance anyway."

"Seeing that we have several similar cases, we can now assume that the counterfeit bars in the deposit boxes are from the transport."

"Undoubtedly," Wieder confirmed Stahl's deduction.

"Incredible. Those guys are real pros. Not only did they manage to give us the slip, they've also evidently managed to launder part of their spoils on the very day of the robbery," the Minister for Special Affairs commented. "Do we know who was stupid enough to exchange stolen counterfeits for clean bars?"

"The boys in Luxembourg have arrested the manager in charge of the vaults. But as far as I know he hasn't confessed yet."

"Was this the first transport with forged bars?"

"Most certainly. Gold content and weight are checked on arrival as a matter of routine. Forgeries would have been detected immediately," Wieder assured the Minister.

"But the Yanks know that. They would never be dumb enough to send us fakes. We must assume that all major media would jump at a report like that. And then... then the shit hits the fan! With a vengeance!"

"Exactly," Wieder agreed. "The public will start doubting the authenticity of the gold stocked in the pyramid and all the painstakingly established trust in our German gold reserves will be jeopardized. Followed by everyone speculating who has planted the counterfeits on us."

"We can't let that happen," Stahl exclaimed. "We need a plausible explanation for the forgeries. Right now especially we can't afford to have the public's trust and that of the financial markets further undermined."

"Any suggestions?"

"Why don't you claim that your gold transports are always doubly protected? One transport with the real gold and one with forgeries."

Wieder seemed skeptical while evaluating the idea.

"Listen, Jürgen," Stahl reiterated his proposal, "tomorrow you post a surveillance video on the internet showing the arrival and unloading of one of the last genuine gold transports. Make it look like the robbers got the wrong vehicle and bingo."

"Christ, Sven, you're a genius!" Wieder's relief was written in his face."

"And before that you send a copy of the surveillance footage to the papers and all the news channels," Stahl added.

"Consider it done. This way we nip any suspicion right in the bud... But we still have another problem. As always, the Bavarians want more. Their Central Bank wants their share of the gold holdings physically displayed in Munich."

"I'll be there tomorrow, Jürgen, and I'll take care of it. So don't worry!"

Just before midnight two black limousines left the village of Iphofen.

*

The Minister's chauffeur steered the Audi safely through the darkness towards the freeway. Stahl sank back into the heated backseat, glancing out the window into the night, two as yet unread draft bills for the next Cabinet meeting beside him. Deep in thought, he sat like that for a while. Nobody could afford to lose their nerves now…

Stahl well recalled how everything had started that time in Frankfurt just about ten years ago at the Central Bank. Back then he had been one of his party's young, aspiring undersecretaries in the Treasury Department. When the post of Central Bank President had become vacant, he had been the first candidate to be considered by the Finance Minster. A fantastic career jump. Stahl had accepted without hesitation.

He had been in the job for about a year when his immediate subordinate, the director in charge of the gold deposits, had unexpectedly died.

He had immediately promoted Dr. Jürgen Wieder as his successor. Even then he had valued his abilities. Stahl stretched his legs in the spacious back of the limo. Yes, he had definitely appointed the right man. He opened the electric window. Cool, refreshing night air flowed into the car through the gap.

In those days, just after taking up his new post, a very worried Wieder had come to him. A spot check had revealed a counterfeit 12.5 kilo gold bar. What was even more worrying was that the forgery had been made less than two years previously as confirmed by the material analysis.

They had a thief and forger within their own ranks in the Central Bank! Stahl had kept his head, instigated a task force and had everyone implied checked. The result was quickly forthcoming. But surprising! The thief had been the deceased department head himself. Assisted by two of his colleagues he had been defrauding the bank for many years. Three hundred kilos of gold altogether were missing and had been replaced by worthless copies. The Central Bank's security standards were generally acknowledged to be exemplary, yet nobody had noticed anything. The incident couldn't have been more embarrassing.

The perps' method had been ingenious. Remelting old gold bars in order to correspond to the London Good Delivery Standard had been mere routine. Occasionally small excess quantities accumulated whenever the old inventories had listed bars with deviating fine gold content or weight. These tiny amounts had been misappropriated. When the fraud remained undetected, they had stolen whole bars and replaced them with forgeries. It had all been so simple. Opportunity makes the thief.

At that stage, Sven Stahl had already been in office for a year. Had the security gaps become public knowledge, it would have seriously damaged the Central Bank's reputation. The responsibility rested with him, so Stahl had decided to conceal the whole affair. The counterfeits remained where they were and nobody noticed anything. Stahl's political career remained unblemished.

At the time, three men had been in on the secret: Stahl, Wieder and his assistant Bernd Brandner, who had discovered the forgeries. More or less to the day, a year later,

Wieder had talked to him. Stahl was sure he had told him not even to think about it. But the temptation was great. Why shouldn't they do it? Senior executives in the private industry earned considerably more than they did. So they went ahead.

Their greed grew over the years and with it the amount of counterfeits. It had been easy to grow accustomed to the higher standard of living. But they mustn't lose their nerves if it came to an audit. Stahl shivered in the cold night air still blowing into the car. He closed the window. They had reached the freeway. It was pitch-dark outside. He picked up the first draft bill and started to read.

Wednesday

Hofheim, Lena's Apartment, 0710 Hours. Two bowls and spoons as well as low-fat milk and the current edition of the *Frankfurter Rundschau* were waiting for the muesli and bananas Lena was serving for breakfast.

"Good morning," she said and kissed his cheek.

"Good morning."

"Last night was wonderful," she tenderly purred into his ear.

Markus nodded, but didn't quite agree.

"That was an understatement. Last night was sensational."

Lena beamed at him.

"I'm hoping you'll stay for breakfast."

"You've just talked me into it," he grinned.

They sat down at the table.

"Are you busy today?" Lena enquired while handing him a cup of coffee.

He took a big sip and deposited the cup in front of him. *Porcelain*, he registered, *minimalist design*, *off-white and conical.* He appreciatively and carefully turned the cup by 180 degrees, then raised his eyebrows in amusement. The back of the cup subtly displayed the word 'sexy'. Curious, he turned Lena's cup around, too, and laughed out loud when he read 'Tiger'. He blew her a kiss and nodded.

Lena, also amused and half apologetically, told him: "A present from my best friend. So, are you busy today?" she repeated her question.

"Well, kind of. I've got to finish another article for the *HNP* by three o'clock," he said while skimming through the paper.

"But we'll see each other tonight, won't we?"

"Damn, I don't believe it!" Markus exclaimed.

"What's wrong?" Lena asked.

"I just don't believe it… It can't be…"

"Would you ever tell me what's up?"

"Felix Armbrüster is dead!"

"Who is dead? I don't understand."

Markus spread out the paper and pointed to a prominent, quarter page obituary.

We mourn the loss of our colleague Felix Armbrüster.
The recipient of the prestigious Zurich Journalist Award Felix Armbrüster died suddenly and unexpectedly.
We extend our heartfelt condolences to his wife and two children.

"It says here that Felix Armbrüster is dead," Markus commented incredulously.

"A colleague of yours?"

"We met at the School of Journalism. Felix also occasionally worked for the *Rundschau*. He was roughly my age."

"Was he sick?"

Markus scanned the obituary for the third time. "…suddenly and unexpectedly," he read out loud. "Sounds more like an accident."

"How terrible. The poor family," Lena said with compassion. Do you know them?"

"Not the children, but Melinda, his wife. She was also at college with us. She and Felix fell in love at first sight. They were together since they were freshmen."

"You should contact her," Lena suggested. "I'm sure she could do with a shoulder to lean on."

"You're right. Good idea."

Markus' cell signaled an incoming email

To: mmanx@gmx.de
Subject: Central Bank Security Measures
From: info@bundesbank.de

Dear Mr. Manx,
Due to the current public interest we have decided to publicize some of the Central Bank's security measures for gold transports. We therefore reply to your press inquiry as follows:
For gold transports we always employ two armored vehicles. One contains the genuine cargo, the second one is stocked with outwardly identical, but worthless duplicates. Neither the personnel loading the transports nor the security team know which vehicle carries the real gold.
Fortunately the ambushed transport two days ago contained only the copies. The real gold arrived safely at the Central Bank.
CCTV footage showing the arrival of the transport with the genuine cargo can be viewed at:
www.bundesbank.de/de/presse/gold

Yours sincerely,
Rose de Jong
Press Spokesperson

German Central Bank
P.O. Box 10 06 02
60006 Frankfurt

A click on the link, another click on the icon with the triangle and the video was running.

"Look at this, Lena," Markus said.

"Is that the gold transport?"

They could see an armored van slowly passing through

the Central Bank's security check. The outlines of the escort jeep were hazily visible in the background before the gates closed.

"That's the van you saw on the airfield?"

"Well, it looks identical."

"Did you recognize anyone inside?"

"No," Markus said. "But look here, down on the right. The surveillance cameras always datestamp every frame." Both of them watched the centiseconds ticking over on the clock beside the date.

"Of course," Lena observed, "otherwise the recording would be worthless.

"OK, now I need your expertise: how many shots does a surveillance camera take?"

"Simple domestic models are designed to capture ten to thirty images per second. You still see movement and it saves storage space."

"And professional equipment?"

"Five hundred fps or more."

"Fp what?" Markus asked.

"Frames per second, you know."

After several changes of the cameras' perspective, they both saw the van being unloaded. The datestamp read 06.59.

"Where does the Central Bank actually load the second vehicle?" Markus wondered.

"Why are you asking me? I've no idea."

"Because I only ever saw one van being loaded," he replied.

"Perhaps when the plane's in the hangar afterwards."

Markus was still skeptical.

"Strange…"

The surveillance video's last frame showed the unloaded armored van. Half lost in thought, Markus gazed at the still.

The kitchen light flickered and came back on.

"A power dip," Lena explained.

"A what?"

"A power dip. A power failure for a fraction of a second. That's why the light flickered."

"At least the power failure didn't last as long as it did two days ago. Remember, I told you about the fifty cent eating coffee maker that cheated me out of my wake-up coffee."

"I do. And I'm extremely grateful for that power cut," Lena remarked with a chuckle. "Otherwise you may not have gone to the café and we would never have met."

"True. I didn't look at it that way. I hereby apologize to the coffee machine and promise never to complain about it snitching my hard-earned money again."

They both laughed.

While Lena cleared the table, Markus was still staring at the still with the unloaded armored van.

"Damn it. That's the end of my groundbreaking story about the counterfeit gold from the transport. Their version with the two vans makes the Central Bank look squeaky clean. And the robbers have been reduced to nothing but a pitiful bunch of guys who have stolen three tons of counterfeits."

"That nearly sounds as if you're siding with them."

"I'm not, but somehow I get the feeling that the Central Bank got off more lightly than it should have."

Lena closed the dishwasher when Markus asked: "That power cut two days ago, it would have affected the Central Bank as well, wouldn't it?"

"No, they're equipped with a perfect backup system."

"You're right, of course, otherwise there'd presumably be ten seconds missing in their footage," Markus concluded.

"Wait," Lena interrupted. "I've got an idea. Even with the emergency supply, it will take a few milliseconds before the batteries and the backup generators kick in. The voltage fluctuations aren't apparent to the naked eye, but they are measurable," she explained.

"How long does it take before the emergency system reacts?"

"Generally between fifteen and fifty milliseconds. I guess just fifteen with the Central Bank's system. That means five to ten frames should be missing in the case of professional surveillance equipment with five hundred images per second."

Markus nodded. He still needed a little while to follow the calculation.

Lena extracted her laptop from its bag and plugged in Markus' power cable. Half a minute later she had loaded the surveillance video in maximum resolution.

"Do you know the exact time of the blackout?"

"Six fifty seven or fifty eight," he told her.

"Are you a blackout databank?" Lena asked, amazed by the precise reply.

"Impressed?" Markus grinned. "It was actually just a coincidence. I had to reset my clock radio after the power cut. At six fifty nine."

"That will make the search easier. We'll narrow it down to the minutes around the blackout."

Fascinated Markus stared at Lena's screen displaying the surveillance footage in slow motion. Lena deftly controlled the speed, varying between fast and slow.

"Do you see it?"

"See what?"

"Look at the timestamp. We really are dealing with a 500 fps camera. A new image every two milliseconds."

"That's good for us, isn't it?" Markus probed.

"Absolutely. There should be at least five frames missing."

The video had played to the end and Lena started it again. After the third time it was obvious:

"There are no missing frames."

"That means there was no power cut at the Central Bank," Markus concluded.

"That would be one possibility," Lena agreed.

"And the second one?"

"The video was recorded at a different time when there was no blackout."

"The first option can be easily checked," Markus suggested. The home insurance companies maintain a blackout databank. After some freeloaders tried to cheat their insurers with false blackout damage claims, the companies reacted by setting up a databank containing verifiable date for every household."

It didn't take long before a phone call to Markus' insurance company had clarified the matter and validated his speculations once again.

"My office and the Central Bank definitely had a power cut at six fifty seven."

"That eliminates option one," Lena rejoiced, "and the footage is not from the day of the heist."

"Bingo!"

They both jumped up and high-fived.

"But what the hell is the Central Bank trying to hide?" Markus wondered.

*

Berlin, American Embassy, 0730 Hours. Aaron hastily went through the Brandenburg Gate. The chilly air in the fall in Berlin always badly affected his joints. He had to be careful. Suddenly, he turned around and carefully scanned his surroundings. Nothing conspicuous. Soon after he entered the US Embassy, a compact building complex reminiscent of a fortress. In the foyer Aaron slipped out of his winter coat – a little too warm for the season – and draped it over his left arm. To ease his tension he rolled his shoulders back and forth. His neck vertebrae audibly snapped into place.

"Hi, Peter," he said as he stepped into the office.

He had already been expected.

"Hi, Aaron, you OK?" Peter Redman asked without waiting for an answer. They sat down opposite each other at the conference table. Neither of them carried any written documents.

"Let's quickly go through the main points," Redman began and added, "starting with the leak concerning operation *Brilliance*. We have ruled out Glenmore, the Rocky Mines Corporation's CFO, as a suspect. Did interviewing their directors turn up anything?"

Aaron pulled an email printout from his jacket pocket. He smoothed the unfolded page and pushed it over to Redman. Langley had thoroughly vetted the director in charge of production and unearthed nothing to arouse suspicion regarding him or his family. The CIA had even been able to justify every dollar the man had spent compared to his official salary. The email contained the verified facts and a conclusion. Silence prevailed as Redman intensively studied his CIA colleagues' evaluation.

"We can forget about him as the leak as well," Aaron answered the still open question when Redman lifted his eyes from the printout.

"That leaves three more suspects."

"Actually only two," Aaron corrected him. "The agency also cleared Judy Stevens, Glenmore's PA. We've now narrowed it down to Ray Hampton, chief of the internal audit department and Byron Lapeng, the mine director's PA. Both have access to the relevant data. Lapeng evidently went into hiding yesterday."

Although he had just been informed that one of the suspects had disappeared, Redman didn't show any emotion.

"He won't be able to hide for long. The agency will track him down anywhere on this planet no matter which hole he crawls into!"

He knew very well that a director's assistant wouldn't last very long without sufficient funds. Tapping the phones and emails of his parents, his sister and his current girlfriend would presumably yield results very soon. Moreover, his name and various personal data such as his social security number, cell number and mail addresses were listed on the NSA's records. Should they appear anywhere in the worldwide data traffic, Redman's colleagues would be informed instantly and cast their nets.

The next steps to finally close the leak were quickly discussed.

"OK, let's continue with operation *Snow White*."

Redman got up and walked over to the wall safe behind his desk. Four mechanical locks secured the old-fashioned appliance. He entered the number combination and they could hear the steel lock pins disengaging and releasing the door. Redman opened it, extracted a file holding roughly a hundred pages and placed it in front of Aaron.

"Time's running out, Aaron. The threat level is becoming critical."

Without taking a closer look, Aaron knew what was contained in the documents before him – the highly confidential CIA security report. Those who followed current politics realized what caused such a headache for the two agents without knowing what was in the report. Since the end of the cold war, the European Allies had reduced the size of their armies to such an extent that they were no longer functional. Especially right now, when the USA was facing three powerful enemies simultaneously, the Allies were more of a hindrance than a help. The threat of three separate wars was imminent. If Europe remained as unprepared as it was now, none of them could be won.

The Russian's massive military buildup was upsetting the European power balance. They had already used their new strength to annex the Crimea and parts of the Ukraine. Now the Russians were massing troops in the Baltic to prepare for an invasion.

Meanwhile China had utilized its economic prosperity to reinforce its armies and threatened the global balance with the building of artificial islands and the blocking of important waterways in the Pacific. The CIA assumed that a war in the South China Sea would be unavoidable one or two years hence at the latest.

The third threat, the Islamist or so-called Islamic State's takeover of the Arabic world, had greatly changed the global distribution of oil resources and thereby hugely affected financial transactions. Yet another non-acceptable situation for the USA.

America had to fight back. It needed the European allies and, damn it, they just had to adequately contribute. Something had to give. And fast.

"Our worst-case-scenario has just been replaced by a worst-worst-case-scenario. The European democracies are nothing but a bad joke!" Redman summarized the current status.

"What have you decided?"

"We're going to bring *Snow White* forward," Redman replied. His expression didn't betray that this would permanently seal the fate of many people.

"When?" Aaron asked.

"Immediately. We shall use the first opportunity," Redmond said, placed the file back in the safe and locked it.

The sound of his concluding sentence also carried a threat: "Make sure that gold business doesn't get in our way, Aaron!"

*

Frankfurt, Situation Center of the German Federal Police, 0850 Hours. Following a short knock on the door, Gmeiner had stepped into the office of Police Chief Hartmann, who had greeted him with a puzzled expression. Gmeiner had never come to see him outside official meetings before. It simply wasn't his way.

"We checked out that Manx guy," Gmeiner came straight to the point. "So far he's just an insignificant reporter who's not produced anything out of the ordinary of late. He's divorced and has two kids. His earnings just about finance him and his family. I believe he was just lucky yesterday."

"Let's hope so," Hartmann said, still irritated by Gmeiner's forthright manner. "He's already published two articles about the sequence of events with more inside information than all the other, larger media. This thing is evidently right up his alley. It's quite incredible that a small little rag like the *HNP* commands the opinion leadership in the whole of Germany. I've instructed my press officer to inform me immediately if he rings again for another statement. We shouldn't underestimate him."

"I agree," Gmeiner said congenially. "I'll stay on his trail, so he won't get out of hand."

It was already five to nine when the two of them went over to the conference room next door. *Gmeiner can be quite pleasant when he wants to be,* Hartmann mused. *I guess he's trying on the friendly approach because he still hasn't got anything to show for his efforts. But the old rule still stands: never trust the BND...*

A Federal Police IT specialist and his counterpart in Stahl's office in Berlin were setting up the video link for the conference which was about to start. Feedback noises were still buzzing from the speakers and the experts were feverishly restarting the connection. Everyone who knew Stahl was aware that every second of a delay would presumably have the man throwing a fit. Two minutes to nine the link was functioning. Gmeiner and Hartmann were still alone in the room.

One minute to nine Bernd Brandner showed up.

"Good morning, gentlemen."

"Good morning," was the near instant reply from monitor 2. Stahl, the Minister for Special Affairs, was also punctual.

"Let's start."

The feedback was gone, but had been replaced by a deep humming sound emanating from the speakers. As Stahl didn't throw a tantrum in light of the technical glitch, the humming might not be heard in Berlin and the conference members in Frankfurt endured it without mentioning it.

"General Steiner isn't here yet," Hartmann observed, "but I think we'll start without him."

"Any news?" Stahl impatiently interrupted him.

Hans-Joachim Hartmann first summarized the latest results of the police investigations. The previous night they had discovered the body of the soldier who had driven the escort van. The autopsy had shown that he had already died at the crime scene itself. Shooting him in the head in front of the two passengers of the armored van had merely served to create a credible threat.

The forensic analysis of the traces found in the Rödermark warehouse hadn't produced anything pointing to the perps. All those involved had apparently been completely masked and left no hairs or fingerprints.

Hartmann gave the floor to Brandner who informed them about the video which confirmed the official version of the successful gold transport. To the assembled inner circle he admitted that the Central Bank had uploaded an old video on the net.

"We have to ensure that the counterfeit bar from Luxembourg doesn't lead to bigger problems."

"A wise decision," Stahl commented.

"And what about the real gold?" urged General Steiner, who had just arrived.

"Our colleagues from the Fed didn't tell us much. They said they had to clarify the matter internally first. Although I don't understand what there is to clarify," Brandner replied. "If they don't report back promptly, the Central Bank President will personally contact the chairman of the American Federal Bank."

Not to appear empty-handed once again, Gmeiner informed them about several intercepted emails and phone calls that may have been connected to the robbery. He delivered his unsubstantial contribution with his usual eloquence. His agency was well known for its pomposity and doing things for the sake of doing them.

"If nobody has anything else to add, I now terminate this meeting. What time suits you for our next session this afternoon, Minister?" Hartmann asked in the direction of the camera.

"Five o'clock." Without considering any possible objections, Stahl vanished from the screen with a: "Good luck, gentleman."

The annoying humming noise disappeared with him.
Luck? We could use a bit of luck, Hartmann thought.

*

Frankfurt, Ulmenstraße, 1115 Hours. Markus closed his office door behind him. Exhilarated by the events of the previous night, he skipped down the stairs to the entrance. Once he'd reached the bottom, he found himself out of breath. *I really need to work out more,* he thought.

In the lobby he opened the mailbox, one of twelve, with his name on a neatly printed label. He well remembered the far too small, always overflowing boxes they'd had before and how the landlord had finally installed a more modern and spacious version after several complaints. The considerable costs for this and the individual nametags he had added to his tenants' rent.

Markus found four letters. A short glance at the senders and three of them went straight into the trash basket specially provided for the purpose. Junk mail advertising office supplies, clothing and expensive cars. Not so the fourth letter - no stamp, addressed to him in handwriting and evidently personally delivered. Markus inserted his index finger under the self-sealing flap and tore the envelope open to read the following lines penned in a spidery scrawl:

Hello, Mr. Manx,
I have some explosive information about the missing gold for you.
I shall call you today at 3 p.m. under the name of Miller

and will then tell you at which of the following places to meet me and when. Be careful.
1. Minerva Fountain at the Römerberg
2. St. Catherine's Church at the Guardhouse
3. Main Entrance of the Zeilgalerie Mall
There I will ask you for a chewing gum.
Please hand me some gum if everything is fine or tell me you don't have any if you're being followed or you feel suspicious.
Please be on time. It's important for you!

No signature! Deep in thought, he climbed up the stairs to his office. *Just like a bad spy thriller. What does he want from me? Should I really meet him? Why should I be careful? Explosive information about gold... What does he know?* Back in his office he pushed the envelope under his computer keyboard.

Holding the phone receiver, he contemplated his next move. How much information about the false video should he divulge during his inquiries at the Central Bank? Would five or ten missing frames per seconds be noticed? Or was Lena mistaken after all?

Markus dialed the number he knew by heart at this stage.

"German Central Bank Press Office, Marie Schneider speaking. Good morning."

"Hello, my name is Markus Manx. May I speak to Ms. de Jong please?"

"I am sorry, but she is not here at the moment. Can I help you?"

Darn it! His strategy wouldn't work with an employee he didn't know. He had planned to confront Rose de Jong directly with his suspicions. She wasn't a good actress and Markus believed her reaction would show him if he was on the right track.

"I'm afraid you can't," he told the woman. "I've already been on the phone to Mrs. de Jong several times about the issue and need to talk to her in person.

Rose de Jong's colleague was persistent. She had obviously been instructed not to connect anyone to her immediate superior without good reason.

"Could you at least indicate what this is in connection with, Mr. Manx?"

"It's about a video she sent me earlier this morning."

"OK, I shall pass on the message and ask her to call you back."

"Many thanks. Please also tell her that it's extremely important. She has my number."

Markus hung up, convinced he was onto something.

*

Frankfurt, Central Bank, 1145 Hours. "A Mr. Marx called looking for you, Mrs. de Jong," Marie Schneider told her boss when the lady returned to the press office.

"Did you mean Manx?"

"Could be."

"Did he say why he was calling?"

"He said it was about a video you sent him this morning. Also that he wanted to speak to you personally and that it was very important."

"Can I have a quick word with you, Jürgen?" Rose de Jong asked the President of the Central Bank soon after.

"Come in. What's up?"

"That Markus Manx guy phoned again. He's waiting for me to return his call. I think he doesn't buy our story about the double transports."

"OK. I want to learn more about him. Ring him from

here and we put you on speakerphone. I need to hear everything he says and how he says it. But don't mention that I'm listening in. He mustn't know how important this is for us."

Rose de Jong dialed Markus' number and activated the speech amplification. Markus wouldn't be able to recognize the actual phone because outgoing calls only ever displayed the switchboard number.

"Markus Manx."

"Hello, Mr. Manx, this is Rose de Jong from the Central Bank. You were urgently looking for me. What can I do for you?"

"Thank you so much for returning my call so quickly. This is about the link you sent me earlier."

"I hope it answered all your queries," Rose de Jong interrupted him in an attempt to take charge of the conversation.

"Not entirely, to be honest…"

"How do you mean? We're glad to have foiled a major gold robbery with our admittedly somewhat elaborate strategy."

"I'm not so sure about that," Markus approached the critical point. "I showed the video to an expert and that person doubts that it was recorded on the day of the heist."

Rose de Jong wondered how to react. That cocky, crummy little reporter was questioning an official Central Bank video! She settled for moderate indignation.

"Mr. Manx, it wasn't an easy decision to publicize our security strategy involving the double transports and expose our cover. It saved us, and therefore the Federal Republic of Germany, 100 million Euros. How dare you doubt the authenticity of the footage?"

"I'm familiar with your explanation," Markus retorted confidently. If his suspicions were correct, de Jong's indignation was clearly an act. He felt even more reassured by the fact that he could hear a slight echo on the line. Another person was obviously listening in. That would certainly not be the case if this was a trivial matter.

"What surprises me is that you only published the double transport strategy after I called you. Shouldn't you have announced such a triumph right from the start? Instead you idly stood by while those cheeky robbers were downright idolized."

OK, Markus thought, *she didn't deny my implied allegations straight away. She pretends to be outraged, yet she's quizzing me. I must be on the right track!*

"The expert I presented with the video can disprove its authenticity. Please don't ask me about the technical details because I know less than nothing about those. All I want is an official statement regarding my accusations."

Another brief silence. Rose de Jong looked at Wieder who shook his head – deny everything!

"Mr. Manx, I would urge you to seriously reconsider publishing such unfounded allegations. Our video is authentic, as I already assured you, and proves the successful delivery of three tons of genuine gold bars. All the robbers got were counterfeits."

"I acknowledge what you say," Markus said, "but I still have another question: how does one of the bars stolen on Monday from the gold transport show up the very next day in a safe deposit box in Luxembourg?"

Rose de Jong hesitated again and glanced at her boss. Wieder just shrugged his shoulders. She decided to play for time.

"What makes you think that the gold bar in a Luxembourg safe come from our transport?"

Markus simply said: "I have a photo of the loading operation at the airport which distinctly shows the very same gold bar also depicted on the photos issued by the police in Luxembourg.

He now went for broke. "If the video turns out to be false and the counterfeit bar in Luxembourg is actually from the transport, it means the American Federal Reserve sent us counterfeits, doesn't it?"

Now Rose de Jong was definitely dumbstruck and looked at her boss for help. Wieder reacted instantly by writing *deny everything!* on the first piece of paper to hand.

"Mr. Manx, your theory is pure speculation and devoid of any foundation. I repeat that the video we published shows the successful transport of the real gold. The previously returned gold from foreign storage was always checked by us for authenticity. Of course, there were never any complaints. I can only advise you to reconsider what you are about to publish," she ended the call.

"How can he possibly prove that our video is a forgery? We used the recording of the next to last transport that arrived at the same time. The footage is real, just not from that particular transport."

"Was there anything to indicate a different date?" Wieder asked. "Is there anything we overlooked?"

"I don't think so. We checked it several times. Should I consult an external expert?"

"Don't. It's too late. It would just upset the apple cart. All we can do is wait right now. Please keep me informed in case that Manx guy publishes anything or rings gain."

"Will do. See you later." Rose de Jong left, leaving a pensive Central Bank President behind.

*

Frankfurt, Ulmenstraße, 1345 Hours. Markus checked the internet for the latest updates on the gold heist. None of the major news portals had anything to report.

He rang Manfred Krüger at the Federal Police to be told that they were still none the wiser. Krüger denied they would abandon their manhunt because no actual gold had been stolen. They were, after all, still investigating the murder of the escort jeep's driver.

Markus was concerned that he would be facing the biggest embarrassment of his life if his allegations proved to be untenable. He rang Jonathan Schreiber, his present editor. Jonathan had to approve his speculations and back him up. But the editor seemed incredibly relaxed. His comment was that the Central Bank wouldn't sue anyone on the strength of a suspicion alone. Should his theory prove to be false, Markus would have to carry the blame, he informed him. He would be the one whose name would appear under the article.

Half an hour later, Markus read his online article for a last proof. He had decided on a compromise and omitted his conclusion about the false gold delivery.

CENTRAL BANK'S FAKES
DID THE ROBBERS ONLY GET AWAY WITH COUNTERFEITS?
INVESTIGATIONS INTO THE RAID OF THE THREE TON CENTRAL BANK GOLD TRANSPORT TWO DAYS AGO ARE STILL ONGOING.

MEANWHILE THE CENTRAL BANK ANNOUNCED THAT THEY ALWAYS DEPLOY SEPARATE TRANSPORTS FOR SECURITY REASONS. ONE VEHICLE CARRIES THE ACTUAL GOLD WHILE THE OTHER ONE IS STOCKED WITH OUTWARDLY IDENTICAL, YET WORTHLESS DUPLICATES, ACCORDING TO A CENTRAL BANK SPOKESPERSON.

This was apparently also the case in the recent raid. The Central Bank uploaded a surveillance video documenting the arrival and unloading of the real gold.

However, the authenticity of the footage is being questioned by a security expert. During the recorded unloading process a power cut occurred at the Central Bank. Until the emergency power supply was activated, some images should be missing for several milliseconds. But this is not the case. The Central Bank still maintains that the footage is a genuine recording of the gold being unloaded.

*

Frankfurt, Ulmenstraße, 1455 Hours. Markus was sitting at his desk checking if his article was still online on the *HNP's* website. It had been on the net for the last hour and the Central Bank hadn't issued a counterstatement. *A good omen! They've read the article, I know they have. What channels will they use to make it disappear? Will Jonathan's boss or his boss back down if the Central Bank puts pressure on them? Let's see if the HNP will honor its journalistic integrity when it comes to it.*

His phone was ringing. A suppressed number.

"Markus Manx."

"This is Miller. Did you get my letter?"

"I did."

"Good. Let's meet in thirty minutes at venue two."

The caller hung up without waiting for a reply.

What a strange guy. Just hangs up and expects me to have time for him. Markus wasn't sure if he should go. He'd actually forgotten about this morning's letter. He read it again. The whole set up was just like the plot of a cheap spy movie. But he was curious and decided to meet the man after all. What could possibly happen to him, out in the open, right beside Frankfurt's St. Catherine's Church…

*

Berlin, American Embassy, 1510 Hours. Peter Redman was beside himself with rage. "What the fuck!!"

"We should have never shipped the old duplicates from the Fed to Germany, Peter. An inexcusable mistake," Aaron said.

"We can't afford any mistakes right now. None, you hear me!" Peter hissed.

"I know."

"Who fucked up?"

The procedure is always the same. Whenever Germany requests gold deliveries, the duplicates are taken from the Fed and disposed of. At the same time we produce identical, genuine bars for the delivery."

"Are the real bars ready?" Redman asked.

"Of course."

"That still doesn't explain the mistake.

"I can only assume that both pallets were temporarily placed beside each other and they got mixed up. Our boys slipped up," Aaron said.

"And the real bars?"

"We managed to save them just in time before they were dumped."

"Did the Germans smell a rat?" Redman asked.

"Not as far as we know."

"What will we tell the Germans to calm them down? We can't arouse any suspicion."

"The Krauts lied to their own press. They told them they

used two transports. But they didn't."

"So?"

"We use the same story. That we also routinely use two transports for security reasons. One with the real stuff and the other with duplicates. That would at least explain the existence of the counterfeits. The Germans won't query anything because they don't want their own fairy tale investigated."

"When do we deliver the real bars?" asked Redman.

"They're already in Germany, at our airbase in Ramstein. We have the German army collect it. As an explanation we'll state quite openly that we mixed up the pallets when we loaded the bars and the real gold was accidentally delivered to Ramstein. That should do the trick. The Krauts won't suspect anything," Aaron tried to end the unpleasant conversation.

"By the way, Aaron, do you have an update on the information leak in our mine? Any news about the two suspects?"

There were times when it wasn't advisable to be in the same room with Peter Redman – when something rubbed him up the wrong way or when something didn't work out according to plan. Aaron was aware of this and tried to phrase his answer as concisely as possible. "The agency is checking the internal auditor, Ray Hampton, as we speak. They promised us a report by tomorrow."

"And did they catch Lapeng?" Redman interrupted him.

"Not yet. He's still at large. The director of the mine has no idea why his PA so suddenly disappeared. Lapeng wasn't scheduled for a vacation or a business trip."

Redman turned his attention to his computer, a clear sign that their conversation was over. When Aaron didn't leave the room fast enough, Redman looked up: "Anything else?"

"Yeah, there's this reporter who's getting more and more annoying and he's putting himself in danger," Redman complained.

"Are you talking about our gold fan from Frankfurt?"

"That's him, Markus Manx. He's gotten deeply into the gold heist story. We don't really mind that, but he's starting to connect the robbery to Felix Armbrüster."

"Where did you get that intelligence?"

"Wire taps," Aaron replied.

"OK. And is there a connection?" Redman asked.

"There isn't, but we can hardly tell him that."

"Is there a way to get him off the story?"

"I don't think so."

"Then have him shadowed around the clock," Redman ordered brusquely.

"Right, we'll plant a Trojan on his PC so we know what he's researching and writing."

"If you can't keep that guy in check, let me know. We can't let him get in the way, you hear me?"

After Aaron had left the room, Peter Redman put on his coat and walked out of the American Embassy.

*

Two hours later. Peter Redman couldn't tell anyone about his forthcoming meeting. It was too important. One wrong word and the deal would fall through. The man he was about to see needed sensitive handling. But then he also desperately wanted to show that the deal had been successful. A sure way to advance fast in his organization's hierarchy.

They had arranged to meet at a former playground, now rundown, somewhere in Berlin Hellersdorf. Not a great neighborhood and therefore perfect for the purpose. Peter

Redman was unrecognizable. Instead of his customary suit he now wore jeans, a slightly shabby leather jacket and an old gym bag slung over his shoulder in an effort to blend in with the general population of the area, like the teenagers hanging out close by. He sat down on a bench and put the bag down on the ground.

He didn't have to wait long. With his Arab looks, Mohamed wasn't conspicuous around here. "Salam alaikum, Allah be with you," he greeted Redman and sat down beside him on the bench.

"Wa alaikum Salam," Redman replied.

The formalities over with, they got straight down to business, both wanting to conclude the deal as quickly as possible.

"How far are you with your preparations?"

"We are ready. I have six brothers in faith who are prepared to fight."

"How far will they go? How much do they know should they get caught?"

"They are prepared to die to go straight to paradise. But if they should still get caught, they can't reveal anything. They don't know either of us. There are three groups of two fighters each who also don't know about each other. Should any of them be exposed beforehand, it won't jeopardize the operation."

"Good. What do you need?"

"Did you bring the money?" Mohamed said, lowering his voice, presumably out of habit. Discussing money could easily result in a sudden death in his circles.

Redman pushed the gym bag over to him.

"Three million US Dollars, the agreed down payment. You'll get the other seven afterwards."

Mohamed pulled the bag onto the bench without opening it. "Here is a list of the equipment we need," he said.

Redman unfolded the paper and quickly skimmed through the list: Kalashnikovs, hand grenades, plastic explosives. The quantities sufficed for more than one operation. They were evidently using the opportunity to stock up. He didn't care. Procuring the stuff would be no problem. And he actually welcomed the idea of supplying the equipment. This way he could be sure that everything would work without a hitch and nobody could trace anything back to them.

"When shall we go ahead?" Mohamed asked.

"Sometime in the next two weeks. I'll let you know," Redman told him.

"Salam." Mohamed got up and quickly left with the bag.

Redman stayed put. He felt confident that operation *Snow White* would be successful.

*

Frankfurt, St. Catherine's Church, 1530 Hours. Markus walked to the church. It wasn't far from his office and the fresh air on this sunny day in the fall would do him good.

Where exactly am I supposed to meet this Miller guy? He asked himself when he was standing outside the building. *Should I go inside?... I'll better wait right here.*

Markus positioned himself beside the main entrance and attentively vetted his surroundings. He watched an old lady going into the church, to pray, he guessed. A young couple came out, the man with a camera around his neck. Presumably tourists.

Markus had been standing there for five minutes eyeing everyone who passed him when a man in his fifties approached him. Sneakers, black pants, a coat and a baseball cap. He looked quite unremarkable. Even the cap didn't attract any attention in Frankfurt.

"Hi, would you have a chewing gum for me?" the man actually asked him.

Markus had come prepared. "I have some spearmint," he said and offered him the open packet.

"Thank you. Can we take a little walk?"

"If you like... You're really keeping up the suspense, aren't you?"

The man didn't seem in the least threatening. But how did someone look who was up to no good? Markus appraised his stature and decided that he would be able to hold his own, at least physically, if it came to a confrontation. He was, after all, at least four inches taller and probably forty pounds heavier.

"You must be wondering about all the secrecy. And I will tell you more in a minute. But let's walk a bit first."

Is that dude plain paranoid? Or is he some freak and I'm just wasting my time?

They walked together in silence. Miller glanced back several times, evidently checking if they were being followed.

"I think the coast is clear," he started. "You know Felix Armbrüster, a colleague of yours?"

Markus hesitated. He'd just read his college friend's obituary in this morning's paper.

"Please don't stop. Walk normally and inconspicuously."

"What about Felix Armbrüster? And how do you know that we were acquainted?" Markus asked. Miller now had his undivided attention.

"I guess you are aware that Felix died two days ago. Apparently not of natural causes."

"Tell me more."

"He was run over by a train. Suicide is definitely out of

the question."

"What makes you say that?" Markus remembered the wording of the obituary: *died suddenly and unexpectedly.*

"It's a long story. Did you know what Felix was working on?"

"Not really, to be honest. After college we both worked for a paper here in Frankfurt. But since he moved to Berlin, we lost sight of each other.

"Have you met Melinda, his wife?"

"I also know her from college. Felix and she were already dating back then… But would you ever tell me what this is all about?"

I can't wait to hear what's coming next, Markus thought. *For a paranoid freak, if he is that, he's pretty well informed.*

"Right so. Roughly a week ago Felix Armbrüster was in the States to do some research in New York and Washington. You may know that he had his own gold blog."

Now Markus remembered. He'd planned on calling Felix for an interview to go with his coverage of the gold pyramid. But his guilty conscience over his short fling with Melinda had stopped him. The affair had been over once Felix and Melinda had gotten over their rough patch, but Markus didn't know if Felix had noticed anything.

"Yeah, I know about the gold blog, but I didn't really read it. And I haven't been in touch with Felix for a while now."

"He was researching quite a sensational story," the stranger continued. "About the European gold reserves in the States, the German gold reserves in particular."

Miller checked again if they were being followed.

"Felix believed that a least a considerable part of the reserves no longer existed."

Markus was quite critical when it came to official authorities, but now he was skeptical. Could this actually be true?

Miller apparently noticed his doubtful expression.

"Let me explain it to you. Felix had been collecting evidence that the USA has been selling substantial amounts of gold on the global markets for decades."

Markus' curiosity was aroused: "How could that work without anyone noticing?"

"The USA cooked the statistics of a large mining corporation and offered the Federal Reserve's gold on the market as newly prospected gold from the mines."

"Why would they do that?"

"The CIA have always needed a lot of financing for operations not approved by Congress. The billions of Allied gold suited their purposes perfectly."

"The CIA? But all hell will break lose if this becomes public knowledge."

"Absolutely. Do you now understand why Felix ended up in front of a train?"

"It's hard to believe. But why are you telling me of all people?"

"You knew him," Miller explained. "Besides, you're also working on a sensational story."

"You mean the robbery of the Central Bank's gold transport? I don't see the connection?"

"Where did the stolen gold come from, Mr. Manx? What do you think?" Without waiting for a reply, Miller continued: "It was gold belonging to the German Central Bank the Fed stored for the republic of Germany in New York. The CIA has been helping themselves to Germany's gold holdings for decades."

"Are you seriously trying to tell me that the German gold in the US is fake?"

"Felix was very close to proving exactly that."

"But how would he have done that? He couldn't simply have walked into the Fed's vaults and checked if the gold was real. Not even our Central Bank or our Government has managed to inspect our reserves in the States."

"True, but be honest. How far would you go to make a story like that public?"

"What do you mean? Of course I would publish it without hesitation. It would be the scoop of the century."

"I'm not asking without reason. A few years ago you stopped your research into the red-light district in Offenbach after your family was presumably threatened."

How does he know that?

"I ask you again. How far are you prepared to go?"

"What choice do I have? If what you're telling me is true, I'm in it up to my neck already," Markus replied.

"I agree, but in this instance we're dealing with the CIA!"

"Once we've exposed their secrets, we have nothing more to fear from the CIA. They'd have no more reason to eliminate us. Am I right?"

"Correct." For the first time Markus detected Miller's slight American accent. "Before we get onto the big story, let's talk about the article you published this afternoon. You totally nailed that one."

"What? You mean the video was a fake? How would you know that?"

"Your conclusion about the missing frames was real good. But there is another piece of evidence. On the video one can faintly see the tire marks of the armored van. That means it had been driven over a wet road. But there was no rain when the heist happened two days ago. Unlike the transport before it when it rained during the night. There could be a connection."

"Incredible. You're slowly starting to impress me."

"I can't tell you any more today, only that there are people in the background who have an interest in exposing these crimes."

"And how am I supposed to verify what you've just told me. I'm a journalist. I need proof."

"That does present a problem. Felix Armbrüster kept his documents safe somewhere. You have to talk to his wife and find out where. She will trust you."

"I see. That's why you need me. I'm supposed to abuse our friendship to get his research."

"I'm sure Mrs. Armbrüster would also like the public to know the truth about her husband's death, don't you think?"

"Alright so. I'll ask her to meet me."

"Good… There's something else, Mr. Manx. From now on you'll have to be extremely careful. Don't underestimate the risk. The CIA won't hesitate for a second to prevent their dirty secret coming to light. And they'll do whatever it takes, believe me."

"OK, I'll be careful. But how can I contact you?" Markus asked.

"Here is a list of instructions how to encipher messages between us. Don't be offended by the terminology. There are zillions of spam messages in cyberspace every day. With these code words any contact between us will look just like one of them."

Markus was appalled when he read the list of code words. "You're telling me to use this porno terms to send you encrypted messages?"

"You've got it. Nobody will suspect anything if our messages are intercepted. And we are definitely under surveillance, you can depend on it!"

"Before I forget," Miller continued, "here are five unused cell phones and prepaid cards. They are numbered. A new cell and a new card for each day. Only ever switch on the cell for that day for a few minutes to check if I've sent you a text or to text me. In the evening you destroy both the phone and the card. At the bottom of the list you'll find five cell numbers. One for each day."

Markus looked at the list. Impeccable planning, he had to admit. But he was still a little wary.

"Isn't that a bit over the top?"

"Believe me. You'll understand soon. Don't trust anyone. Nobody can know about our meeting." Miller paused to emphasize his words. "Switch on the first phone tomorrow. I will text you a new meeting place and the time. Also try to arrange seeing Mrs. Armbrüster in Berlin tomorrow. Send me a coded message if she agrees. In that case I'll reschedule our meeting for Berlin and text you. Good luck. We can pull this off." With those words Miller left a very shocked Markus Manx.

*

Frankfurt, Ulmenstraße, 1635 Hours. Markus was still confused over his conversation with Miller. To get back into his daily routine he had another look at the Central Bank's video. He needed to check if Miller's assertion about the tire marks was correct. And yes, at close inspection he could see the armored van's marks.

The van must definitely have driven over wet ground. But it didn't rain on Monday. I was at the gold pyramid shortly before myself and I walked back to the office. Incredible. That Miller guy was right!

Then Markus looked up when the previous gold transport had taken place. Exactly four weeks before the last one. Also on a Monday and at the same time of day.

It took Markus a few minutes to find a weather history

and data archive to verify the conditions on the day of the previous transport. Markus knew the answer before he saw the result.

It's true. The rain had stopped at the time, but the streets must still have been wet. The Central Bank really is pulling a fast one.

Markus felt more and more convinced that Miller's allegations had been right.

But he really is slightly paranoid, he thought while dialing Melinda Armbrüster's number, hoping that his battery wouldn't die. A quiet female voice answered:

"Yes…?"

"Hi, Melinda, this is Markus… Markus Manx."

He didn't quite know how to start.

"Markus! We haven't talked in ages," was her surprised reply.

"You're right." Markus felt extremely uncomfortable. "We've lost sight of each other since you and Felix moved to Berlin." Markus cringed when he said *Felix*, but he simply had to put his emotions behind him. "I read in the papers that Felix died. That's just terrible."

Melinda was audibly fighting back the tears.

"We… we can't yet believe it ourselves… Felix threw himself in front of a train… and we…" she started to sob, "we never noticed any signs… nothing at all."

Markus hardly knew what to say.

"Is there anything I can do for you?"

"We… we have no idea… how to go on, Markus," Melinda cried. "Nobody can help us. Nobody can bring Felix back."

The conversation was getting out of hand. Melinda was obviously completely beside herself. Markus tried to get back to the facts.

"Start at the beginning again, Melinda. You said Markus

threw himself in front of that train. Did he actually commit suicide?"

"I find it so hard to believe... but they did an autopsy."

"Was Felix working on a particularly explosive story lately?" Markus tried to gently turn the conversation around.

"He may have been. He was in the States last week, on important research, he said. But I've no idea what he was looking into. I've never been interested in those gold stories."

Melinda was slowly starting to regain her composure.

"But why are you asking? Have you two been in touch lately? Felix didn't mention anything."

"No, I'm afraid I haven't been talking to him. I'd planned to call him about a story I was writing. I never got around to it though. But I did regularly read his blog," Markus lied to pretend he had been interested in Felix's work.

"That stupid blog. We've had so many rows about it. Ever since he started it, he spent far too much time on it. And the last few weeks it was particularly bad."

"I heard that Felix was onto a huge scoop, Melinda." Markus tried to approach the all decisive question. "Did you know anything about really important documents that may be connected to his death?"

After a long pause Melinda finally replied. "There was a time when I actually liked you, Markus. But now you're being terribly crude."

Melinda talked herself into a rage. "We don't hear from you in years. Then Felix dies and you call with your feigned condolences while all you really want is to pump me for information to get at some documents. Do you know how much that hurts me? It's hard enough trying to get over a suicide. No, Markus, go away and leave me in peace!"

"Melinda," Markus tried to vindicate himself, but she had hung up.

That sure backfired! OK, I can understand that Melinda is pissed at me. But now we may never know why Felix died.

*

Frankfurt, Situation Center of the German Federal Police, 1700 Hours. Chief of Police Hartmann wasn't feeling very well. More mentally than physically. Late-life depression, his wife had been convinced for a long time. It was common knowledge that people were susceptible to the affliction in their mid-fifties. Those close to Hartmann frequently suffered the effects. His resilience towards stress was decreasing all the time while his surliness increased in inverse proportion.

Today was just one of those days. Nothing negative had happened so far and yet his mood was about as bad as could be. And he still had to face the crisis committee meeting…

Minister Stahl didn't waste much time on pleasantries and asked those present if they had finally come up with some results. Hartmann said nothing, glad that Stahl had relieved him of the burden of making the cumbersome introductions. Instead he started listlessly doodling on his papers.

Brandner from the Central Bank was the first to speak up. This was his chance to shine with the news about the genuine gold.

"The real gold is on its way to us. The Americans organized two transports. The one with the counterfeits was the one that was hijacked and the one with the genuine bars will arrive in a few hours."

"And you actually buy that?" Hartmann instantly argued. "Is that their usual procedure or was this the world premiere?"

"The Americans told us they had been tipped off about a raid and that's why they used the strategy for the first time."

"And why weren't we warned as well? Or at least informed right after the robbery?"

Police Chief Hartmann's foul mood was obvious. He realized that the different sides were trying to hide something. There was far too much politics involved for his liking. In cases like these people were always looking for a scapegoat. And he had no intention to be the one shouldering the blame.

Finally putting his cards on the table he said: "I trust the Yank's story about the double transport as little as that reporter believes in ours."

Contrary to his usual pro-American stance, Gmeiner from the Federal Intelligence Service now sided with Hartmann.

"None of this surprises me. I've been working closely with the CIA, the NSA and all the rest for twenty years, but I doubt they've ever considered me their equal. They let you play as long as it suits their plans. Yet they drop you instantly when you're no longer of any use to them."

"That's been my experience, too," General Steiner concurred. "A lot of problems could be tackled far more successfully through mutual cooperation. But the Yanks are only interested in their own concerns."

"Gentlemen," Stahl intervened. "None of this is getting us any further. First of all we should be glad that the gold turned up. And secondly what do we care why the Americans made the right decision in hindsight."

"With all due respect, Minister," but that's not enough to convince the public. That journalist, Manx, has already published an article doubting the authenticity of the Central Bank's video. But perhaps Mr. Brandner can enlighten us further."

"What can I say? Just because a few frames are allegedly missing because of a power cut doesn't necessarily mean that the video is a fake. Perhaps our backup generator reacted fast enough and nothing is missing after all. What do I know? I'm not a technician."

"You see," Hartmann remarked, noticeably more aggressive towards Brandner, "You say things like *What do I know* and make it obvious that you don't want to know. You're starting to make mistakes and you're recklessly undermining our credibility!"

"Stop right here," Stahl intervened. "We'll accomplish nothing by fighting with each other. We could do with some results from the investigations to come to grips with the problem."

The shot was clearly aimed at Hartmann. Stahl's face briefly disappeared from the monitor, conveying the impression that he was whispering instructions to somebody. The assembled men now had a clear view of Stahl's stately office; his background decoration as it were.

Seconds later Stahl's face reappeared and Hartmann reported about the discovery of a getaway vehicle, but without any suspicious fingerprints and merely a single hair that may have belonged to one of the robbers. But the police databank hadn't found a match. Just like the VW Touareg, the vehicle had been stolen two days before the heist and the license plate the night before.

Then Gmeiner tried to impress with the news of a phone call his agency had intercepted. A possible perp had rang somebody in the gold laundering business, but hadn't revealed any useable names and then turned off his cell. They were hopeful about the number of the man he had called, which they had been able to identify. The BND had promptly passed the number to Hartmann's staff.

While Gmeiner was presenting his findings to the camera, Hartman had finished decorating his paperwork. Not to annoy Gmeiner for once, but because his thoughts kept drifting to his retirement. His line drawing depicted an allotment with a little summer house and fruit trees sheltering a bench underneath plus various fantasy flowers. The door to the summer house flaunted a sign which read HARTMANN HERMITAGE in large letters. He was aware that not only his professional life was drawing to a close, but also his marriage. All he wanted was peace.

"At least something," Stahl complimented Gmeiner and propelled Hartmann back to reality. They all agreed to meet again the next day.

I wonder if the previous transports carried genuine gold or just counterfeits like this time, Hartmann thought as he left the conference room.

*

Hofheim, Lena's Apartment, 1850 Hours. As arranged, Markus had brought the wine for their dinner. He'd managed to get hold of a particularly special one, a Brunello di Montalcino from the Castelgiocondo estate. The last bottle from their 2010 vintage. The wine merchant had even given him a ten percent discount. Markus loved the pure Sangiovese grape from Tuscany. Sadly his paltry income didn't often allow him to splash out like this.

He took the stairs instead of the elevator to Lena's fourth floor apartment, his first humble effort to improve his fitness once again. The door was invitingly unlocked and he could see her working behind the open kitchen door as he went inside.

"Hi, Markus," she welcomed him, "I'll be with you in a minute."

From the lounge he watched her pushing something into the oven. Once again, she looked stunning! High heels and black stockings under a red, knee-length, silk kimono with a beige floral print.

"That kimono looks great, so Japanese."

"I'm glad you like it. I bought it in Tokyo. But that was a good few years ago… Dinner will take a while. We'll have dessert first and the lasagna after."

"What do you mean dessert first?"

Lena took his hand and pulled him into the bedroom.

"Follow me and I'll show you."

About half an hour later Markus knew exactly what she had meant.

"After that dessert I can hardly wait for the main course," he commented, his hair all tousled.

"You won't be disappointed either. I've cooked a lasagna with salmon, prawns and spinach."

"Wonderful. And the wine's just perfect for it!"

Markus helped her set the table.

"I just have to tell you what happened to me today. Somehow I still can't believe it myself. Guess who rang me this morning?" Lena grinned.

"No idea. You got a new assignment?"

"Exactly. People always say that technical lectures never lead to real commissions and then: B-I-N-G-O!"

"The way you're acting, I take it you caught quite a big fish," Markus concluded.

"Correct, detective. One could say a golden opportunity."

She laughed in the Lena way he loved.

"Come on," Markus prompted. "Some major corporation, am I right?"

"Not quite so big, but very special," Lena told him proudly.

"Out with it. Who is it?"

"Geißen & Mapitier. Yes, the guys who print the Euro notes."

"Really? They work closely with the Central Bank, don't they?"

"They do."

"Are you going to tell me more or do you need another glass of wine first?"

"OK so. This morning some secretary to the board of directors called to arrange a meeting with me at short notice," Lena started.

"Why did they pick you?"

"I asked her exactly that myself and guess what: her boss saw me at the IT symposium on Monday and apparently he'd been real impressed. I agreed to meet him."

"That's the spontaneous Lena I love. Always straight to the point," Markus laughed. "And when?"

"The secretary suggested I have lunch with him today. Apparently her boss and some other people who make the decisions would only be in Frankfurt for another day."

"You already had the meeting?"

"Yeah, at the airport. Twelve thirty at the Sheraton. When I got there, some assistant had already been expecting me and brought me to a specially booked conference room. Everything was perfectly organized. Five people immediately joined me and we had the usual round of introductions," Lena described.

"That was all super fast. And what are you supposed to do for them?"

"They want me to work out a concept to check possible

weaknesses in their security systems. They're even giving me a team."

"Sounds exciting. Especially since their systems are presumably already quite foolproof."

"I assume they are. But they want to make absolutely sure any potential weak points won't develop into a problem at some stage. At any price."

"Got it. And when you say at any price, I gather they made you a first class offer you couldn't refuse and you accepted instantly," Markus teased her.

"Precisely. They offered me twice as much as I would have asked them for. I signed the contract there and then."

"Congratulations, well done! And there are no snags?"

"There is one: we're starting right away. I've got to be in Munich tomorrow. They were worried because they only just about managed to prevent someone hacking into their personal data last week."

Markus swallowed hard.

"Hey, you're supposed to be happy for me."

"Munich," he said visibly downcast. "That means I'll only see you at the weekends… Snoopy."

"You're calling me Snoopy?"

Markus didn't answer her. *Perhaps that was the wrong timing,* he mentally scolded himself.

"Sure, I'm delighted for you. It's a great opportunity."

"Don't be silly. We've only known each other for three days and you already act as if we were married. Tell me what *you* did today. I want to know how the gold robbery story developed."

After Markus had digested her accusation of acting like a possessive husband, he turned back into the professional journalist.

"I'll tell you about the video first," he started. "I confronted the Central Bank with our suspicions about it and they once again insisted on its authenticity. The conversation with their press officer seemed quite strange. As if she'd turned on the speakerphone. So I decided to write an article about my speculations. It was online at noon on the *HNP's* homepage, at least until this evening."

"Why do you think they might take it off the net?"

"Well with explosive subjects like this it's not always easy for the smaller papers to stick to their guns. Some of them choose the easy option when the pressure gets too much."

"Any other news on the gold front?"

"I noticed something else in the video." In view of Lena's unusual contract, Markus didn't want to mention the ominous Miller for the time being. So he pretended that he'd spotted the tire marks himself.

"That's brilliant, Markus," Lena praised him. "Now you can not only prove that the video doesn't show Monday's transport, you can also substantiate that the Central Bank presumably tried to fool the public. You've got them!"

"That shall be tomorrow's article. There was also something else."

"Go on, tell me!" Lena urged him. But Markus first took a leisurely sip of red wine.

"Do you remember the obituary of my college friend Felix Armbrüster?"

"Sure, weren't you going to ring his wife to express your condolences?"

"I called her and she told me that Felix threw himself in front of a train."

"What?" Lena was incredulous.

"His wife didn't understand why he did it."

Markus now mixed Miller's stories with what he had learned from the phone call to fill Lena in on the latest information.

"She can't believe it was suicide. And, wait for it: Felix was researching some really explosive business for his gold blog. He was in the States last week to look into his suspicion that the gold reserves held there are only counterfeits."

"Incredible. Did he have any proof?"

"Possibly, yes," Markus said.

"If that should be the case, Felix really was in danger. But it's very hard to believe…. What did his wife say?"

"She wasn't interested in Felix's projects and didn't really know anything. But she did say that they had argued a lot lately because his gold blog was often more important to him than his family."

"If your suspicions are right, we're dealing with a major conspiracy: the gold heist, the looted US gold reserves and Felix's nasty murder."

"Any ideas how to prove it?" Markus asked.

"Let me think…"

Lena chewed on her lower lip, as always when she was trying to solve a puzzle.

Eventually she asked: "Do you know where he was supposed to have killed himself?"

"Not exactly. Somewhere in Berlin, I guess."

"I've just thought of something. A few years ago I hacked into the system of the Charité teaching hospital in Berlin. If we're lucky, that's were Felix was brought for the post mortem. I know that every suicide has to be checked by a forensic pathologist in case of foul play. If the medical examiners find anything, the autopsy report and the death cert are lodged in their databank."

"It would be worth a try to see if they found any external factors," Markus agreed. "Although his research documents would be far more fascinating…"

"One step at the time, Sherlock!" she said.

"Sherlock?" Markus grinned.

Lena opened her laptop and started typing. Her fingers danced across the keyboard while Markus enjoyed the rest of the red wine in his glass.

He started dreaming about lounging on a sandy beach with Lena, listening to the sound of the waves, sipping their cocktails and chatting about his childhood.

"I found it," Lena tore him away from his daydream. "The hospital actually didn't upgrade its security and I easily got into their system. Locating Felix's data was no problem."

Markus jumped up.

"What did you find?"

"Look. This is his death cert. It says time the time of death was four p.m. and the apparent cause of death was suicide."

"But that doesn't really shed any more light on the matter."

"True, but that may not be all. Let's take a closer look at the document's properties. OK, it was originally created by a Dr. Müller at thirty four minutes past three yesterday. Then a Prof. Dr. Hellbrügge revised it at five fifty two."

"And what does that prove?"

"Nothing so far, but let's see what that man Hellbrügge changed." She paused for a moment. "Now it gets interesting. In Müller's version the time of death was specified as between *eight and eleven a.m.* As cause of death he listed *non natural.* There's another field regarding indications about unnatural causes and he ticked it. He entered: *because the subject had already been dead hours before the accident occurred.*"

"That's incredible!" Markus exclaimed. "They actually changed the death cert so the whole thing would be treated as a suicide!"

He was absolutely shocked. "Who the hell is powerful

enough to be able to change a death cert?... And who murdered Felix?"

Lena couldn't take her eyes off the decisive entry in the original cert when she replied:

"Considering the suspicion of fake gold reserves in the US, I can only think of the CIA. And should that be true, this whole affair is deadly serious, Markus. You have to be extremely careful from now on," she pleaded.

"I could do with some fresh air," he said. "Want to go for a walk?"

"No, thanks. I have to check something else. Just take my keys from the hall table so you don't have to ring when you want to get back in."

She gave him a kiss.

"See you in a bit. Just knock at the door when you're on the landing."

The walk revived him. The fresh air helped to get his thoughts in order. *Felix was killed after researching the US gold reserves. What evidence did he have that they are fakes? What is the connection with the transport of counterfeits to Germany? If the Fed had also previously delivered fakes, the German Central Bank must have noticed. Who is that Miller guy? Does he work on his own or who does he work for? What's his motive? Is it a coincidence that one of the Central Bank's close associates hired Lena right at this point or is it all linked to the gold heist and my research?* A lot of questions he urgently needed to answer.

Back from his walk, he knocked and Lena opened the door. Then she went straight back to her laptop. She was staring at the screen, slightly pursing her lips.

That unmistakable sign that she's concentrating hard, Markus thought and waited.

A little later, Lena looked up. "Sorry, but I haven't any news yet."

"Why the 'yet'? What are you trying to do?"

"It's only a hunch. But nowadays a lot of people use cloud storage. Perhaps Felix did, too. I'm trying to find out if that's the case."

"Um…How?"

"Seeing that Felix had his own blog, it's likely that he used the same service provider for his homepage and his cloud."

"Makes sense," Markus nodded.

"It wasn't difficult to find out who hosts his homepage and they also offer cloud services. I just have to break into his cloud and check if Felix stored any data there. And if so, what exactly."

Lena pressed the Enter key.

"Now we'll have to wait. I've activated a tool to find a password. But that can take the whole night, I'm afraid… By the way, I've got an idea how we could pass the time while we're waiting," she smiled encouragingly.

"Have you any idea how incredible you are? Attractive, intelligent, and always surprising. Every man's dream."

"Don't say that. A lot of men don't like smart women. But I'm glad you're not one of them," she said and took his hand.

Thursday

Hofheim, Lena's Apartment, 0730 Hours. When Markus woke up, Lena was no longer lying beside him. He pulled on his T-shirt and stepped into the lounge where she was already sitting at the dining table with her laptop.

"Good morning," he said, "you're up bright and early."

"Give us a kiss," she said and demonstratively offered her lips."

Markus gladly obliged before asking her why she was already up.

"At some stage during the night my program alerted me that it had hit paydirt."

"Does that mean you got in? What did you find?"

"I can answer your first question with a yes. But I still have to say no to the second one. So far."

"Will I get us something for breakfast?"

"That would be great. But I suggest you put on some clothes before you go. It will be quite cold outside in just a T-shirt."

"OK, smarty-pants. I'll grab a quick shower first. Any suggestions in the food line?"

Lena described the way to her favorite bakery, then concentrated on her task again. She didn't have much time seeing that she still had to pack her overnight bag and be on her way to the airport by ten at the latest. Her new clients were already expecting her in Munich.

When Markus returned with fresh bread rolls, he found Lena's laptop abandoned on the table, copying some file onto a USB drive, and the sound of water gushing in the shower.He deposited his bag of groceries in the kitchen and tried to prepare an intimate breakfast for two.

Not that easy considering that I usually snack at the nearest deli, he thought. *But she has a coffee maker that works and an automatic egg cooker…*

Lena floated into the room draped in a lilywhite dressing gown.

"Voilà! Just like breakfast at Tiffany's," she beamed.

"Do I detect a hint of irony in your voice?" he reprimanded her playfully. "I don't think this is too bad, considering we're in Frankfurt…"

"Full marks to the bachelor!" Lena gave him the thumbs up. "Just what I needed." She heartily tucked into the rolls. "And the coffee smells fantastic…"

Markus could no longer contain his curiosity.

"So, what did you discover?"

"I can't tell you much yet. I found an account belonging to Felix. It contains an awful lot of documents. Eighteen gigabytes altogether. Now you'll have to go through them."

"Sounds like an incredible amount of work."

"Absolutely, but you can narrow it down chronologically. I take it you're primarily interested in the more recent documents."

"How much longer will your computer take to download the data?"

"Another half hour, I guess. The download speed is significantly slower than usual because I had to use various hubs so nobody can trace me."

"Is it safe? Or can we be caught?"

"There's never a 100 percent guarantee. But I know what I'm doing…"

"That wasn't meant to be a criticism. I'm just curious."

Lena smiled.

"Don't worry. By the way, I've got a little something for you… Wait…"

She took a scotch tape dispenser from her desk and put it in front of him.

"Just for emergencies."

"Scotch tape for emergencies? What am I supposed to do with that?"

"It might save your life if it comes to it. The dispenser is actually just camouflage for an emergency kit. The bottom is detachable, but you can only look inside when I ask you to. The contents can help us if we find ourselves in danger."

"Are you scared of something?"

"No," Lena replied, "but my job is to create the most ingenious security precautions. I guess it affects my private life as well."

Markus eyed the heavy desk dispenser with its functional design and serrated cutting edge. The plastic housing was usually filled with sand to provide stability. It was quite clever to fill it with an emergency kit instead.

"You really are an extraordinary woman."

Lena lapped up the compliment.

After their extensive breakfast, the download was finally complete. Lena handed Markus the USB drive with the data before she retired to her room to pack. She wanted to make it to the airport in time. Markus went back to his office where he intended to phone the Central Bank. He was looking forward to confronting Rose the Jong with the tire marks on the video.

*

Frankfurt, Situation Center of the German Federal Police, 0745 Hours. Hartmann reversed his Mercedes into his reserved parking space. A plane was taking off above him. He looked up at the Lufthansa airbus. How he would love to be on that plane... Where to? It didn't matter. Just anywhere but here. *People really are no longer meant to be married for more than a quarter of a century*, he thought, sick and tired of his wife's constant nagging, his headaches... *Why couldn't she just leave him alone?*

Hartmann walked through the long corridor to his field office where he collapsed into his chair. Its squeaking sound indicated that it had also had just about enough. He faced the three new folders on his desk. His staff had been busy and that meant he had to work his way through a mountain of paper.

He opened the first file - transcripts of the interviews with the three soldiers. The second file contained photos of the warehouse in Rödermark. Hartmann quickly came to the conclusion that they all looked the same. File three held Manx's article. A waste of time. What could a small-time reporter from a mediocre newspaper possibly contribute to the case? The Police Chief closed the files again.

Retirement and a garden are no solution either, it echoed through his head while he got up and walked over to the conference room. *Ingrid will just pester me 24/7...*

This morning Sven Stahl was exactly on time. Hartmann forced himself to greet him and the rest of the assembly before handing the chair to Brandner.

"Just a few minutes ago that journalist Manx contacted our press office again," Brandner said. "He asked for a statement outlining why the Central Bank is lying about the video of the gold transport."

"What?" Stahl asked, taken aback. "Is he just chancing his arm or does he have proof?"

"Our spokesperson also asked him for evidence and he told her about tire marks left by the armored van in the video. He claims this proves that the recording is not from Monday, but from the previous gold transport a month ago when it rained the night before. And that there was no rain on Monday."

"Damn it!" Stahl cursed, who had instantly grasped the magnitude of the problem. "How could you possibly make such a rookie mistake?" He worked himself up into a proper rage. He'd never been one to tolerate failure easily. Once he had calmed down again, he quizzed Brandner about the Central Bank's forthcoming reaction to the allegation.

Brandner wasn't prepared with a convincing answer. The Central Bank was working on a strategy under the direction of its President, he claimed miserably.

"It's vital," Gmeiner started," to take the incriminating footage off the net immediately. We can't let other journalists check up on Manx's theory. Perhaps we have an even older tape of a gold transport without tire marks we can use as a substitute."

"Not a bad idea," Stahl conceded. "On the other hand it would show even more clearly that something is being hushed up."

"We could always say that we accidently hyperlinked the wrong video," Gmeiner elaborated.

"Do you seriously believe the media are that easily fooled?" Harmann pointed out.

"Of course there'll be speculations," Gmeiner attempted to defend his idea. "But I'd rather have people speculating and mocking us over a stupid mistake than having a massive scandal on our hands."

The crisis committee were still discussing Gmeiner's proposal when there was a knock on the door.

"Come in!" Hartmann shouted testily.

"Please excuse the interruption," one of Hartmann's executives stuttered, evidently feeling pretty stressed. "I just received an urgent email for Mr. Gmeiner."

Gmeiner realized at a glance why the message really did justify an interruption of the proceedings.

"You have to listen to this, gentlemen. It's an article Manx published a few minutes ago about the Central Bank's video."

WHY IS THE CENTRAL BANK LYING?
INTENDED EXONERATING FOOTAGE TURNS OUT TO BE INCRIMINATING

FOUR DAYS AFTER THE SPECTACULAR THEFT OF THREE TONS OF GOLD THE ROBBERS ARE STILL AT LARGE. THE POLICE ARE STILL GROPING IN THE DARK ALTHOUGH IT IS NOW OBVIOUS THAT THE PERPETRATORS STOLE COUNTERFEIT BARS. THE CENTRAL BANK EXPLAINED THIS BY STATING THAT THEY EMPLOYED A SECRET STRATEGY WHEREBY THEY ALWAYS USE TWO TRANSPORTS FOR OUR RETURNED GOLD FROM THE STATES, ONE WITH GENUINE BARS, THE OTHER WITH FORGED DUPLICATES. THE ROBBERS, THEY CLAIM, HAD ONLY GOTTEN AWAY WITH THE COUNTERFEITS.

MEANWHILE THE CENTRAL BANK'S SURVEILLANCE VIDEO THEY RELEASED TO PROVE THAT THE REAL GOLD HAD BEEN SUCCESSFULLY DELIVERED TURNED OUT TO BE FAKED. YESTERDAY WE REPORTED EXCLUSIVELY THAT SOME FRAMES OF THE VIDEO SHOULD HAVE BEEN MISSING DUE TO A POWER CUT AT THE RELEVANT TIME. THIS INITIAL DOUBT ABOUT ITS AUTHENTICITY HAS NOW BEEN AUGMENTED BY FURTHER EVIDENCE. ON THE FOOTAGE IT SHOWS THE ARMORED VAN LEAVING TIRE MARKS WHEN ENTERING THE CENTRAL BANK'S GATES. IT SHOULD THEREFORE HAVE RAINED ON THE DAY. LAST MONDAY, HOWEVER, IT DIDN'T.

ALTHOUGH THE CENTRAL BANK'S SPOKESPERSON STILL INSISTS THAT THE VIDEO IS GENUINE, SHE WAS UNABLE TO PROVIDE A PLAUSIBLE EXPLANATION FOR THOSE TIRE TRACKS.

THIS POSES THE QUESTION WHY THE CENTRAL BANK LIED. WHY WAS THE PUBLIC NOT IMMEDIATELY INFORMED THAT THE ROBBERS HAD STOLEN COUNTERFEITS? THERE IS

ONLY ONE CONCLUSION: THE USA INTENTIONALLY SUPPLIED US WITH FORGERIES. IF THIS IS TRUE, WE MUST ASK OURSELVES IF THEIR PREVIOUS DELIVERIES ALSO CONTAINED FAKES. IS IT POSSIBLE THAT NONE OF OUR GOLD RESERVES IN AMERICA ARE REAL? AND ARE THE BARS IN THE BRILLIANTLY SPARKLING GOLD PYRAMID REAL? IT IS TIME THE CENTRAL BANK FINALLY ADMITS THE TRUTH!

The article also included several photographs. One of them showed a still from the video with clearly recognizable tire marks. Another the counterfeit bar from Luxembourg, which was also included in a shot of the gold transfer at the airport in Frankfurt. The inscription on both bars was identical. Most prominent was a photo of the gold pyramid. Underneath it in bold letters: *All that glitters may not be gold!*

After Gmeiner had read out the article and shown the photos around, Stahl was suddenly in a desperate rush to excuse himself from the meeting, claiming he had to attend some important talks. Brandner, too, apparently needed to get back to the Central Bank immediately. The meeting ended abruptly…

*

Frankfurt, Central Station, 1013 Hours. Markus was waiting for his train. Following the sensational copy he had supplied over the past few days, his friend Jonathan Schreiber was eager to publish his latest article as well. In this respect at least his commitment had already paid off. The HNP was sure to supply him with constant employment for the foreseeable future – they had never before been as frequently quoted in other newspapers. Markus' research had made the small regional paper the opinion leader regarding the gold heist.

After Markus had briefly sketched the contents of his latest story, Jonathan could hardly wait to get his hands on the finished article. The hits on their homepage had already doubled the previous day. A new revelation and the figures would shoot through the roof.

Markus seized the moment to have Jonathan agree to cover his expenses for some special research in Berlin. Despite her unwelcoming manner on the phone the day before, he had still decided to visit Melinda. Even if only for the sake of their longstanding friendship. He didn't want to leave her with the bad impression she must have formed of him. At half past ten he boarded the Intercity Express from Frankfurt to the capital, scheduled to arrive at twenty past two.

On the train Markus started going through the data on Lena's USB drive. He had purposely reserved a seat facing the opposite direction of travel to increase the likelihood that nobody would join him. He certainly didn't need a nosy neighbor to peep at his material.

He had also wisely selected a time outside rush hour when the train would be less than half full. As an added precaution he demonstratively piled his jacket and bag on the seat beside him so he could work in peace.

Lena had copied thousands of files from Armbrüster's

cloud. The four hour trip would just about suffice to scan through the most recent ones.

Before he began, he transferred the entire contents of the USB onto his harddrive. This would make it easier and quicker to access the data. He also wanted to ensure that he didn't accidentally delete anything. When all the files had finally been copied, he started his search for the proverbial needle in the haystack.

That's weird, he thought when he discovered some folders in a directory called *d-LOG*. *Why did Felix use fish names for his folders? Could he have developed a passion for fishing in recent years?*

He was about to close the directory when he noticed the name *Moray*. *Fishing for moray eels? That doesn't make sense! And, on reflection, Felix would never have taken up angling.*

He now viewed the other folder names from a different perspective and wondered which one he should read first. *Moray* sounded interesting. *Herring* was boring. *Goldfish* fascinated him most of all.

That particular one contained various sub-folders, some PDFs and a large Excel file called *Summary.xlsx*. More than 2 MB. Markus opened this one first.

He found several tabs, one of them filled with rows of figures. This was apparently where Felix had chronologically charted transactions on the gold markets. He also found the production quotas of large mining corporations. *It must have taken him months.*

Another tab revealed a pivot table with a graph showing figures spanning two years and several peaks evidently representing unusually high turnovers.

After he had browsed through the other tabs, he closed the file and looked at the PDFs. Screenshots of Felix' research. He had evidently neatly documented his Excel entries. But Markus didn't understand what his former college friend had been trying to convey. *What could possibly be explosive enough to justify a murder?* he wondered while Lower Saxony's countryside passed by his window without him noticing.

He closed the *Goldfish* folder and contemplated which one to open next. When he read *Herring* again, he remembered how he and some of his buddies at the School of Journalism had occasionally passed each other information with code names. *Red herring*, he thought. *A false trail or diversion.*

Sounds promising. Let's have a look. Markus clicked through the folders until he landed on the Word document *Research Paper.docx.* But it wouldn't open. Instead a window popped up: *Research Paper.docx. is protected. Enter password.*

Damn! Markus thought. *Why did Felix use a password for this one? The information must be especially important.*

He would have loved to jump up and pace up and down the train to concentrate his thoughts. But at this stage the compartment was pretty crowded, although most of the other passengers were too engrossed in themselves, reading, eating or playing with their cells. Nobody paid any attention to him. Good…

After he had calmed down a little, he tried to figure out the password. His first attempt was *Armbrüster.* No go. Another window popped up: *The password you entered is invalid. Make sure that the Caps Lock key is not enabled and use the correct upper/lower case.*

Markus clicked on *ok* and the window closed. He went back to *Open File* and the cursor flashed expectantly in anticipation of a new password.

What could Felix have used? The names of his children or his wife combined with their dates of birth? Perhaps the name of some pet? His parents'? It's useless. This could take forever. Besides, I don't know if Microsoft will at some stage completely bar any access to the file if I enter to many wrong passwords.

Then he remembered that he had Lena's expertise at his disposal. A hacker like her would presumably find a way to open the document in no time.

He switched on his cell phone to send her an email:

DARLING LENA,

I'M ON THE TRAIN TO BERLIN LOOKING THROUGH THE FILES ON YOUR USB DRIVE. ONE OF THEM LOOKS PARTICULARLY PROMISING. I SUSPECT THIS IS WHERE FELIX SUMMARIZED THE RESULTS OF HIS RESEARCH. SO FAR I HAVEN'T FOUND ANYTHING EXPLOSIVE IN THE OTHER DOCUMENTS, SO I REALLY NEED TO KNOW THE CONTENTS OF THIS FILE. UNFORTUNATELY IT'S PASSWORD PROTECTED. CAN YOU HELP, PLEASE? IT'S EXTREMELY IMPORTANT.

MARKUS (WHO ALREADY MISSES YOU TERRIBLY)

He attached the document and sent the email. It would still take over an hour before the train reached its destination and Markus was no longer in the mood to read more files. His index finger already felt half numb from all the clicking.

He closed his laptop and gazed out the window. He started daydreaming about Lena and their past two nights together. But he also remembered Melinda. Their two week affair had left a lasting impression and could have turned into something more serious if she and Felix hadn't made up.

But that was in the past and things had worked out differently. Now he had to absolutely convince her to listen to him. She had always been extremely emotional and it wouldn't be easy to get her to forgive him. He wouldn't have a hope over the phone, but meeting her in person might provide him with a chance to change her mind. His trump card, the original autopsy report clearly indicating that Felix had been murdered, should do the trick. And Markus swore to himself he would not ask her again where Felix might have hidden his papers. If she listened to him, she may just volunteer the information. But he would definitely not mention the subject again.

*

Berlin, American Embassy, 1430 Hours. *To achieve greatness, one has to be prepared to make sacrifices,* Peter Redman thought. The document in front of him was marked *Top Secret* and only intended for his eyes. The phone rang. The tap-proof line. A call from Langley.

"Hi," was all he said after picking up the receiver.

"Hello, Peter," was the reply. "We have a problem!"

That didn't bode well. Redman was getting sick and tired of problems. But it was his job to take care of them and produce solutions.

"What's up?" he barked.

"Markus Manx has Armbrüster's files."

"What!?" Redman was speechless.

"Your man fucked up again. When he searched Armbrüster's office he apparently didn't erase all the data."

"What a jerk! What has Manx got?"

"We're not exactly sure yet, but we know that he has the crucial file. Armbrüster password-protected it. And because Manx couldn't open it, he sent it to his girlfriend, that hacker lady."

"So he doesn't yet know the content!" Redman surmised.

"Correct, but I guess it won't be long before he does. His girlfriend will crack the password in no time. Perhaps she even knows the master password."

"What is actually in that document?"

"It contains a precise description of the turnovers on the goldmarkets and the correct conclusions based on the revenue peaks. If that gets published, all eyes will instantly be on us. There is more than one person who could ask awkward questions. We could get busted."

"I'll make sure that won't happen." Redman said.

Ever since that phone call Redman had been incredibly angry. Manx had actually managed to get at Armbrüster's files. "Shit! Shit! Shit!" he cursed and banged the receiver so forcefully on the top of his desk that the black plastic cover burst.

Furious, he ordered Aaron to come to his office. When he came in a few minutes later, Redman roared at him: "Am I surrounded by nothing but amateurs? Are you all too fucking stupid to erase simple files? How did Manx get his hands on Armbrüster's documents? One should…"

Aaron remained surprisingly composed in the face of Redman's explosion.

"We wiped everything on Armbrüster's computer. Our eraser program deleted every single bite of the incriminating files. Permanently. His office was also clean. I checked.

"You must have overlooked a second computer." Redman was still roaring. He didn't intend to calm down until he had found whoever was responsible.

"In the meantime we've also checked Armbrüster's internet and phone connections. Nothing indicates he had a second PC. And he would have also admitted it when we interrogated him!"

"So we still don't know how Manx got the files."

Even if the analysis of the communication data doesn't reveal a link between that damned journalist and Armbrüster, he thought, *the two of them may have been in contact through another channel. Or are there already more people in the know than we think?*

"Shit!"

Aaron was lucky that he hadn't been the one who'd messed up. But the suspicion that several people were in the know was frightening. They had to check everything again. Somewhere there was a connection between Manx and Armbrüster they had overlooked.

"Did you at least make some headway with the suspects from the mine," Redman changed the subject.

They had. Seven hours earlier at 2327 hours local time in the US State Nevada, on the Interstate 80, a police patrol had spotted a car which had exceeded the speed limit of 65 miles an hour by at least 20. Just outside the small town of Sparks they had caught up with the driver and forced him to stop. He had appeared unusually nervous to the cops. The arrest warrant issued in his name may have been the reason.

According to the officers' report the man had behaved impeccably. He hadn't moved from his position in the driver's seat, both hands visible on the steering wheel at all times. Being questioned by specialists from the agency, Byron Lapeng, assistant to the Rocky Mines Corporation's director for many years, had been ready to talk.

He told them that he'd been on his way to Carson City where he had planned to hide in his sister's place for a while Lapeng had been on the run for two days. When the CIA had started to check out the mine on Monday, he had panicked. He assumed that somebody had denounced him and he feared the worst. The audit would inevitably reveal his misconduct.

It had all started when an ex-employee had blackmailed

him, threatening to report him for sexual aussault. She could proof two of his advances. Lapeng had no choice. He had to pay up if he didn't want to ruin his promising career and lose his family. So he urgently needed money. In the past few months he had managed to procure a six figure sum by taking bribes for awarding contracts. He was now actually relieved that it was all over and had provided a detailed statement at the very first interview.

The agency had checked his statement. Lapeng had told the truth.

"The leak must be somewhere else," Aaron said. "We've handed Lapeng's case over to the local police. The internal auditor Ray Hampton is our only remaining suspect. We're still waiting for the report that was promised for today."

The phone rang. The same voice from CIA headquarters as earlier.

"Manx is in Berlin right now. He has his cell on him, so you can locate him easily."

A nasty grin crossed Redman's face. *That should make it easy. Manx' time is up.* He gave the necessary instructions.

Aaron nodded and left the room without a word. He had no problem getting his hands dirty.

*

Berlin, Subway, 14:50 Hours. Ironically most of Berlin's subway lines are above ground. Therefore cell phones receive a much better signal than they would on an actual underground transport system. Luckily for Markus, who was on his way to Melinda when his cell rang. He answered it although the caller ID was withheld.

"Hi, Markus." The voice sounded tinny.

At first he thought it was the reception, but then he realized that wasn't the reason.

"Don't say anything, please. Just listen carefully, Snoopy."

Although the voice was distorted through a voice changer, he instantly knew who he was talking to. Lena seemed extremely worried.

"After you've hung up, switch your cell off immediately and take out the battery. Whatever you do, don't turn it on again or reinsert the battery or they'll be able to trace you. I'm afraid this is extremely serious, Markus! Finish your job as quickly as possible, if you absolutely have to do it, and get out of Berlin. But be super careful and don't use any predictable routes. Use detours. And absolutely no more emails, you hear me?! Get the Scotch tape dispenser, but don't go back to your apartment. As of now also don't use any of your credit cards or ATM machines. Do everything exactly as I said… Did you get all that?"

"Yes, but…" That was as far as he got. The line was dead.

She called me Snoopy, so I'd know who I was talking to. That was clever. Strangely enough he'd only just this morning assigned a place of honor in his office to the heavy tape dispenser, beside his clock radio on the shelf. Now he would have to use it sooner than expected. He switched off the phone, took out the battery and left the subway at the Nollendorfplatz where he decided to take a taxi to get to Melinda's as fast as possible.

Fifteen minutes later he found himself outside her apartment block. *Will she be in? Will she even want to see me? What's the best way to start the conversation?*

Markus was leaning against the panel with the doorbells. He had long spotted the one with the sign *Melinda und Felix Armbrüster,* but still hesitated. Finding the right words was just too important. He finally braced himself and pressed the bell with his index finger It reminded him of a friend's daughter who always used her thumb when she rang the bell. *Excessive use of smartphones, no doubt*, he thought.

Nobody answered. Markus tried again and this time he heard the longed for "Yes, who is this?" through the intercom.

"Hi, Melinda, it's Markus. Can I come up?"

"What do you want?" was the gruff reply.

"I have to talk to you. Please, Melinda! And I have to show you something that concerns Felix. It's incredibly important, believe me!"

"OK, fourth floor. The first door on your left."

Markus heaved a heartfelt sigh of relief. She was giving him a chance. He took the stairs instead of the elevator.

Melinda was already waiting for him at the door. She looked completely worn out, with red rings under her eyes, presumably from crying. But apart from that Markus could still discern her passion for fashion. The black turtleneck sweater and grey pants fitted her perfectly and emphasized her fantastic figure.

"Hi, Melinda," Markus said a little out of breath.

"Hi, Markus, are you in Berlin on business or to what do I owe the honor?" The sarcastic undertone in her voice was unmistakable. She was obviously still piqued and wouldn't make this easy for him.

From the outside the building hadn't looked particularly inviting, but Melinda and Felix had tastefully furnished their apartment. The entrance hall had evidently been decorated by Melinda. She'd always had a flair for simple, harmonious lines.

"I actually came to Berlin just to see you," Markus started a little clumsily. "I didn't mean to upset you with my phone call. I'm truly sorry, Melinda." He looked deep into her eyes. "Felix death has shocked me to the core."

Melinda's eyes glazed over while she was fighting back the tears. Then she came closer and hugged him.

"It's just so terrible. I've no idea how to deal with it all."

Silently, and with a lump in his throat, Markus hugged her back. Trying to come to terms with her loss would surely take a long time. Everybody knew how much she had loved her husband.

"Where are the kids?" he tried to divert her.

"They're playing in their room. They don't really understand that he'll never come back," she replied.

She invited him into the living room where he sat on a brown leather couch opposite Melinda who looked very lost in her large armchair.

"Be honest," she said, "what brought you to Berlin?"

"I wanted to apologize."

"And you travelled all that distance just for that?"

"Yes." The ensuing silence made his succinct *yes* believable. He'd actually meant it. Their old friendship mattered to him.

"I have to show you something, Melinda," he began after a pause during which they intensely gazed into each other's eyes. "I already mentioned it on the phone." He extracted two pieces of paper from his jacket pocket – printouts of the two death certificates.

"This is the official autopsy report confirming Felix's suicide," he told her.

Melinda took the report and glanced at it.

"Why should I look at this?"

"Because there are two post mortem reports. Now take a look at the other one. It was written a few hours before by the pathologist who had actually examined Felix."

Melinda was totally baffled when she read that Felix had already been dead hours before the train accident and therefore couldn't have committed suicide.

She looked at Markus.

"Where did you get this?"

"Both certs are from the Charité Hospital's internal administration programs. My girlfriend knows a lot about computer systems. She got them for me."

Melinda was fighting back the tears again.

"Felix was always my ideal man. I've always loved him. It's so hard to believe he's gone... What am I supposed to do with these papers, Markus?" she asked and held the autopsy reports up to him.

"I believe you're entitled to the truth. At the School of Journalism you were always the one who absolutely couldn't stand lies. I've never understood why you didn't become an investigative journalist with one of the big magazines or newspapers."

"That was, and still is, a male dominated field. And as the mother of two kids... Forget it!"

Markus looked at her.

"It's not so bad. Working for the fashion mags is fun, really. I also have more time for my family that way."

"I'm sure you excel in that job. Just look at your apartment, it's real tasteful and cozy."

"Thank you for the compliment."

Again she looked at the copies of the death certificates. "What am I supposed to do about them now?"

"Nothing for the time being. I just needed you to know that Felix did not leave you voluntarily."

"But should the killer just get away with it? Who's behind all this, anyway? Who is powerful enough to forge a death certificate?"

"I don't know. Presumably some government organization. Possibly the CIA."

Melinda looked at him critically. "The CIA? What makes you think that?" Melinda asked.

Markus filled her in on what had happened so far, beginning with his perfunctory coverage of the gold exchange on Monday, right up to his research into the robbery. He even mentioned his meeting with the mysterious Miller. And the documents Lena had downloaded from Felix's cloud. He wanted Melinda to know everything.

"Whatever did Felix get involved in?"

"I don't know. But I'm concerned about your and the children's safety, to be honest," Markus told her.

"Don't exaggerate. Who could possibly be interested in a fashion writer and her kids?"

"Look, Melinda, I was wrong to ask you about Felix's research. You must have gotten a totally wrong impression of me. And I won't ask you again. But Felix's killer will want to know if there are still some of his documents about. And that is exactly what's so dangerous for you."

Silence. Melinda sat in her armchair, deep in thought, apparently wrestling with a decision. Then she determinedly got up and went to the kitchen to return with an envelope.

"This letter came in the mail today, Markus. It's addressed to Felix and me. The strange thing is that Felix must have mailed it to himself from the States a week and a half ago. It's his handwriting.

Markus didn't ask her about the content; presumably the documents in question. Melinda alone should decide what to do about them.

"Here, take it."

"Are you quite sure?"

Markus suddenly doubted if he actually wanted the papers. *If they were the reason Felix had to die, then I'm also in real danger right now…*

*

Berlin, American Embassy, 1635 Hours. Peter Redman was standing at the window, letting his gaze drift over the Holocaust Memorial. He imagined running through the concrete blocks, forever fascinated by the endless ways through the stone labyrinth. For him it symbolized a path through life itself where one had to continuously make decisions that would change everything.

He suddenly felt overpowered by his stressful job. *Hampton! That miserable piece of shit!* He cursed to himself. About an hour earlier the Ray Hampton dossier had arrived. As head of the internal audit department Hampton was responsible for the control and monitoring of all internal financial processes. This included preventing fraud by mine personnel.

Redman knew him well and was therefore deeply disappointed in him. With Hampton they had obviously put the fox in charge of the henhouse! Instead of putting a stop to any criminal activities, the man himself had been the one to leak the information. There was obviously no doubt; the agency had checked him out thoroughly. At first they hadn't unearthed anything at all until somebody had discovered a second bank account. The transactions on this one clearly showed two large lodgments of several hundred thousand US Dollars over the period in question and numerous cash withdrawals. Hampton had sold the information for a lot of money and put the company in grave danger.

Hampton was a traitor! His more or less weekly flights to Las Vegas betrayed his motive. The man was presumably a gambling addict and chronically broke. The mine had confirmed that Hampton had reported for work today as usual. Apparently he didn't suspect that they were investigating him.

What an overconfident idiot! Redman summed up.

The telephone conference half an hour ago had led to a unanimous agreement. There was only one response to high treason: Ray Hampton had to be taken out of circulation at once. Redman consulted his watch. His colleagues were presumably taking care of it right now…

More difficult was the second job for the guys investigating the financial transactions. Who had paid? Who was behind it all? What did he want?

Aaron entered the office, audibly cracking his neck vertebrae.

"Hi, Peter!"

"Hi, Aaron… Everything OK? Redman enquired routinely.

"No!" was Aaron's surprising reply.

He now had Redman's full attention. "Talk!"

After our last chat, I personally attended to the matter. The boys from surveillance passed on Manx's location. He was on the subway. But shortly before the Nollendorfplatz his cell's signal was gone. He must have switched it off."

"But just because it's in offline mode doesn't mean we can't trace it," Redman countered.

"True. But it was completely gone. Perhaps he took the battery out. Or he still has one of the old models.

"And then?" Redman urged.

"I could only guess where he'd disappeared to. The most promising idea was to search the subway. I caught up with it on the Ernst-Reuter-Platz and got on. But Manx was gone. He must have got off before that stop. And there's still no trace of his cell signal."

"Damn! Somebody must have warned him. Why else

would he deactivate his phone all of a sudden?"

"Redman thought for a minute. "What is he doing in Berlin?"

"He might want to visit that Armbrüster's wife."

"Possible. Send a couple of the boys to keep an eye on her apartment. But no more than that. It's presumably too late anyway and Manx is already miles away."

"Where could he be gone?" asked Aaron, desperate to make up for his recent mistakes.

"It depends on how emphatically he's been warned. Perhaps he's driving straight back to Frankfurt. Go there immediately and keep watch outside his house. And no more fuck-ups!"

Aaron was well aware of the underlying threat, knowing how quickly he'd be relegated to some boring desk job if he didn't finally prove himself.

"Is everything else in hand? We have to know where Manx is and what he's doing if he's not heading straight back to his apartment."

"Yes, we're keeping tabs on everything." Aaron assured him.

"Everything? Credit cards, use of ATMs, flights, computers?"

"Yes, and all the data from his IT bitch," Aaron confirmed.

"Then we'll get him."

The agency had set the wheels in motion.

Now we'll have Manx by the short and curlies, Aaron thought…

*

Hamburg, Harburg Railroad Station, 1955 Hours. After Markus had left Melinda, he walked westwards without a concrete destination, trying to ensure he wasn't being shadowed. He frequently changed direction, crossed through a shopping mall and left through the back exit. Then he grabbed a cab to chauffeur him to Spandau train station where he took the intercity express to Hamburg Harburg at 18 minutes past five. He paid for the ticket and the taxi in cash.

The train arrived at the Harburg station on time and Markus started looking out for Miller. During the cab ride to Melinda's place he had sent him a text from the prepaid disposable cell Miller had given him the day before.

HOT ASS MIGHTY BIG UNDER RAUNCHY GEAR – HORNY AND ROUND BOOBS ULTIMATE ROCKER GIRL. ONLY 20.00 EURO.

Markus was still irritated by the way the messages were coded, but he understood why. Texts like that would be instantly dismissed as spam. Even a random check wouldn't reveal the true content. And yet, it was so simple. The meeting place was revealed by the initial letters of the individual words; the price was the time. HAMBURG HARBURG 20:00.

Are there really people who reply to that kind of trash? Markus wondered, thinking about all the spam which now provided the perfected cover for his messages.

He strolled through the station, still trying to spot his contact person. Ten minutes later there was still no sign of Miller. Markus now doubted he'd show up although the man had confirmed the time and venue. Markus had checked during his train ride to Hamburg.

FUNTIME IRENE NAUGHTY EXHIBITIONIST, 20 EURO OK.

It was already a quarter past eight by now and Markus went over to the departure timetable to look for a connection to Frankfurt. There was an Intercity at 22.57 scheduled to arrive at 07.02.

Unexpectedly, somebody touched his shoulder from behind and said: "Hi!"

Markus turned around with a jump. It was Miller.

"You really startled me. Did you have to creep up like that?"

Miller just smiled instead of answering.

"Come with me. My car's at the main entrance."

They got into a dark blue BMW 3 Series with a German registration. Presumably a rental.

"Show me your cell phones, please," Miller said.

Markus extracted the individual components of the phones from his pocket. He realized that Miller just tried to check they weren't being traced.

"Happy?"

"You learn fast."

But Miller still wasn't satisfied. He produced a strange measuring device to gauge some kind of emissions.

"I'm just making sure that you haven't been bugged."

"Don't you trust me?" Markus wanted to know.

"It's not about that. But somebody may have planted a bug on you without you noticing."

"And?"

"Nothing. You're clean. We can drive off."

"Are all those precautions just for show or are you plain paranoid?"

Markus was getting sick and tired of the spy antics. And he was annoyed that Miller had let him wait in the cold for 15 minutes.

"Mr. Manx, I've been trained for years not to take risks and it has frequently saved my life. A healthy dose of paranoia is as important to me as a nose for a good story is to you."

"So, would you ever tell me who you work for and why you're acting like James Bond?"

"One thing at the time. We have a long drive ahead of us. But I'll tell you this much. We both share the same interests, and that is to expose what's actually behind the gold robbery."

"You're talking in riddles again."

"I'm referring to your friend Felix Armbrüster's research… Did you get anything out of his wife?"

"What makes you think I talked to her?"

"Who else would you have visited in Berlin? And, of course, that's where you've come from seeing that the train from Berlin arrived at Harburg just before eight."

The atmosphere between them became increasingly tense. They were both running circles round each other.

"Mr. Miller, or whatever your name is, I've had enough of this cat and mouse game! I'll ride with you as far as Frankfurt and then I never want to hear from you again. And I won't say another word to you either unless it's about the weather or something equally trivial. If you don't like it, you'd better start telling me your story."

"You're playing for high stakes, Mr. Manx, do you realize that? If I would work for the KGB or another intelligence service, I would have made you talk long ago. And you don't want to know what methods I would have used."

"Stop dodging the subject. Who *do* you work for?"

"I've had many clients. Right now it's an American company."

"Which one?"

"Infinite Gains."

"Never heard of them. What do they do?"

"No, it's my turn now. Did you get any of Armbrüster's research?"

"I've got a file which apparently contains all his material."

"Why apparently. Don't you know what's in it?"

"Not yet. It's password protected. I couldn't open it."

"What kind of a file is it?"

"A word document."

"Do you have it on you?"

"It's here on my laptop."

"Good. Let me make a quick phone call."

They stopped at the nearest rest area just outside Soltau where Miller talked to someone in English. Markus couldn't hear what he was saying because Miller had walked away a little.

"We'll soon have the master password."

"What master password?"

"One with which we can open any password protected file. In the past it was even easier, but they've lately improved the security. We also have a special program which checks all the possible combinations, but that would be too time-consuming. And I'm sure we both want to know what's in that file as soon as possible." Miller smiled as he said this.

"It's my turn again. What does that company *Infinite whatever* want from me?"

"They collect money from investors and speculate with it to increase the original capital."

"A hedge fund?"

"Exactly. One that's banking on rising gold prices right now." Miller briefly paused before he continued.

"And the publication of Armbrüster's story will drive the price right up."

Markus was as irritated as he was impressed.

"They speculate and then help things along so they get the results they need..."

"You're pretty naïve for a reporter. Do you seriously believe nobody has done it before when billions are at stake? And that's actually nothing compared to how so-called leading politicians manipulate things in the desired direction. You can guess who ultimately pays for that. But the tax payer generally doesn't notice their dirty tricks. Or even believes the State's doing him a favor."

"And you're ruthless enough to take the money to act as their henchman?"

"Do you really want to discuss morals with me, Mr. Manx? Do you only write stories for the benefit of mankind?"

"I do what I do for the common good by exposing what's wrong."

"That's a pretty simplistic version, don't you agree? As I see it, when somebody feeds you information, he does it because he expects some payoff. Whatever is an advantage for some is a disadvantage for others. If you publish the gold story, some people will profit, accidentally or by design. Would that stop you from writing about the scandal?"

"Of course, it wouldn't," Markus acknowledged. Journalism, too, was often an uncompromising business, he knew that. Only the toughest and most dedicated made it to the very top. And the way to the top was paved with ethical stumbling blocks.

A *pling* ended the discussion, much to Markus' relief. Miller had received a text message.

"Please switch on your laptop and call up the password protected document."

Markus was no longer interested how Miller had got the password or who would profit. His curiosity and journalistic instincts were taking over. He needed to find out why Felix had to die…

*

Frankfurt, Central Bank, 2030 Hours. Less than two days had passed since their meeting in Iphofen. Minister Stahl's suggested strategy of claiming there had been two transports for security purposes had backfired. The video meant to prove the assertion had failed; the implementation of the face-saving exercise had been botched.

Dr. Jürgen Wieder was pondering at his desk when a call from Stahl was put through to him.

"Good evening, Sven," he started, "Iphofen was…"

The audibly stressed Stahl interrupted him.

"Forget Iphofen, Jürgen. We need a new idea. They're on to us."

"I don't get it. The gold showed up, after all," the Central Bank President replied, now more subdued.

"Listen, Jürgen," Stahl said testily. "The Chancellor was put under pressure by several delegates and the Federal Audit Office. So she's just ordered a random check of the Central Bank's gold reserves."

His words left their mark.

"Where are they doing the checks?" Wieder asked gravely.

The Audit Office wanted New York and Frankfurt, but the Yanks made it quite clear again five minutes ago that they won't have it."

"That means the gold pyramid!" Wieder concluded.

"Exactly. And immediately."

Wieder gulped.

"How much time do we have to get ready?"

"Basically none! The Audit Office has already assembled a team. They're starting tomorrow," Stahl told him.

"But the Central Bank operates independently. We still have to agree to the audit, don't we?" Wieder stuttered.

"Show a little self-control, Jürgen. You're only independent on paper. And that's that."

Wieder was silent.

The Minister for Special Affairs lowered his voice: "Do I have to remind you who suggested you as President and appointed you? I've already advised the Chancellor of your consent. But you should still inform her in writing, as a matter of form. Right away. And, Jürgen, see you get it done. And no mistakes!"

End of call. They had a long night ahead of them. Time was running out. The stakes were high…

*

Munich, Hotel Angelo Hotel, 2210 Hours. It had been a long day and Lena was exhausted. Her new client paid well, but expected a lot for his money. At the hotel at last, she dropped onto the bed in her executive room. The Angelo was modern and easily reached on foot. The high-speed internet access had been another reason she had picked it. Pity there was only a shower though. She would have loved a relaxing, hot bath. But she'd make do. At least the bathrobe included in the executive deal embraced her like a fluffy cloud.

Lena was lying on her stomach, her laptop open in front of her. She had cracked the password of Markus' Word document. Although her computer had had to try several million possibilities, it had only taken a few short minutes until it produced the result: *GOL-d.*

Lena felt a little restless. She had to wait until Markus got in touch and didn't know when he'd be back and open the Scotch tape dispenser. But it didn't matter when he called. Her cell with its active crypto app was within reach. She checked her laptop again. In the afternoon it had acted up when she had entered the command to decode the password by systematically trying all the different options.

While she was lying there and the laptop was running through a customized search, it suddenly alerted her that it had detected an unidentified program which had evidently cropped up of its own accord!

That's weird! Where did that come from? Lena wondered as she read the warning. She immediately called up the source code to analyze the application of the program. Unusually complex and extremely well hidden. Definitely not the work of a rookie. These people were specialists.

Her tiredness disappeared in a flash while the adrenaline quickened her pulse. She had been the victim of a hacker attack. She of all people. It was absolutely vital to find out who was behind it. Her professional standing was threatened.

Lena opened a VPN connection to a server which then directed her via several more servers until she ended up with her old friends in the hacker community. She needed help.

Around midnight she checked her other laptop. Only a few minutes later it was clear that her security precautions had worked on this one. It was clean.

The stressful day finally took its toll. Dead tired, Lena yawned, checked her cell once more and put the volume of her alarm signal on full blast so it would wake her, no matter what, if her old friends had any news. Or Markus. Despite her tiredness she didn't fall asleep for ages. She harbored a suspicion which made it impossible for her thoughts to unwind. She protectively put her arms around Snoopy, her cuddly toy, and her laptop.

Friday

Freeway A66, just outside Frankfurt. Not far from Hanau Markus was close to having a major argument with Miller. Markus wanted to stop at his apartment, despite Lena's warning, and his office to grab a few things. But Miller was strongly against it. It was far too dangerous, he claimed. In his opinion they should stay at a hotel. But Markus insisted. He was particularly anxious to fetch Lena's tape dispenser although he wasn't quite sure what it was for. Eventually they compromised and booked into a hotel in Hanau just after one in the morning.

After a few short hours sleep they continued on their way to Frankfurt. It had started to rain. During the ride Miller pushed again for Armbrüster's files. So far Markus had refused to hand them over before doing some research himself and then deciding about their fate. He silently watched the windshield wipers dispersing the increasingly heavy rain.

"OK, Mr. Manx, I'll offer you a deal if Armbrüster's information is spectacular enough to inflate the gold price by at least ten percent."

"What kind of deal?"

Miller considered for a moment. Then he abruptly uttered four words: "One million US Dollars."

Markus, who had still been a little sleepy after the insufficient rest, was suddenly wide awake and could only stare at Miller.

"You're seriously offering me one million Dollars if I publish the biggest scoop of my career?"

"You've got it. The story will change your life. With that kind of financial security, your future is assured. Think about it. My offer stands!"

Neither of them said a word for the rest of the journey.

The only sounds to be heard were the engine noises and the windshield wipers laboriously fighting against the torrential rain.

Once they'd reached Frankfurt, Miller slowly drove past Markus' house and carefully watched the surroundings. Following another tour round the block, he dropped Markus off right outside his front door. Keys ready, the reported sprinted through the rain while Miller waited for his return. Ten minutes later Markus got back into the car, clutching a bag.

"You see, there was no need to worry."

"Better safe than sorry," Miller retorted, pretty annoyed with Markus' recklessness.

His concern was more than justified. Aaron and two of his sidekicks had been lying in wait the whole night. One of them outside's Lena's apartment, Aaron himself at Markus' office and another man right here.

Obviously a pro. Even Miller hadn't noticed him. As soon as Aaron's henchman recognized Markus, he alerted his colleagues. Aaron had already arrived at the scene when Markus jumped back into the car. But with an unwelcome witness inside the waiting BMW they couldn't carry out their orders to eliminate the journalist.

Aaron remembered the old proverb: *perseverance leads to success*, so they patiently bided their time. Their prey had absolutely no idea how close they were.

At half past seven Miller and Markus arrived at the Ulmenstraße. Once again Miller circled the block first. Nothing suspicious.

Markus would have liked to stretch his legs to clear his thoughts. The persistent rain, however, stopped him although the manufacturer's ads for the raincoat he had grabbed in his apartment pitched the material as breathable and able to withstand the worst of storms. Not so. The shoulder seams were drenched through in no time.

Markus pulled the neon-yellow hood up and braved the inclement weather. A few fast steps saw him inside the hall where he opened his mailbox. After a quick glance, the entire contents landed in the trash basket.

He trudged up the stairs.

"Morning, Markus," his colleague Klaus greeted him. "I had nothing but junk mail, too."

"Hi, Klaus," Markus said, "you're early today."

"Yeah, I got some photos from the office. Now I'm off to the Taunusanlage. What's it like outside?" he asked with a grin. A purely rhetorical question considering the dripping-wet Markus.

"Your umbrella won't be any good. The rain's nearly horizontal. You'll be soaked to the bone. You can borrow my raincoat if you like," Markus offered generously. "But I'll need it back by lunchtime."

Klaus hesitated. The jacket was extremely flashy. Its upper half bright yellow and the bottom part a frog-like green. Both slightly fluorescent. The designer must have been pretty coked-up.

"I'll take it," Klaus decided, in the end more concerned about his comfort than his appearance. Seconds later he left to face the torrential rain.

Markus went up to the office. The light was already on and he could smell the coffee. Klaus had really been unusually early today. Markus filled himself a coffee and quickly checked his news portals.

*

Frankfurt, Central Bank, 0730 Hours. Bernd Brandner, the Central Bank President's right hand, personally welcomed the visitors. He had coordinated the preparations right through the night and only managed two hours sleep. Those who knew him well could see the exhaustion in his eyes. The area underneath his lower lids wasn't dark but pale – nearly white. His eye muscles were twitching slightly.

Brandner greeted the men and women from the Federal Audit Office and escorted them to the large conference room.

"Ladies and gentlemen, I'm glad that everything's proceeding so quickly," he lied, actually surprised that the colleagues from the Audit Office, he liked to call them sleepwalkers, had turned up well organized at such short notice. Remarkable!

One of his staff briefly outlined the safety regulations. Then everyone was presented with a copy of the requested inventory lists. The audit could start.

The group reached the underground security gate to the gold pyramid. The massive entrance closed behind them, then the inner doors opened. The subsequent individual checks were reminiscent of airport security controls, the only difference being that the persons being checked were individually kept in a small room they couldn't leave until after the procedure was finished. The full body scans ensured that no piece of metal could enter or leave the pyramid undetected.

The entire time Brand had asked himself what those people could possibly be carrying in their heavy cases. He couldn't believe his eyes when the content was finally revealed. Their highly sophisticated, professional equipment surprised him even more than their prompt appearance had. Mobile ultrasound devices, X-ray machines, precision scales, digital calipers and cameras. Three of each. The Audit Office staff briefly conferred amongst themselves, then set off in three teams of two, each of them perfectly equipped. To be on the safe side, Brandner had arranged that each of the small groups was accompanied by a Central Bank employee. Nobody got inside the pyramid without the strictest surveillance.

Brandner took his leave.

Those guys seemed unusually focused and competent, he thought on his way to the Gold Crisis Committee. Naked fear crept up on him. Had somebody tipped them off?

*

Frankfurt, Ulmenstraße, 0745 Hours. Michaela, his congenial office neighbor, abruptly tore his door open. Soaked through, she simply stood there staring at Markus without being able to utter a single word. Tears were streaming down her face.

Markus jumped up and went over to her.

"Michaela, you're shaking. What happened?"

He put his arms around her and hugged her reassuringly.

She started to sob, blew her nose several times and tried to regain her composure.

Markus didn't know what to do.

"Would you like some hot tea?" he asked and handed her some paper towels from the kitchen roll used for all kinds of emergencies.

Michaela dried her face.

Markus tried again.

"What happened, Michaela?"

Eventually she began: "Right outside our front door a pedestrian was run over by a car."

"Is it bad?" Markus asked.

"Ambulance! Police! It's mayhem down there."

"Did you see the accident?"

"No," she said quietly. "I just heard a muffled thud and then a car drove off at full speed. A hit and run... We immediately called the cops and an ambulance. The ambulance guys were with the victim until the emergency doctor came. The doc tried to resuscitate him. But it was no good, the man died," Michaela sighed and blew her nose again.

Markus started to harbor a nasty suspicion. "What did he look like?" The color was draining from Markus' face. He was scared of the reply.

"I was standing too far away when I was calling the emergency services. I couldn't see anything through all that rain. There was so much blood."

She faltered at the thought of the blood-smeared accident victim.

"But I remember he was wearing a weird raincoat with a hood covering his face."

"Klaus!" Markus screamed and bolted down the stairs. Michaela ran after him, but couldn't keep up.

It was still lashing outside. The doctor and his paramedics were absolutely soaked to the skin. They had already packed away their gear and were talking to one of the policemen. The corpse had been covered with a sheet. Markus was horrified when he saw the hem of his raincoat protruding from under the covering. *Damn it! That must be Klaus!* Totally numb he stood beside the front door until Michaela joined him.

"Is that really Klaus?" she asked, her voice trembling.

"I... I so much hoped it... it wouldn't be," Markus stammered, "... but now I'm sure it is... I lent him my raincoat. And now he's dead."

Michaela wept uncontrollably. The victim was no longer just anybody. The dead man lying there in the rain was an intimate friend.

They silently climbed up the stairs to the communal kitchen. Markus put peppermint teabags into two mugs and poured hot water over them. He handed Michaela one of the cups.

"Careful. It's hot."

He couldn't think of anything else to say.

Markus heard the phone ringing in his office. He briefly considered if he should answer it. It kept on ringing. Somebody was pretty persistent. *No more bad news, please!*

He ran to his office, lunged at the phone and instantly recognized the number.

"Hi, Lena. Sorry, but I'm not feeling very well right now. Can I call you back in an hour?"

Markus anticipated Lena would be sympathetic. Instead she said firmly: "No, Markus, you can't. It's extremely important."

"Klaus is dead," he said sadly.

"Markus?"

"Yes."

"This is really incredibly important! Why haven't you opened the tape dispenser yet?"

"One of my buddies has just been killed in a car accident," Markus tried to explain.

"Unscrew it. Everything you need is inside," Lena said.

"Right now?" Markus was still trying to get a grip. He didn't understand why Lean was so short with him.

"Yes, right now! Inside is a piece of paper with instructions. Follow them to the letter," she demanded. "Talk to you soon." Then she hung up.

Markus opened the top drawer of his desk. It was filled with useful gadgets. He picked out a small screwdriver and placed Lena's tape dispenser upside down on the table top. No screws, only four rubber anti-slip pads, one on each corner.

He punctured the first pad with the screwdriver and tried to ease it off. It actually came loose and exposed subjacent flat-headed screws. They were easy to release and so was the plastic bottom panel. Markus spread out what he found inside: a HTC smartphone, a prepaid phone card with 50 Euro credit and a charger as well as two hundred Euros in cash bundled in ten new twenty bills and small a piece of paper. Markus unfolded the note:

MARKUS – IN AN EMERGENCY
- *ABSOLUTELY DON'T USE YOUR LANDLINE. TURN YOUR CELL OFF AND TAKE THE BATTERY OUT.*
- *ONLY USE THE CELL WITH THE NEW SIM CARD I GAVE YOU.*
- *IF YOU GET A CHANCE TO TALK UNOBSERVED, CALL ME IMMEDIATELY ON THE LISTED NUMBER. BUT MAKE SURE TO USE THE CRYPTO APP. ACTIVATE IT AND THEN DIAL.*
- *I'LL TELL YOU EVERYTHING ELSE OVER THE PHONE.*

YOUR LENA

Suddenly his restlessness turned to fear. He wondered if he should fill Michaela in on what was happening. Or call Lena right away. He decided to ring Lena and inserted the SIM. The battery was ninety percent charged, ready to use. The app worked like an ordinary phone, it just took a little longer to get connected.

"Markus?" He instantly recognized Lena's voice despite the tinny sound. "Listen carefully, OK? I'm quite sure that any of your normal calls are being monitored. This app prevents that and that's why my voice sounds so strange. Always wait a few seconds before saying anything. There's a slight delay because of the scrambling. If you don't wait, we talk over each other. And now tell me what happened to your friend."

Markus told her about lending Klaus his raincoat, about the hit and run and that the victim had been Klaus.

Although Markus' voice also sounded weird, Lena still sensed how shocked he was. But she still couldn't avoid being the bearer of more bad news.

"Somebody installed a Trojan on my computer," she said.

"You mean someone is spying on you?"

"The program is professional enough to be from the BND or the CIA."

He heard a phone ringing in the background.

"Wait a minute, Markus."

LENA: "BORIS?"

...

LENA: "PRIVET BORIS."

...

LENA: "ETO SOYEDINENIYE ZASCHCHISCHCHENO OT PROSLU-SCHKI?"

...

LENA: "BORIS , MNE NUZHNA VASHA POMOSHCH'."

...

LENA: "KTO-TO RAZMESTIL U MENYA TROYAN. MOZHETE LI VI VZLOMAT' KOD?"

...

LENA: "MNE NEOBHODIMO VIASNIT', OT KOGO TROYAN I CHTO ON DELAYET NA MOYEM KOMP'YUTERE."

...

LENA: "YA PREDOSTAVLU VAM SEYCAS UDALENNYY DOSTUP K MOYEMU KOMP'YUTERU."

...

LENA: "SPASIBO ZA POMOSHCH'."

"Are you still there, Markus?" Lena asked when she had finished the other call.

"I'm here. Who was that?"

"Boris, my contact in St. Petersburg. I asked him for help."

"And can he?"

"Yes, he's trying to delete the Trojan. He's linked to several hundred hackers. They're much faster and effective together. Especially if they suspect it could be an American Trojan. It's a point of honor with the Russians," she explained. "We have to check if your PC is also infected."

"How do you intend to do that from Munich?"

"My friends in St. Petersburg will take care of it. We'll give them remote access to your computer. Then they can use it as if they were sitting right in front of it."

The thought of Russian hackers manipulating his computer made Markus feel uneasy. But his trust in Lena won in the end.

"OK, what do I have to do?"

Lena explained how he had to click a link on a particular website and download a small program. It only took him a few seconds. Then he entered the password Lena told him.

Now the distance between St. Petersburg and Frankfurt was immaterial. His PC was controlled by invisible hands.

*

Frankfurt, Federal Police Situation Center, 0900 Hours. Bernd Brander drove through the city like a mad man. The crisis committee meeting was scheduled for nine o'clock. *If I only had one of those flashing blue lights!* he thought when he was stuck at a traffic light. On the freeway his

Golf GTI would be able to make up for some lost time. Relentlessly aggressive he overtook any car in his way. Twice he had to take the right lane for this maneuver when some obstinate drivers refused to give way.

In the end he arrived on time, though he appeared a little harried to the other committee members. Yet nobody noticed the pressure he was under because of the gold reserves inspection.

Brandner was the first to address the meeting. Markus Manx's speculations had triggered a virtual avalanche. A lot of the media had picked up on the *HNP's* story and discussed why the Central Bank wanted to spread a major lie with the video they had released. The whole affair threatened to get out of hand.

Central Bank President Dr. Jürgen Wieder had had no choice and decided on a new strategy. Manx's speculations were confirmed as correct while the Central Bank tried to point the finger at him for exposing their security strategy and increasing future risks as they claimed.

According to their latest account all the gold transports so far publicly documented by the press had contained counterfeits. The real bars were secretly processed via the US airbase in Ramstein on different days.

To make the lie more plausible they invited ten specially selected journalists to witness the handover of the real gold in Ramstein. Markus Manx had been deliberately excluded, but the *HNP* was allowed to send one of their permanent staff. They chose Jonathan Schreiber.

So none of the journalists would doubt the gold's authenticity, some of the bars were even examined in front of their eyes and cameras. Each of the reporters was allowed to pick one out of the 240 bars which was then checked by an expert on the spot. Brandner described how the press representatives had been particularly interested in the bars from the melt numbered 20863 which had started the whole thing in the first place. As expected, there had been no complaints that the gold was forged.

A general sigh of relief. The dreaded scandal had been avoided and the real gold was safe and sound inside the pyramid.

"Well done," Stahl actually praised Wieder's deputy. But then he probed further: "And what about the inspection of the gold pyramid by the Federal Audit Office?"

"It started at half seven this morning," Brandner reported. "We let the inspectors choose random samples."

"How long will it take?" Stahl enquired. His tone of voice didn't indicate that he already knew all the details.

"Just a day. The gold's authenticity will be confirmed by this evening."

Brandner surprised himself by how confidently he anticipated the outcome.

"Good," Stahl commented on the latest developments. "As all the gold has now been accounted for, I hereby dissolve this crisis committee. Mr. Hartmann, you will, of course, continue the investigations into the robbery and especially the murder of the soldier. You can depend on the support of everyone assembled here. I expect results by next week."

They all nodded quietly.

"Right, gentlemen. I thank you for your cooperation. If you will now excuse me. I've got to see the Chancellor."

That was the end of the crisis committee.

Two men left the situation center feeling uneasy. Hartmann was expected to finally produce results and Brandner had to get back to the gold inspection.

*

Berlin, American Embassy, 1030 Hours. As so often before, Peter Redman was standing by the window gazing across the gray concrete blocks of the Holocaust Memorial. But today he didn't have the leisure to mentally plan new routes through the columns. His boss was right beside him.

"How do you intend to finally solve the problem with that Manx pest?" the Director of the CIA wanted to know.

We're monitoring his accounts, credit card movements, landline, his cells and the Sat Nav in his girlfriend's car. The surveillance is airtight. It's only a matter of time before we catch him."

"Let's hope so! I don't want to jeopardize all our work because of a German reporter. It's embarrassing enough that the wrong man was run over."

Redman was fed up being reproached for Aaron's sloppy work. Next chance he'd get, he would start looking for a more capable man. He tried to stir the conversation in a different direction.

"Do you have reliable information that the right-wing Polish government is heavily investing in armament?"

"We do. Next month they'll be ordering tanks and equipment for their ground forces. Mainly from US companies. Admittedly, we're financing their new administration with three billion dollars.

"So Poland is on the right track, I take it?"

"Definitely."

"What about France?" Redman continued.

"The Islamists' attacks have greatly undermined the left-wing government. We're still counting on the Front National for a military buildup. According to the latest opionion polls the FN nearly has an absolute majority."

"How much did that cost us?"

"We paid ISIS a hundred million dollars for the Paris attack. That includes weapons and cash. Then there was another 700 million dollars to the FN for their election campaign."

"So France will also be a reliable partner?" Redman asked.

"We're pretty sure, yes," the CIA Director boasted. "We expect the according results at the next elections."

"And then Germany…," Redman said.

The Director snorted disdainfully: "Germany! Germany's still a dead loss. They've decided on further cutbacks for defense and troops despite a budget surplus. Our lobbyists don't predict any turnaround from the Krauts."

"Then *Snow White* will have to turn the tide," Redman remarked.

"Absolutely! Due to the flood of refugees, the right-wingers are at nearly fifteen percent. One major incident and we'll get the swing to the right we need."

"How good are our contacts?"

"Extremely good. We're also actively supporting their election campaign."

"Hopefully the operation will be successful so," Redman commented.

It was his superior's turn again. The reason for his trip to Germany was after all to personally satisfy himself that the preparations were progressing smoothly.

"So where are you at?"

"Conditions here in Berlin are ideal for our operation. Even better than Paris," Redman explained. "I've just had a look on site myself."

"When's *Snow White* going ahead?"

"We'll be using the state funeral of one of the old Federal Presidents. We'll decide the timing!"

"Do the operators need any help to go underground?"

"No, they want to be martyrs. We guaranteed to take care of their families and they themselves believe that they're going straight to paradise anyway."

"Perfect! Are they willing to officially claim responsibility for the act?"

"Yes. They've already prepared an announcement to that effect. They're proud of the whole thing," Redman said.

"So the who and the where have been established. Just the when needs to be decided now," the head of the CIA summarized. "The proper timing and flawless execution of the operation are in your hands now, Peter. I'm counting on you!"

"And so you can! Europe will become a reliable partner before long, you'll see."

The price everybody would pay for a better world seemed justifiable to Redman...

*

Frankfurt, Ulmenstraße, 0930 Hours. Markus left his office unobserved through the back door. The rain had finally stopped. The ambulance and police cars were gone.

Markus was scared and kept looking back over his shoulder until he reached the Rothschildpark. Nobody was following him. The park was deserted. He wiped the rain from one of the benches and sat down, not noticing that the dampness of the wood was soaking through his jeans. Trembling slightly, he activated the encryption app and dialed the specified number.

Lena got straight to the point.

"Markus, I've just received a message from Boris. Your PC is infected. They know everything that's on it, including Felix's files. My friends suspect that the CIA planted the virus."

Markus was speechless. He felt the cold dampness

slowly creeping up his legs.

"It looks like the Trojan is communicating with a server in Berlin," Lena continued. "At the American Embassy. If Felix was killed because of his investigations, you're in grave danger, Markus. Your friend's death was no coincidence. That hit and run was definitely meant for you!"

Markus still couldn't think straight. "What now?"

"We absolutely need to know who's after us and how much information they have!"

Lena outlined her idea and their next steps.

Markus sneaked back into his office through the back entrance. So as not to arouse any suspicion, he made a few irrelevant phone calls. Then he bought a train ticket to Munich on the net and printed it out. At a quarter past twelve he left the building though the front door after checking his mailbox and scanning his surroundings. Everything appeared to be OK. Constantly taking advantage of any available recess and shelter he swiftly made it to the train station.

Five minutes before Markus, Michaela had left the office through the back exit. With a scarf covering her head and a slightly too long black coat she looked like a Turkish woman. Even her friends wouldn't have recognized her.

Markus was aboard the 12:54 train to Munich, reading the *Hessische Neueste Presse*. Michaela was sitting four rows behind him. He didn't acknowledge her presence and used the time until the train would reach its destination to ring the Central Bank and the police in Frankfurt. He was restless.

The conductor checked the tickets. Michaela bought a return ticket from Frankfurt to Munich, going back the same day. She paid in cash instead of using her discount railcard.

The conductor announced Würzburg Station and the

train came to a stop. Apparently indifferent, Markus stared out of the window, but just before the train started moving again, he quickly grabbed his backpack and jumped onto the platform at the very last second. The carriage door closed behind him and the train continued to Munich without him.

Michaela observed Markus' hasty exit. Nobody had followed him. His smartphone and wallet were still lying on the table.

She got up and sat down on his seat where she covered the phone and the wallet with her purse and coat.

An hour later the train rolled into Nürnberg central terminal.

Until then Michaela hadn't moved and pretended to be bored watching the other passengers. Shortly before the departure signal, she hurriedly picked up her coat and purse. During the rush, the phone and wallet were left behind.

Once the train started moving again, an elderly man occupied Michaela's seat. He furtively glanced around the carriage, but the owner of the objects was gone. A few minutes later he started examining the wallet: cash, valid debit card in the name of Markus Manx, discount railcard and a small piece of paper with phone numbers.

The stranger removed the cash and the cards and stuffed the empty wallet into the garbage can. Then he scrutinized the smartphone and the slip of paper. He recognized none of the names... except one! *Markus Manx*, the stranger thought, *that was the name on the debit card. Nobody writes down his own phone number...*

The number was interesting:

The Frankfurt prefix, a gap, four digits, another gap followed by another four digits. He held the smartphone and entered the first four digits to unlock it. Wrong entry! His attempt with the next four numbers worked. What a lucky break! The first number sequence was presumably the debit card PIN, he guessed. With a satisfied grin, the man stowed everything away in his coat pocket.

Munich, the next stop was announced. Some rows behind the man, Michaela, who hadn't left the train, surveyed the situation. She saw the dishonest stranger putting on his coat and hat and disembarking with his new treasures. She followed him at a distance as he immediately made for the nearest ATM.

His transaction was evidently extremely successful. With a pleased expression the man counted his money and walked away.

Michaela was amazed how quickly things happened. As soon as the stranger had crossed the Karlsplatz square close to the station he was nabbed by two younger men who had been lying in wait for him. At that moment a minivan appeared and all three men got in. There had been no struggle. None of the people around had noticed anything.

Lena's hunch had been right.

*

Just a few blocks from the Karlsplatz the minivan had driven into the yard of a large building. The front, matching the style of the Karlsplatz rotundas, represented the Neo-Baroque with its ornate balustrades. In the center of the building a large, sandstone-colored steel gate which had opened automatically and closed again without a sound after the van had entered. High-tech sensors protected the whole place.

The basement, equipped with state-of-the art technology, was abuzz with activity. At least a dozen people were busy monitoring screens or making phone calls. In the adjacent room sat the abducted target with a black sack over his head. The interrogation hadn't started yet.

Ted Branigan attentively looked at the large, wall-mounted screen. The man to his right excitedly pointed at it. Branigan's expression froze. Another colleague produced a clipboard with a computer printout. Angrily, Branigan sent them both away.

The interrogation specialist picked up his satellite phone and demanded that his boss urgently call him back on a secure line.

Redman rang back immediately. "What went wrong, Ted?"

The guy we got is definitely not Markus Manx," Branigan replied.

"Are you sure?" Redman asked.

"His blood group and iris scan left no doubt. It's not Manx, just some bum."

"What facts did you base your chase on?"

"We have his internet booking for the train to Munich, the credit card payment, his phone data up to Munich and a cash withdrawal here! We also had a team at the station and one at the Karlsplatz," Ted apologized.

"He tricked us, damn it! He must have smelled a rat," Redman exclaimed furiously.

"What now?" Branigan wanted to know.

"Just get rid of the bum somewhere in the city. But alive!"

Redman had the sinking feeling that the rules had just changed to his disadvantage. The situation could hardly be more embarrassing. Manx had slipped through their fingers again. The agency had lost the element of surprise. Manx had been warned!

*

450 miles from Munich an Intercity Express sped towards Hamburg at 124 miles an hour. Markus glanced at his ringing prepaid cell.

"Yes," he said."

"The eel has bitten," he heard Michaela's voice using the agreed code. Then she just hung up, as arranged.

As if in a trance, Markus stared out the window. He could no longer deny the suspicion. Only a government organization like the BND or the CIA could have organized such expert surveillance. It was now obvious that they were monitoring his phone, his PC and his credit card transactions and immediately analyzed the data. He had just about fooled them and gotten away. This time!

Lower Saxony's scenic landscape passing by his window provided a mocking contrast to the reality of his existence. Inside a week his sedate, nearly boring professional life had dramatically changed. And now he was even being chased. Because of Felix Armbrüster's gold story he had accidentally got involved in. If Lena's information was correct and the Trojan was communicating with the US Embassy, it was presumably the CIA who had tried to take him out.

The thought sent chills down his spine. He hardly registered the door to his compartment opening. A young black man carrying a large IKEA bag entered and sat down opposite him at the table. Just like Markus he gazed out the window when the train rolled on again.

After a while Markus had calmed down a little, but the feeling of being unsafe remained. He didn't know how to handle the situation. What should he do next? Where should he go? He glanced at the ticket in front of him. Why had he booked as far as Hamburg Altona? Probably because that was the last stop and he wanted to get as far away as possible. He had no concrete plan and hardly knew anyone in Hamburg. Apart from a certain Stefan Wallner he had been friends with during their student days and who now worked for a news magazine. But could he stay with him? Out of the question! Stefan lived with his wife and two small kids in a small three room apartment in the city. There'd hardly be enough space. Besides, Markus hadn't contacted him for at least two years. Not even on Stefan's birthday.

But where will I spend the night? Markus pondered. It was too risky to stay at a hotel. He'd have to produce some ID even if he paid in cash. And the hotel booking systems may also be monitored.

Suddenly the voice of the black man opposite him tore him away from his thoughts.

"Hello."

"Hello," Markus replied uncertainly, not knowing to which language the internationally standard hello belonged.

"Are you also going to Hamburg?" the man enquired.

"I am," Markus replied. "How come you speak our language so well?"

"I learned it on the way over and I've lived in Munich."

"What's your name?

"I am Rahuaa, and you?"

"I'm Markus. And where are you from Rahuaa?" Markus asked, quite happy to be diverted from his problem.

"From Eritrea. I've already been in Germany for two years. I'm looking forward to Hamburg. Do you live there, too?"

Markus guessed the young African was about eighteen, twenty at a stretch. He seemed quite likeable with his open manner. "No, I don't live in Hamburg," he told him.

"So why are you going there?" Rahuaa wanted to know.

Markus hesitated and Rahuaa noticed.

"You don't have to…"

"No, no," Markus quickly assured him. He didn't want him to think that he'd been impolite. "I don't really know, to be honest. I just got onto this train to get away."

"I understand. I also wanted to get away from Eritrea."

"Well, it's not quite the same," Markus started to explain. He didn't want to to confide in a stranger why he was actually on the run. So he told him something about occasionally being seized by the spirit of adventure. Whenever that happened he would just get on a train and head off, he claimed.

Despite the substantial age difference between them they entered into a conversation and took to each other more and more.

"So what will you do when you get there?" Rahuaa asked.

"I don't actually have a plan yet."

"You can come with me to my best friend Amanuel. We escaped from Eritrea together. Then we lost sight of each other in Hungary. Last week I heard he's at a refugee camp in Hamburg.

In view of a missing alternative, Markus decided to accept the offer. He had never been to a refugee camp. *Will I even get in?* he wondered. *But I'm also a kind of refugee. In my own country.*

Once they'd reached their destination, Rahuaa phoned his friend who apparently gave him directions. They trudged northwards across a beaten track. It was pitch dark and beginning to drizzle. Markus was extremely glad when they finally saw a brightly lit parking lot beyond the darkness with tent after tent provided by the Federal Relief Agency. Hundreds of them arranged in neat rows. They hadn't quite reached the place when a young man came sprinting towards them and joyfully embraced Rahuaa.

*

Frankfurt, Central Bank, 1730 Hour. "Can I have a quick word, Jürgen," Rose de Jong asked her boss urgently while peeping through the door into the Central Bank President's office.

"Come in. What's up?"

"I've just been at the closing meeting of the Audit Court," she replied. "Would you like a short summary?"

"Go ahead."

The way Wieder was sitting behind his desk gave the impression he wasn't terribly interested. In reality he had thought about nothing else all day.

"Do you want the bad news or the good news first?" Rose asked caustically.

"The good news first," Wieder said.

"The audit showed that our organization, procedures and safety precautions are beyond reproach."

"That sounds fine."

"Now the bad news?"

It wasn't noticeable that Wieder was inwardly on tenterhooks.

"Yeah, shoot."

"Their high-tech equipment found nine bars which aren't genuine, counterfeits, in other words. But that was considerably below one percent of the random samples."

"Did they say what they're going to do next?" Wieder asked, slightly nervous.

"No, but the Chancellery's authorization for the audit was only valid for one day. And that's now over."

"What about the forgeries? Will they be reexamined?"

"That wasn't discussed."

Rose de Jong was about to leave the room when Wieder

stopped her.

"Would you like to see the forgeries they found in Luxembourg, Rose?" he asked, pointing at two 440 ounce bars the size of a child's shoe. Each 8.5 inches long, 3 inches wide and 2 inches high.

"Interesting."

She picked up one of the bars with both hands, but quickly put it down again. It was heavy. Then she took a closer look.

"Seems pretty real to me."

"But it isn't. Cheap lead sheathed with gold," Wieder explained. "Our colleagues in Luxembourg sent them over."

He pointed to a prepared package of similar size beside the two bars, wrapped in brown paper and sealed with tape.

"Can you please send that off by mail tomorrow morning? It's one of the Luxembourg counterfeits. It's going to the guys at the Federal Audit Office. I know it's heavy, but none of the men were available right now."

"No problem. I can even mail it today."

"No, do it in the morning, or they'll come back too fast with an analysis," Wieder told her with a smile, but determined. "And get a receipt, please."

"Rose de Jong picked up the package.

"Do you want me to get it insured?"

"No need. It's just a forgery."

Rose the Jong left the office. The small parcel was addressed to:

Federal Audit Office, Adenauerallee 81, 53113 Bonn.

*

Hamburg, Refugee Processing Center at the Volkspark Stadium, 2000 Hours. The camp was surrounded by a makeshift fence with a hole towards the freeway. That's how Amanuel had smuggled his friend Rahuaa and Markus inside. It was unlikely that Markus as a German would have been allowed past the security guards at the entrance.

One of the tents had several folding tables. Amanuel organized some tea for the two newcomers who gratefully accepted the reviving beverage. The refugees around the other tables ignored them.

Amanuel found it difficult to express himself in German and frequently reverted to his native tongue. Rahuaa answered him in German, presumably so Markus wouldn't feel excluded. At some stage Rahuaa started talking about his escape from Eritrea.

His story started in a simple hut on the northeast coast of Africa. They had known they were coming, but it had been too late to flee, Rahuaa related. His father, his mother, his three sisters and he had been sitting around the fire in their one simple room. Suddenly the door had burst open and three soldiers stormed inside, their weapons at the ready. His father jumped up and protectively positioned himself in front of his family, but only seconds later he was hit on the head by the butt of one of their rifles. His attempts to defend himself with his hands from the consistent beatings only prolonged the inevitable.

Tears brimming in his eyes, Rahuaa admitted that he hadn't dared to help his father.

Then the biggest of the three soldiers had grabbed his mother and torn her away from her daughters. His mother pleaded to spare her children and the soldiers yelled at her and his sisters.

His voice faltering, Rahuaa told Markus that he'd been too scared to scream. He grabbed his littled sisters and protectively threw his arms around them. He didn't know if his father was still alive or lying dead in front of them.

In the end the ringleader commanded Rahuaa to get up and follow him. He didn't roar, but spoke in an alarmingly calm voice. Rahuaa got up. He knew they had come for him. They wanted to make him one of theirs. But Rahuaa swore to himself that he would never turn into one of the animals they were. He'd rather die.

Suddenly it was very quiet in the tent apart from the breathing of the roughly ten people who had gathered around them. Markus hadn't noticed their presence; he had been too engrossed in Rahuaa's story. He unobtrusively wiped a tear from his eyes. He couldn't believe how calm the young black man seemed to be.

"Any idea what happened to your family?" Markus asked.

Rahuaa told him that he hadn't known for ages until a friend had told him that his father was dead. His mother and sisters were OK. They were now living with another man. A good man.

"And how did you escape from the soldiers?"

The soldiers took him to a training camp where they instructed him and other boys in the use of firearms. But because he didn't want to shoot at women and children, he had fled with a friend of his.

He recounted how they had somehow made it to Ethiopia, always picturing their end-destination, Germany, the country all the refugees raved about.

What Rahuaa said next made Markus wince.

"The police here are trustworthy. There are many bad people back at home."

Just a week ago Markus would have wholeheartedly agreed. Right now he didn't know what to think.

It was late by now. Once some of the men had started to

retire, Markus remembered that he'd still no idea where he'd spend the night. But Rahuaa had already worked it out with Amanuel, who had offered his bed to both of them. They'd just have to move close together.

Overwhelmed by the hospitality of these people who didn't know him and had nothing, he finally fell asleep. A refugee amongst refugees.

*

Hofheim, Lena's Apartment, 2120 Hours. Just a few hours ago Lena had received Michaela's text message at the offices of Geißen & Mapitier in Munich: *The eel has bitten*. She was extremely worried, but didn't let on; just continued working as usual, although she repeatedly scanned for any movements through one of the office windows. Nothing seemed suspicious, however.

After her flight had landed in Frankfurt, she'd taken a taxi to Hofheim. Now she was standing outside her apartment where she swiped her hand over a switch to the right of the entrance without touching it. The finger veins scanner recognized her blood flow and opened the apartment door with a slight click. *Finger vein scanners are safer than iris recognition*, she reassured herself.

Once inside, one of the diodes of her Smart Home system flashed. An alarm signal! Lena entered her code into the display and called up the video recording. The motion sensor had detected an attempted break-in at 15:10. A person in a parcel service uniform had tried to break into her apartment. He had unpacked professional locksmith tools. His equipment hadn't been stowed in the usual toolbox, however, but in a DHL package. The guy knew what he was doing.

The main entrance downstairs wasn't particularly well

secured and had been no obstacle. But Lena's front door was far more difficult to open. The state-of-the-art locking cylinder was nothing but camouflage. The steel bolts could only be opened via the vein scanner. But the imposter DHL guy's composure inferred that he knew Lena wouldn't disturb him. And perhaps another man had been keeping a lookout downstairs. Neither of them had evidently noticed Lena's video surveillance of the staircase. Four minutes later the man gave up without leaving any traces of an attempted break-in.

The Smart Home system had instantly alerted Lena on her cell phone. Because she had switched it off in Munich, the message hadn't reached her until now.

Are they trying to bug my apartment or are they looking for files?

Lena usually enjoyed spending time on her own in her apartment, but now, after the attempted break-in, and especially after what had happened to Markus, she didn't feel safe there anymore. She quickly packed a pair of jeans, a T-shirt, underwear and toiletries to last her for the next couple of days in a gym bag. After a brief glance at her watch, she left her apartment. The Smart Home display was switched to *Simulate Occupancy*. She left all the lights on.

Her Fiat remained parked outside her house as she ran to catch the next city train. The S2 was just coming in, the doors opened and Lena hopped on.

There were no other passengers in her compartment. She put the gym bag on the seat beside her, pulled her ancient Nokia cell with a new prepaid card out of her pocket and dialed Petra's, her best friend's number.

At least those old models have one advantage, no Bluetooth, GPS or WLAN. She smiled, if a little tortured. *Just phone and text. Non trackable, old-fashioned technology. Drug dealers and other criminals swear by it...*

"Yes?" said Petra's voice after several rings.

"It's me, Lena."

"Hi, Lena. Good to hear from you. Did you change your number? My phone didn't recognize you."

"Yeah, I've got a new number. Do you have time today, Petra?"

"Sure, are you in the area?"

"Not yet. But I can be at the station in Kassel by half twelve. Can I stay at yours?"

"No problem. I collect you from the train. It'll be great to catch up." Petra sounded delighted.

"I'm also looking forward to it. We'll talk when I get there. See you later," Lena quickly finished the call when other passengers got into the compartment.

*

The train arrived on time. Lena had barely stepped onto the platform when Petra threw her arms around her. "I'm so glad you're here. And completely out of the blue."

"Yeah, the timing was pretty perfect."

"Just this afternoon I was pissed that there's absolutely nothing happening this weekend."

"Must have been telepathy," Lena smile.

Petra's apartment in Kassel's inner city was only a few minutes by car. There was virtually no traffic at this hour.

Lena and Petra had known each other since they had started school together. Petra had never left Kassel and was now teaching first graders.

"Christ, Lena, it must be three years since we last got together. And it's only two hours by train."

"Nothing much seems to have changed around here."

"True. Kassel isn't exactly a boomtown."

At the apartment Petra fetched two glasses of red wine

and a hunk of cheese.

"Right, Lena, come on, you still haven't told me the reason for your unexpected visit."

Petra's still as inquisitive as ever, Lena thought. "The reason is called Markus."

"I see. A guy thing," Petra grinned.

"Well, but not the way you might think…"

"Spit it out!"

Lena told her at length about her new boyfriend, the meeting at the café and a little about her job.

Petra listened attentively, especially to the part of how Markus and Lena had met.

"That's brilliant, Lena! I googled you an hour ago. You're pretty famous now, aren't you?"

"Don't get too carried away."

"Really? The trade press is lauding you as *the* IT security specialist in Germany," Petra added, highly impressed by Lena's career.

"I'm doing OK," Lena admitted. She consciously concealed the story about the gold.

"But you've still not told me why you're here."

"You don't miss a thing, do you?"

"Pure curiosity, honey."

"Can I tell you some other time? Right now it's so wonderfully relaxing here with you.

"Sure, I was just nosy. But you have to promise not to leave it for so long again the next time.

"I promise," Lena said. "We see far too little of each other, I agree."

"Come for a long weekend when it's warmer and we'll go on day trips like we used to do. We could go hiking again."

"Sounds good. Or we stroll hand in hand along the river, have a bite to eat and then take in a show."

It's great having such a friend, Petra thought. *But I can't help thinking there's something weighing her down...*

Saturday

Frankfurt, Sachsenhausen, 0730 Hours. The past few days had been extremely exhausting. But today... *who could possible call this early on a Saturday*, thought Central Bank President Dr. Jürgen Wieder. He was sitting in his 500 square feet lounge, dominated by a massive mahogany table which could easily seat ten people. Wieder's position afforded him a perfect view of the whole room - the glass wall facing the garden and the perfect furnishings chosen by an interior decorator. Without doubt his favorite spot in the magnificent Art Nouveau villa in Frankfurt's posh district Sachsenhausen.

He was reading an article in a Swiss financial magazine, one he particularly liked for its in-depth, far from mainstream coverage.

And then the phone rang.

"He could hear his wife talking to the caller.

"Good morning, Mr. Brandner. Yes, he is. Just a minute, please."

The caller had to wait a few seconds while she crossed the generous living room and handed the phone to her husband.

"What's so important that it couldn't wait, Mr. Brandner," Wieder asked deliberately gruff although he had a pretty good idea.

Brandner sounded nervous.

"They... they've arrested Rose de Jong, Dr. Wieder."

"Slow down, Mr. Brandner. What exactly happened?"

"They found her with a genuine gold bar from the Central Bank's reserves. She'll be charged with grand theft."

"Do they have any proof?"

"Yes, the evidence is apparently overwhelming. After an anonymous tip-off, the police searched her house last night and discovered a gold bar. Well hidden inside a parcel. It clearly has Ms. de Jong's fingerprints on it."

"Is there no exculpatory evidence?"

"No," Brandner said, "everything seems to be stacked against her. The prosecution claims that she... she had some inside knowledge."

Brandner seemed baffled.

"But... Ms. de Jong isn't one of those in the know!" His voice was starting to fail him. "There must be something we can do for her!"

"Get a grip, Mr. Brandner and think. Yesterday the Audit Office found nine forgeries in our holdings. We had to act and quickly come up with a plausible story."

"But... but Ms. de Jong of all people?"

"Are you offering yourself instead?" Wieder barked, who was now in his study with the door firmly closed.

One could only guess at the *no* coming from the other end of the line.

"We'll get her the best lawyers and pay her off handsomely once she gets out."

The Federal Central Bank President ended the conversation. At that moment nobody anticipated that his solution would have a deadly outcome.

*

Kassel, Petra's Apartment, 0740 Hours. Lena found it hard to wake up properly when her phone rang. *Who the heck...* It felt like she'd only just gone to sleep.

Snoopy had fallen out of the bed. She picked him up and covered him with a corner of the blanket.

The phone was persistent.

The display showed *Unknown Caller* when she finally picked up, struggling to open her eyes.

"Yes," she said in a tired voice.

"Lena?"

"Ah, it's you Boris... And?" she asked still half asleep.

"Lena, you took your time! Listen, my friends did an intensive net search last night. The Americans have lodged an arrest warrant with Interpol for you and your boyfriend."

"Whaaat?"

Lena was suddenly wide awake.

"The warrant has already been valid since midnight. We found it with Interpol and Europol."

"Damn! Why would they do that? It makes no sense."

"Don't ask us," Boris replied. "A lot of stuff doesn't make sense."

"Did you find out what they're charging us with?"

"High treason! Imagine. They'll catch anyone on those grounds. If you're captured outside Germany, they'll instantly extradite you to the States!"

Then Boris told her the name and coordinates of the person responsible for the arrest warrant.

"Thank you, Boris!"

Lena's mind was in a whirl. Sleep was out of the question now. And she had to keep Petra out of it, no matter what. No more communication from Petra's apartment. No phone, no emails, no surfing the net.

She was close to a nervous breakdown. An arrest warrant! What now? *I should take a shower to clear my head....*

Petra's bathroom could have belonged to a teenage girl. Everything was pink: pink towels, pink shower curtain, pink soap. Even the shower hose was pink.

What a bizarre contrast, Lena thought. *Petra's idyllic world while I'm being chased by Interpol. I've got to get out of here. And fast.* Leaving the bathroom, she could smell freshly brewed coffee and bread rolls.

"Good morning," Petra greeted her. "You still don't need much sleep, do you?"

"I could have done with some more this morning. Did the phone ringing wake you?"

"It doesn't matter. I had some bad dreams and not a particularly good rest anyway."

"However did you manage to get fresh rolls that quickly?"

"Pre-baked from the freezer. I just popped them in the oven."

"Great!"

Lena didn't intend to stay any longer than necessary. She didn't want to risk getting Petra involved. So she fibbed that the call had been from Markus. He wanted to meet up and show her Hamburg.

After breakfast Petra drove Lena to the station. The Intercity Express arrived on time. Lena flopped down on her seat and tried to gather her thoughts. She was scared of what the future had in store for her. More scared than even during her time as an active hacker. So far it had been just some kind of a game, but now it was dangerous.

Lena got up to have a good look around the open coach. Nobody apart from her. *Smiling is easy,* claimed a poster advertising a major bank. *Easy for some,* Lena thought sarcastically. She systematically analyzed her conversation with Boris earlier. He had given her the IP address of a computer and a name. The PC was inside the US Embassy in Berlin. The name sounded American: Peter Redman. Her enemies were more or less at her own doorstep. Evidently extremely powerful enemies.

The CIA was notorious for its cyber attacks. So were the Israelis. But the Russians were by no means rookies anymore either. This was once more confirmed when she opened her mailbox. Boris had sent enough information for her to visit the American Embassy, virtually, of course.

You guys are the greatest, Lena thought, *St. Petersburg always delivers.*

Who was that Peter Redman? What was he so desperately trying to conceal to justify an arrest warrant or even a cold-blooded murder? And most of all: how could they get out of this mess in one piece?

The train was still at the WLAN hotspot at the station in Göttingen, twenty minutes after Kassel, when she had managed to hack into the embassy's intranet via the printer's internet address. The IP address was correct. Just as well network printers were like computers, but frequently without protection.

Figuring out the administrator passport had also been a cinch for her. It was more or less always predictable. When dozens of printers were used in three shift operation, they usually chose passwords easily remembered by the systems administrators. *Germany One* was yet another proof of that.

First Lena downloaded everything that had gone through this printer over the last few days using the reprint function. The reprint trap was a much loved topic for IT specialist. Everyone was glad when his cancelled print job was automatically terminated at a later stage. Hardly anyone considered that the printer would save the jobs for any length of time.

Once the train had left Göttingen and gathered speed, she had downloaded the whole history. She went through it starting with the latest documents.

When Hannover main station was announced, she'd looked at them all. A lot of general stuff related to embassy business, but nothing of much use to her. She saved all the documents in a folder and let a search program she had written herself scan the data. Felix Armbrüster? Nothing… Redman? Nothing… Gold? Nothing… Manx? Nothing.

What about herself? Eck? Lena immediately opened the texts the program had located. But again nothing. The highlighted passages contained similar names, but not hers. The analysis hadn't helped. No hints regarding a guy called Redman or the gold heist.

After Hannover Lena tried to get into the staff members' individual computers via the printer. It would take quite some time as the embassy's internal firewalls effectively shielded the PCs. The recorded calls of that Redman person would help. But quickly accessing those data was impossible.

Lena felt extremely uneasy. This was a David and Goliath battle. But reality hardly ever turned out in favor of the little guy.

*

At 13:15 the Intercity reached Hamburg Altona only three minutes behind schedule. The final stop.

Lena grabbed her gym bag, quickly left the train and scanned her surroundings. No sign of Markus anywhere. She slowly walked towards the line of stalls where they were supposed to meet. Why hadn't they arranged an alternative meeting point, just in case? Just before the end of the platform she spotted him after all. He waved, ran over to here and took her into his arms.

"Lena, at last!"

"Don't squeeze me to death," she commented on his enthusiastic embrace.

"You've no idea how much I missed you," Markus said gravely and kissed her cheek. "Will I take your bag?"

"Thank you, but no need." Lena had quickly converted the gym bag into a rucksack and now carried it on her back.

"You don't have much luggage either," said Lena, looking at his black laptop bag slung over his shoulder.

"Computer, phone, towel, change of clothes. That's all."

"You forgot your toothbrush?" she tried to cheer him up.

"True, oral hygiene wasn't on yesterday's agenda. But there's a mall here at the station. Let's do some shopping first."

They took the escalator down and quickly bought what they needed: toothbrush, bread rolls, cheese and red wine.

"Where did you sleep last night?"

"I'll tell you later in detail," Markus replied.

"Any idea where we'll stay tonight?"

"Yeah. Stefan, a friend of mine has a empty apartment he's renovating. There's only a matress, bedding and a fridge. Basically a building site, but we can have it for a few nights.

"Still more comfortable than sleeping under a bridge," Lena remarked.

"Stefan is on vacation at the moment," Markus explained. "The caretaker has the keys to let the workmen in. Stefan told him we'd be coming. The apartment is on the Reeperbahn."

"The Reeperbahn? St. Pauli?"

Lena had never been to Hamburg's red light district. But she didn't like any of the smutty stories she'd heard about it.

While they were walking Markus regaled her with Reeperbahn anecdotes from his hormone dominated youth. Lena barely listened. She was too busy studying her surroundings: empty streets, overflowing trash cans from the previous night, seagulls fighting over the garbage piled up on the ground beside them. A pungent stench wafted towards her from some of the alleys.

Three homeless people, wrapped in tattered blankets

were sleeping on the sidewalk. Between them an emaciated Alsatian who dolefully gazed into the distance, his ears flopping down. Diners, bars, restaurants, sex stores – all gray and empty at this time of the day. The party was long over; the red light district seemed dead. Nothing but misery, boredom and disillusion. Amidst all that dreariness the sign *No Weapons* seemed like a mockery. The area was more dirty than offensive, Lena concluded.

Their sleeping quarters were in an old building beside the famous bar *Zum Silbersack*. The janitor handed them the keys: fifth floor, right under the roof, no elevator. A mattress on the floor, fresh sheets and blankets. In the kitchen an ancient refrigerator; the cooker and the rest of the fittings had already been removed. At least the bathroom appeared to be OK.

Lena and Markus spread their shopping on an upturned beer crate they had found in the kitchen. There were no plates or knives. Markus broke a bread roll in half, put a slice of Gouda in between and handed it to Lena.

"We even lived more luxuriously in our student days," she chuckled to cheer herself up a little.

"At least we're safe here! And the lights are working," Markus said when he pressed a switch. A single forty watt bulb dangled from the ceiling, screwed into a cheap hardware store socket and dimly illuminated the room.

"And the heating is working, too," Lena added. "Thank God, or it'd be pretty freezing."

Markus filled her in on his adventures since Thursday afternoon. Then Lena told him about her own odyssey.

"Whatever did we get ourselves into, Markus?", she finally asked him.

Markus just looked at her without a word.

It was getting dark outside. St. Pauli was waking up and prepared itself for the next round.

*

Berlin, American Embassy, 1700 Hours. Peter Redman quickly read the last few paragraphs of his documents.

Aaron enjoyed the view from the floor-to-ceiling windows of Berlin in the twilight. He used the involuntary waiting period to complete his afternoon dental hygiene. The silver clip of his ballpoint pen came in handy as a toothpick. He even still had time to utilize the same tool to attend to his fingernails.

Redman closed his file and scrutinized Aaron.

"Are the preparations complete?"

The agent calmly finished his grooming exercise, pulled up a chair and sat down opposite Redman.

"Yes, Peter. We've deposited the ordered equipment at the arranged locations. Our operators are ready. They're just waiting for us to tell them when?"

"Where are they now?"

"They're already here in Berlin."

"Good," Redman acknowledged curtly. "Have you decided which one of the old boys we'll use as a catalyst?"

"Any of the three former Federal Presidents will do. Each of them qualifies for a state funeral with all the trimmings here in Berlin," Aaron said. "It's definitely Berlin for all three of the guys!"

"Which one did you pick?"

"The one with the convenient pre-existing ailments. It won't be conspicuous. His GP works for us."

"Are there still any points to be addressed?"

"No," Aaron said without the slightest trace of doubt in his voice. "Only the timing is still open."

He waited for a reaction while Redman was thinking. Aaron nearly got the impression the man was fighting with his conscience, but quickly dismissed the idea. Perhaps he just didn't want to disclose when it would all go ahead. Or maybe he didn't know himself yet.

"I shall inform you of the time in due course," Redman said. "How well do we know the exact sequence of *Snow White*?"

"Only roughly," Aaron replied. "The entire Federal Government will presumably be present at the funeral. And many foreign politicians. I guess everyone of distinction."

"Can we distinguish between friend and foe during the operation?" Redman probed.

"No, if we want to ensure its success, we have to allow for the maximum casualties. Particularly in the case of the german government that's necessary to reach our objective."

"Sometimes collateral damage simply can't be avoided," Redman agreed. "We all have to keep our wits about us now! We'll never find such a perfect opportunity again!"

They were closer to their goal than ever before. There was just one more obstacle to take care of…

*

Hamburg, St. Pauli, 1900 Hours. It was pitch dark outside now. The bare walls felt oppressive to Lena and Markus in the faint light of the pathetic bulb. There was nothing to divert them. All they could do was wait. But wait for what? The CIA was after them. The previously hazy sense of threat intensified.

They left the apartment to temporarily forget about their problems although they were aware of the risks. But nobody knew of their whereabouts or would recognize them amongst the hustle and bustle of the Reeperbahn. They were willing to take the chance. The apartment was just too depressing.

Soon after they found themselves outside the bar *Zum Silbersack*. Suddenly everything that had been so dreary in the afternoon looked colorful and sparkly. The neon signs vied with each other to attract the customers' attention. On the other side of the road two platinum blondes, probably Eastern European and underage. Conspicuously white boots trimmed with rabbit fur; the sheer nylon pantyhose emphasizing their long legs. The skimpy jackets seemed impractical for the time of year, but not to the girls – it was their work gear as members of the oldest profession in the world. Markus furtively eyed them up and down. Lena noticed and smiled. She didn't comment.

Hand in hand they strolled through the district. On their right was the Davidwache, Germany's most famous police station. Facing it stood several prostitutes no longer in their first bloom. Their lived-in faces revealed that many a dream was shattered here on the Reeperbahn. More or less in the gutter and for little money.

The garish neon lights were everywhere and glib doormen tried to entice the passing trade into their establishments with their bawdy jokes.

Explicit images of strip joints and sex stores exuded frivolous illusions of erotic encounters and anything goes. Also available for cheap or at a flat rate in the side streets.

A lot of tourists were already swilling beer outside the bars and dance clubs and amused themselves vociferously on the sidewalks. People of all ages; everyone in an exuberant mood. The red light district had put on its finery. It looked downright clean, no thrash and still too early for roaring drunks. The Reeperbahn was unrecognizable. A stark contrast to its hungover daytime face Lena and Mark had seen earlier.

They immersed themselves in the crowd which slowly

made its way through the longest entertainment strip in the world towards a dubious sexual encounter, a drinking bout or an empty wallet.

Lena enjoyed floating with the masses without being recognized. The anonymity made her feel save. She clung tightly to Markus who had put his arm around her shoulder.

They turned right at the Bismarck Memorial and walked towards the St. Pauli Piers. The harbor was aglow with lights and filled with the never-ending noises of the dockyards. They didn't talk, both engrossed in their own thoughts. If somebody had tailed them, it was unlikely they would have even noticed.

They strolled along the river, past the fish market and were frozen to the bone when they got back to the apartment. Markus took the bottle of red wine out of the bag and placed it on their makeshift table.

"It's mad, isn't it," he remarked, "not so long ago we were eating at one of Frankfurt's top restaurants and now we don't even have a bottle opener or wineglasses."

Lena got up and returned with two glasses.

"From the bathroom?"

She nodded, took out her toothbrush and slowly pushed the cork down into the bottle's neck with its hard plastic grip.

"Who would have thought it? Not just an IT expert!" Markus said full of admiration and poured the wine.

"Thank you for the compliment, but let's go over the facts."

Markus started listing things in chronological order, starting with the loading at Frankfurt airport, then the raid at Neu-Isenburg, up to the release of the three hostages and the Central Bank's misleading reports.

"Stop," Lena interrupted him. "We still don't know who the perps behind the raid were, or do we?"

"You're right. All we know is how the heist happened and then the forgeries turned up in Luxembourg."

"And you only started mentioning the Central Bank in your articles when they started releasing false reports. Seems like they only got nervous once the counterfeits appeared. Any idea why that would could be?"

"I can only guess that they don't want to have their reserves inspected. Perhaps some of those guys are not as squeaky clean as they'd like us to believe.

"Are Felix Armbrüster's files somehow connected to the Central Bank?"

"I don't think so. All his research was centered on the States. He didn't investigate the German Central Bank."

"Perhaps the only connection between him and the Central Bank is that they were both concerned with gold," Lena speculated.

Markus nodded.

"Before my talk on Monday I wasn't involved in any of this," she continued and knitted her eyebrows. "I meet you. You tell me about your research and the false videos circulated by the Central Bank. Up to then I don't notice anything suspicious. Once I start helping you look into the whole Felix business, everything changes. First the CIA plants a Trojan, then somebody tries to break into my apartment and now the arrest warrant."

"Do you think the job offer from Geißen & Mapitier might have something to do with all this?" Markus asked.

Lena shrugged her shoulders.

"Everything is connected to Felix and the CIA."

She thought for a moment.

"Boris' information also points to the American Embassy and that Redman guy. There are two coincidences linking us, Markus. Somebody slipped us the same Trojan and there's an arrest warrant out for both of us. And both times the CIA is involved."

Markus agreed. "But what makes us so dangerous for them?"

"Years ago the CIA had their fingers in arms deals and drug smuggling to finance illegal activities. Perhaps Felix and you were about to expose one of their new financing sources…"

"…and they want to stop that, no matter what it takes," Markus picked up on her train of thought.

Lena sipped at her wine.

"But how does the Frankfurt gold heist fit into all this?"

"I don't know."

Lena looked at him. "Is that gold story important enough to you to endanger both our lives, Markus?"

"No, we just happen to be up to our necks in it." After a brief pause he continued: "No scoop in the world is worth risking our lives for."

"Then let's think how to get out of it in one piece. The worst parts are the personal threats and the arrest warrants."

Markus concurred. He held up his glass, sniffed the rest of the wine and emptied it in one gulp. He didn't enjoy it, but the effect helped to loosen his thoughts. They needed a plan.

"The CIA thinks we're dangerous because we know too much," Markus started. "And in their eyes we're a threat as long as we're alive. But once the information becomes public knowledge they've got no more reason to chase us." Another pause and then: "Besides, that Miller might be good for a million."

"Or we get ourselves killed before anything is published."

"So we have to get it out there as fast as we can," Markus concluded.

Lena disagreed. She'd become pensive. Her mindset

was that of a hacker. She didn't believe that they'd be out of danger once the results of their investigations were published. Hatred, revenge and fear could be powerful motives for murder. And it was quite likely that somebody inside a powerful organization like the CIA would cry out for retribution.

"Remember Julian Assange from WikiLeaks and Edward Snowden, the whistleblower. Both of them published their information and neither of them is free to move anymore. I don't want to end up like that! Going public is out of the question," she hissed, shocked by the possible consequences.

"Do we have an alternative?" asked Markus, who wasn't going to budge that easily from his number one option. But being honest with himself, he had to concede that he wasn't willing to let the biggest scoop of his life rot away in some drawer. That's not why he had become a journalist.

"Perhaps we should lie low somewhere for a while. We need a bargaining tool. Something that makes us more valuable alive than dead to the CIA," Lena suggested.

"And what kind of a trump card could we possible come up with?" Markus asked.

Lena didn't answer him. But her gut feeling dictated that was the way to go. How, she had no idea yet. They finished the wine in silence and slid under the blankets while the Reeperbahn outside got into full swing.

*

The danger they were both facing weighed heavily on their minds. Now Markus was lying on his back, wide awake, following the slight swaying of the bulb. Pink colored light reflexes flickered across the ceiling. The neon lights on the other side of the street bathed the room in an unsettling semi-darkness. Music fragments and raucous laughter echoed from the bars.

Markus was far too nervous to sleep. Lena, on the other hand, had turned over on her side and had already nodded off. He could hear her regular breathing. He mentally constructed the next day. Step by step.

First thing in the morning he would contact the American Embassy in Berlin. If Lena's and his suspicions that the CIA was after them were right, the embassy must be the nerve center. There was absolutely no doubt.

They had gone through all the arguments and Markus had eventually accepted Lena's point and ruled out publishing their findings. This left just one option…

Markus decided to travel to Berlin and propose a deal to the agency. Once more he carefully weighed the pros and cons. He would relinquish all the original documents and copies and immediately delete the electronic backups once they had agreed to his proposal. He'd swear not to publish anything about possible shady CIA financing deals as long as they left him in peace and revoked the arrest warrant.

Lena had repeatedly tried to change his mind. She thought it was far too risky for him to go to Berlin and her concerns were justified. What if the CIA wouldn't believe them? What if they'd set a trap? Markus had tried to alleviate her fears. Finally they had agreed to hand over the documents for want of a reasonable alternative. Markus was scared of what was lying ahead.

The street lights had died down. It was just after six in the morning. Not having slept at all, Markus got up and put on his clothes. He silently went over to the window, careful not to wake Lena. The single-glazed panes were fogged over and wet. Markus wiped them with his hand. Outside everything was pitch-black. The street was deserted. Two young men staggered past, trying to prop each other up.

He picked up his cell phone, went into the kitchen, silently closed the door behind him and dialed a number he had already looked up the previous evening. He talked quietly.

That was easy enough. Not as hard as I feared, he thought after he'd hung up. He scribbled a short message on a scrap of paper: *I love you, Lena, Markus. P.S. Please don't worry. I'll be back tonight.*

He took his backpack with the documents and put the note on the kitchen floor. Lena was still asleep as he left the apartment.

Lena's eyes were closed when Markus had checked on her, but nothing escaped her notice. She could hear him getting dressed and making a phone call. Inside the empty, badly soundproofed apartment it was relatively easy to overhear what he was saying inside the kitchen despite the closed door. *The US Embassy! I knew it...*

Once she was sure he was gone, she opened her eyes and slowly walked over to the window. The spot Markus had wiped clean hadn't yet fogged over again. She watched him leave the house. On the opposite site of the street he turned around once more and looked up. But he couldn't see her in the unlit apartment. Once he was out of sight, Lena dialed a number she knew by heart.

"Yes," replied a voice from the other end of the line.

"This is Lena Eck. He's on his way to Berlin to see you. He's got all the written documents on him. I've erased the electronic ones already. The data on his PC automatically delete themselves as soon as he switches it on."

"Good work, Lena. Come to Berlin now."

"I'm sorry, Markus," she murmured as she put the phone back down on the upturned beer crate.

*

"We will shortly arrive at Berlin Central Station," announced the loudspeakers on the train. The exhausted Markus had nodded off and woke up with a start. Damn! He'd been careless. His backpack, he'd placed on the seat beside him, was gone. He panicked.

"I put it on the luggage rack," the passenger beside him said curtly. Markus thanked him, but was profoundly shocked. Abruptly wide awake, he got up, pulled the rucksack down from the rack and walked towards the exit.

Soon after he left the main terminal. He knew the American Embassy. Years ago he had been invited to represent the *Frankfurter Allgemeine* at the Ambassador's reception. He remembered it clearly. The substantial buffet had included Canadian lobster, Norwegian salmon and Russian caviar.

At the Embassy, the receptionist escorted him upstairs in the elevator which stopped on the fifth floor. Where was she taking him? Could the ambassador himself be behind the conspiracy? Markus wasn't quite sure how he felt. Everything seemed threatening. He wiped his sweaty hands on his jeans as he followed the receptionist, unable to think straight. He only hazily took in how she stopped and opened a door. "Please step inside." She closed the door behind him.

He found himself in a dark wood-paneled room and was startled when he noticed a man standing beside the entrance; a beefy kind of guy with a Bluetooth headset, presumably a bodyguard.

The middle of the room was dominated by a huge oval, walnut conference table. Although six people were sitting around it, it still seemed empty.

One of the men stood up and introduced himself as the ambassador. Markus didn't hear what he said and stared at the rest of the assembly as if in a trance. As if somebody had hit him right in the stomach. He had spotted her right away. He couldn't breathe. How could it be? What was she doing here? Lena!

She was sitting at the end of the table, whispering something to her neighbor. Markus didn't detect a trace of fear in her eyes. Quite the opposite, in fact. She seemed very much at ease. Lena had betrayed him! When she saw his desperate expression, she looked away.

They had put Lena on his case right from the start! A lot of things fell into place. It had started like every thriller. Always the same. They had met. They had fallen in love. Then they had been chased and attacked. The agency had always known his immediate location.

Markus was sweating even more profusely now. The rucksack slipped from his grip. He wiped his brow with the back of his hand. *How could I've been such a damn sucker? Her warning not to go to Berlin yesterday was nothing but a diversion.* He had questions he needed to ask her. A lot of questions. His disappointment was just as devastating as his fear. He was trapped.

Another man got up to join him and the ambassador. Markus didn't catch his name. His thoughts were still in turmoil. Everything seemed like a dense fog. Over and over he glanced at Lena. He had never been as disappointed with anyone. But it was obvious that he couldn't expect any help from her side.

Just after the introductions, without offering Markus a seat, the ambassador opened the glass door separating the conference room from the roof terrace. The bodyguard followed them. Markus didn't feel the biting wind. Everything happened as if in slow motion. He wasn't prepared for the bodyguard's attack. The sudden, hefty punch to his chest upset his balance and he staggered backwards, expecting to hit against the stainless steel balustrade. Instead the railing collapsed and Markus fell. Even while he was falling he could hear: "It was an accident. The handymen will have to fix that thing."

Markus was still in midair. It took ages while his whole life was passing him by in fractions of seconds. The terror of what was about to come. Then the inevitable. The collision.

Complete silence. The square in front of the US Embassy was deserted. Markus was lying on his side, his limbs twisted. Breathing with difficulty. Forehead bathed in perspiration. Unable to move. Blood dripping out of his ears. The ground around him gradually turned dark red. Everything that had happened these last few days appeared infinitely far away: Lena, the gold heist, the CIA, everything. He couldn't feel his arms and legs. Then he was freezing. *Death is surreal… I'm so terribly tired…*

The last thing he saw was Lena. His Lena! She was walking out of the embassy and passed him at some distance. Markus couldn't turn his head; only his eyes followed her. A few yards on, she stopped and looked at him one last time. Markus saw her stone-cold expression; then she was gone. Love! Betrayal! Death had ended it all. He closed his eyes…

Sunday

Frankfurt, Sachsenhausen, 0730 Hours. Central Bank President Dr. Jürgen Wieder had just unfolded his Sunday newspaper, his greatest joy at the few weekends he found the leisure to thoroughly enjoy reading it. Most of his weekends were taken up with meetings. But at this hour on a Sunday Sachsenhausen and his own household were still asleep apart from the maid. He could smell the coffee brewing.

He picked up the phone at the first ring.

"Yes?"

"Brandner here."

"Any news?"

"Ms. de Jong denied everything at the first hearing. She claims the bar had been planted on her."

"Did she give any names?"

"Wieder was aware that Rose de Jong could badly incriminate him although more than likely nobody would believe her statement in the end. They had nothing on him. Absolutely nothing. Neither the package nor the gold bar had his fingerprints on them. But he would still have to justify himself. And perhaps some of the dirt would stick.

Wieder hoped Rose wouldn't make any accusations that ultimately wouldn't help her case anyway. He valued her level-headedness; a quality for which he had hired her.

"No, she didn't reveal a single name," Brandner replied.

The Central Bank President breathed more easily. Evidently Rose didn't intend to alienate him unnecessarily. He would show himself grateful. Money wouldn't be an issue.

The prosecutor said that all the evidence is stacked against her," Brandner continued. "The gold bar, her fingerprints, her access authorization. But there are still issues to be addressed."

"OK. What's the DA's angle?"

"He's proceeding on the assumption that Ms. Jong most certainly had accomplices."

"How did she comment on that?"

"She still maintained that she was framed. She didn't answer the question about accomplices. When the DA threatened her sentence would be prolonged if she continued to shield whoever else was involved, she also didn't say anything."

"The situation is highly unpleasant for us," Wieder said.

"True. They're still analyzing her private and professional phone calls and emails. The prosecutor pointed out that her lack of cooperation indicates a planned repeat offense. In his opinion they have sufficient evidence for a conviction."

"Sometimes it is necessary to make sacrifices," Wieder remarked as he ended the call. Sacrificing the innocent Rose de Jong was easier than he would have thought. If she continued to keep her mouth shut, the suspicions surrounding the Central Bank could be quickly removed.

Jürgen Wieder got himself another cup of coffee. His stomach wasn't easily upset. *The simplest solutions are often the most efficient...*

*

Hamburg, St. Pauli, 0734 Hours. His heart beating like mad, Markus woke up to the insistent ringing of his cell phone. He was bathed in sweat, his T-shirt sticking to his body. It took the best part of half a minute to get back to reality. His pulse was racing. He anxiously touched the blanket beside him. Lena was there, fast asleep. He took a deep breath. Falling from that roof terrace had been a nightmare. A horrific nightmare.

His phone was ringing relentlessly. Still pretty dazed, he answered it.

"They've just been at my apartment," Michaela whispered.

"Who?" Markus asked in a hoarse voice. His mouth was still dry after that terrible dream. In vain he tried to shake off his drowsiness.

"Two guys. Judging by their accents and appearance, I'd say they were Americans," Michaela told him. "Obnoxious dudes. They knew about everything that happened. And one of them kept creacking his neck. Nasty."

"What did they want from you?"

Markus folded back the blanket, sat up and dragged his fingers through his damp hair.

"They knew you'd gone into hiding. Presumably they lost your trail. They also knew that you're in touch with me. They want to meet you today."

"Where?" Markus asked, surprised by the developments.

"Your choice, they said. They need two hours notice. If they don't hear from you, they're expecting you at the American Embassy in Berlin at three o'clock."

Michaela gave him a cell phone number.

"I'm supposed to tell you that you'll pay dearly if you publish anything at all or pass on your information."

The unexpected visitors had apparently intimidated her badly. Markus had never heard her so scared. Her fear was even perceptible over the phone. With good reason. He knew only too well what those scumbags were capable of.

"They also mentioned that you should consider your kids."

The implications were unmistakable. Markus was shocked. His brain feverishly searched for a way out. He had to act, had to protect his family, his children. People he loved beyond measure. Nothing in this world would make him put them at risk.

"Please be careful," Michaela pleaded and hung up.

Lena had woken up and was now sitting beside him on the mattress. She noticed his sweat-soaked T-shirt and his incredibly worried expression. When she gently caressed his back, he finally put down the phone and haltingly filled her in on Michaela's news. He didn't mention his nightmare.

Before he had finished, Lena jumped up and urged him to get dressed.

"We've got to get out of here right now!"

Markus was puzzled.

"I'll explain later. Come on."

It took them only a few minutes to get ready. Lena had switched off Markus' phone and taken out the battery. They stormed down the stairs with their few belongings. At the exit Lena briefly glanced to her left and right. She started running and pulled Markus into a bar on the opposite side of the street.

This early in the morning just a few diehards from the night before were still sitting at the tables, sipping their first coffee or last beer. She made straight for the first available window seat which afforded her a comprehensive vantage point over Stefan's front door perhaps 200 feet away.

"OK, Lena, let's calm down. Why that rush out of the apartment?"

Before she could answer him, two cars sped by at a conspicuously high speed and braked with screeching tires just outside the house where they'd been sleeping on the mattress just minutes ago.

Although they couldn't be seen from the outside, they instinctively ducked down.

"This is happening right in front of our eyes" Lena

whispered. "The guys who got Michaela to pass a message to you, made sure she'd ring you. The rest was easy. All they had to do was check what number she called after their visit. They've located us."

Neither of them said a word. They had no idea how to handle what they were facing. Their opponents had endless power. Running away was no long-term solution.

Markus ended the silence. Hiding forever wasn't the answer, for his family and job's sake alone. They had to find another solution. But what solution? They couldn't keep running. Had those henchmen caught them inside the apartment, their one bargaining tool would have been lost. The gold files were their only life insurance.

"Felix must have faced just the same difficulties" Markus said. "We could just mail the documents and collect them from the recipient when we need them."

"But it would have to be someone they can't connect to us. Otherwise the information still wouldn't be safe," Lena interjected. Then she also supplied the solution they'd been looking for.

Markus readily agreed and Lena instantly transferred all the data onto a USB stick and then deleted the remaining traces from her hard drive. They readdressed the envelope Melinda had handed to Markus. The USB and documents would be delivered in the mail over the next few days. Lena could then collect them whenever they needed them.

"They're leaving again," Markus reported when he observed the six men reemerging from the house. One of them angrily kicked the fender of his car before getting in.

"That cheek is unbelievable. They've obviously no respect for German laws."

Lena didn't contradict him. As a former hacker she was only too well aware how far the arm of the American authorities extended into German territory. But how far this also applied in the real world was news to her.

They'd already been at the bar for over an hour. The second cup of coffee tasted as bad as the first one. Time passed slowly. Where should they go now? They hadn't had a shower yet and booking into a hotel was still a no-go area.

"Let's go back to the apartment," Lena suggested. "Nobody will look for us there at this stage."

Markus agreed for want of a better alternative. Right now the apartment could we be their safest bet.

They settled the check and briskly crossed the road. Nothing seemed suspicious. No damage to the main entrance at street level. Perhaps it hadn't properly closed behind them when they'd rushed out of the house. The apartment door, on the other hand, had obviously been kicked in. The frame had splintered through the force and the lock had been released.

They stepped inside. Markus adjusted a brush and pushed it under the door handle.

"How long does it take to get from Hamburg to Berlin by train?" Lena asked.

"Two hours with the Inter City Express from Hamburg Altona. Plus a fifteen minute walk to the American Embassy."

It was now just after half past nine.

"Then we have to leave by twelve at the latest. That gives us just over three hours to come up with a plan."

Markus showered first, grateful that at least a trickle of lukewarm water drizzled from the calcified shower head. When Lena followed him, he was already dressed and about to dash out the door.

"I'll just fetch us some breakfast."

Perhaps the fresh morning air would help him clear his thoughts. When he got back, he heard Lena making a phone call. She answered his quizzical look with a thumbs up sign, assuring him not to worry about the cell.

"Boris has an idea," she told him after finishing the call.

Markus put down the bread rolls on the beer crate. He tore the bag open completely. It now served as a table cloth, just like in his student days.

Lena explained: "Boris believes the CIA will kill us even after the documents have been published. If only as a deterrent to others…"

"That sounds promising…" Markus had lost his appetite.

"We've only one chance, Boris said."

"Being?"

"A massive bluff. The CIA is scared of the documents in our possession. But Boris thinks they don't know exactly what they contain and says not to discuss their contents, no matter what."

"I don't understand the strategy," Markus replied.

"Wait! Boris told me that the CIA has figured that I'm an IT specialist. They respect that. He suggests that I claim I've written a program which automatically sends all our information to the major media unless we don't deactivate it by entering a code once a week."

"I get it. That way we're more valuable alive than dead," Markus concluded and absentmindedly bit into his roll.

"Exactly."

"Does that program already exist?" he asked after a while.

"No, at least not in a format we can show to the CIA. Of course they also have their specialists. If they suspect it's badly encrypted, they'll try to hack into it. And then they'll chase us again."

"But will the CIA believe our story without anything to

show them?"

"No, but Boris promised he'll send me something to impress the agency before twelve. He sounded as if he's already prepared something."

"So you really want to go to Berlin?" Markus said.

"Yes, and I won't talk to them about the gold business, but only about our program."

"I don't like you taking that risk. It's my fault that we're in this mess. My investigations are to blame!" How could he possibly go on if anything happened to her?

"Only I can credibly claim that I know nothing about the information contained in the documents. It's the only way the bluff will work, Markus."

Still Markus insisted he would travel to Berlin on his own. Lena was to keep him informed on what Boris had concocted. As an IT layman they wouldn't expect him to know the ins and outs of the program. He could hide behind Lena.

"How do we keep in touch? How can I be sure you're OK?" Lena asked anxiously and looked at him. She didn't like his decision one bit.

"I'll be back in Hamburg on the train arriving twenty two minutes to seven. If not…"

He didn't finish the sentence. They didn't have a Plan B. Both of them were aware that this one chance was all they'd got and felt accordingly uneasy.

Lena brought Markus to the station. They embraced on the platform.

"I'm scared. For both of us," she said quietly.

Markus quickly kissed her and got on the train. When it started to move and Lena waved at him, he felt more anxious than ever.

Looking for a seat, he went through several passenger cars. He had consciously taken an earlier train to give himself some breathing space. Eventually he found an unoccupied seat without a neighbor. He sat down. Now he had time to think in peace.

Paying for the ticket hadn't been a problem. The day before he had found a pawn store and hocked his Rolex Oyster. The jerk behind the counter had offered him a measly 1,500 Euros for his precious watch. In reality it was easily worth four times as much. But Markus didn't have the time for lengthy discussions and accepted. He would redeem it a few days from now in any case. Paying the hefty commission was still better than selling the heirloom dirt cheap. He didn't have a choice and if the plan didn't work out, he would no longer need it anyway.

Suddenly he remembered his research in the Offenbach red light district. The threats. His family. The fear. Claudia had been so right with her reproaches back then.

Markus missed his family, his kids. Basically, he hadn't learned anything in the past few years. Once again his professional ambitions were about to destroy something immensely important – his relationship with Lena. Perhaps even his whole life. Felix, too, had made that mistake. Why couldn't he stay away from all that damned investigative journalism?

Lost in thought, he glanced through the aisle when the automatic compartment door opened and two Federal police officers entered. The first one immediately checked the passengers' ID cards. He was armed with an automatic handgun and carried a nightstick and handcuffs. The second officer's uniform and posture emphasized his athletic appearance. Holding a submachine gun to provide backup for his colleague, he attentively eyed the passengers. A fierce looking German shepherd underlined the menacing atmosphere.

Markus hadn't been worried about possible police

checks until two colored people got up and hastily left the compartment in the opposite direction. The officers just briefly looked up and continued what they were doing. *Perhaps they're checking on illegal refugees. Their numbers are growing all the time...*

The Inter City Express stopped at Berlin Spandau. Ten more minutes to the main terminal. Markus suddenly started to panic. He had completely forgotten about the arrest warrant in his name. He quickly stuffed his belongings in his backpack and left the passenger car. He carefully peeped into the next compartment. No police, so he sat down in the middle. The time he had gained would have to do until they reached the main station. He hoped the train would soon start rolling again.

The doors closed with the usual squeaky noise, but the Inter City didn't move. Markus put his face so close to the tinted window, the tip of his nose nearly touched the cold glass. Screening his eyes from the light, he tried to see what was happening outside and recoiled in horror. Both sides of the platform were flanked by police officers. Very close to his window they were just leading two handcuffed colored people away. The same two people who had so hastily left the compartment just before him, Markus realized. It didn't bode well; they were checking each and every passenger. At that moment the two officers started the ID card control in his compartment. The train still hadn't moved; its doors were still closed.

Markus grabbed his rucksack and was about to jump up. But he sat right back down again when he saw more officers approaching from the other direction.

He was trapped. Trapped and very scared. What could he possibly do now? He urgently had to make it to the American Embassy. Being arrested was the worst thing that could happen to him now.

Slouching lower into his seat, Markus clumsily extracted his phone from his jeans pocket and dialed Lena's number. He whispered with his hand shielding his mouth when she picked up.

"I'm stuck at a police check…"

At that moment, the first cop had reached him.

"Passport control."

His voice sounded cold and forbidding.

Markus handed him his ID card. Small beads of perspiration were forming on his forehead. He barely resisted the urge to wipe his brow. *Don't draw any attention to yourself.*

The officer swiped Markus' ID through a card reader, no bigger than a notebook, and waited. Calmly, he looked from Markus to the display. Being on the run was absolutely terrifying. Markus shuddered. It felt like an eternity until the scanner produced a result.

The cop turned to his buddy and nodded his head in Markus' direction. The second officer instantly held his body even more erect, fastened his grip of the submachine gun and barred the aisle. The German shepherd also got the hint, sat up and waited for his command.

Markus' stomach was churning.

The officer took a step back and ordered: "Get up very slowly!"

Markus was now between the two cops.

"Slowly raise your arms. Leave the backpack where it is!"

He did as he was told, got up and extended his arms. Resistance was futile.

Then he was frisked: Legs, chest, armpits.

"Now slowly turn around!"

The same procedure.

The body search revealed his wallet, phone and keys.

They all disappeared into a transparent plastic bag.

The officer nodded at his colleague again.

"Follow me!" he summoned Markus, picked up the rucksack and started walking ahead of him. Only now did Markus notice the other passengers staring at him. He had been too scared to perceive the people around him. He followed the cop, his desperation growing with every step. How could he possibly contact Lena now? Or reach the American Embassy on time?

*

Berlin, American Embassy, 1300 Hours. The office of Peter Redman, CIA Coordinator for Europe. Aaron opened the discussion.

"Seeing that he hasn't contacted us by now, he must be coming to Berlin."

"Or he isn't coming at all," Redman retorted.

"Manx is scared enough. He will be here, believe me. I doubt he fancies spending the rest of his life being on the run."

"OK, let's go through everything again so. How can we be sure that he'll hand over all his documents? And how can we check if there aren't any copies?"

"We can't," Aaron said. "We've got two options. We believe him and let him live. Or we believe him and silence him. But we have no choice but to believe him either way. There's no guarantee that he'll hand over everything."

"Our mistakes are coming back to haunt us," Redman commented. "We waited for too long to take him out. Now his girlfriend is in the know. And presumably also his colleague. Who knows, there may be more people."

"There's nothing we can do about it now. All we have is those two options."

"Which of them is the least risky?" Redman wanted to know.

"There's always some residual risk. He's got nothing to lose once he's dead. But he does if we let him live and keep on threatening him."

"I prefer the latter option," Redman said.

Aaron produced two sheets of paper.

"This is a list of all the people Manx presumably cares about, including family and friends."

He pushed the first sheet over to Redman.

"The second page lists names of people close to his girlfriend, Lena Eck. Manx will have to get it into his head that going public won't just have consequences for himself. We could imply that we're prepared to kill every one of those people. Regardless if they're in the know or not. Pure retaliation!"

"Agreed!" Redman concurred.

The door opened and one of his staff members entered the room.

"Langley didn't trace any of your key words on the net over the last twenty four hours," he reported and disappeared again.

"Good," Redman commented. "So far Manx hasn't released anything."

"Option two might just work. Manx is obviously scared," Aaron replied. "I'll be back at three o'clock."

He turned around and left the office.

*

Lena was shocked. A police check. Markus had ended up at a police check! She tried calling him back several times. To no avail. She pocketed her cell and instinctively made for the station where the next train departing for Berlin was just announced over the speakers. Without hesitating, she got on at the last minute. The doors closed immediately behind her. While the train slowly took off towards Hamburg's main terminal, Lena tried to concentrate. Her suggestion this morning to travel to Berlin herself and talk about nothing but the IT program suddenly seemed pretty futile. Why should the CIA believe her bluff? What if the embassy already knew that Markus had been arrested? She had nothing concrete to bargain with.

Boris simply had to deliver now. Not only that, he'd have to perform a small IT miracle. She needed a perfect program. One that would fool the CIA. Boris would do it. He'd never let her down before. But this time? He still hadn't got back, even though he was way overdue. Yet, he was her last hope.

Where are you, Boris?

Lena kept getting up to have a look around. But nothing indicated another police check. How was Markus doing? She was afraid to close her eyes for even a second.

Suddenly she flinched. She hadn't seen the man approaching who was now standing in front of her and asking in a deep voice:

"Your ticket, please!"

Just the conductor!

Lena looked at him with a sigh of relief and finally reached her destination without any more incidents. Yet she was tense and the crowded train had made her feel despondent. She left Berlin's central terminal, crossed the river Spree and followed the road past the Chancellery across the Potsdamer Platz. Just a few feet in front of her towered the Reichstag building. Today the massive Renaissance edifice seemed menacing to her. She turned into the street behind as the unpleasantly cold easterly wind whistled through the Brandenburg Gate.

Lena had absolutely nothing to offer the CIA. *Damn it! Boris promised!* As if on cue, her phone rang. She stopped right inside the Brandenburg Gate. A woman on a bicycle just about managed to avoid her. But Lena didn't notice. She only had eyes for Boris' text message and stared at her phone.

HP: CIA – click: Eye of the Eagle – PW: InTeLlIgEnCe.

She prayed it would work. There was no time to try it out. At three minutes to three Lena put her phone back into her purse and approached the Embassy. Her nerves were in shreds as she walked through the main entrance.

The receptionist greeted her politely. Lena told the woman her name and whom she wanted to see. A glance at the visitors' list revealed that she had no appointment. The receptionist calmly dialed an internal number. Lena couldn't overhear what was said, but was told: "They're expecting you, Mrs. Eck."

She followed the receptionist through the foyer to the elevator which took them two floors down, evidently to a room in the basement. They got out and found themselves inside a brightly lit conference center. Two women were sitting behind a desk, busy on the phone. Beside them stood a tall man in a gray, buttoned up suit who eyed her vigilantly. Lena instantly registered the headset with its twisted cable disappearing behind his back. She kept following the receptionist until the woman stopped soon after to open a door.

A large table provided seating for eight people. Lena sat down and waited. Time was passing slowly; just like a slimy snail caravan gradually passing by.

Are they watching me? Are they trying to ensnare me in some psychological trap? she asked herself and tried to breathe calmly. *Remember what Boris told you: bluff and appear confident.*

She demonstratively placed her return ticket to Hamburg on the table. *If our strategy works, there's no harm them knowing where I'm going.*

Without a knock, the door was opened. Peter Redman and Aaron quickly entered the room. The introductions were short and frosty.

Redman asked why Markus Manx wasn't there.

"I'm here to represent him," Lena stated assertively. She still had a feeling that her voice would fail her. But Redman's question had provided her with a valuable clue.

They don't know about Markus' arrest yet. That makes me feel a little better.

Redman didn't look anything like the stereotypical CIA agent. No trench coat, no shades. A round face framed by a bald head and a double chin instead. Far more like the average American tourist.

His skin color is a sure sign of high blood pressure, Lena thought, *could be a choleric.*

Peter Redman in his dark suit and white open-necked shirt got right down to business. He sounded very calm and determined when he stated that the documents Markus Manx had illegally procured were extremely important to the CIA. They wanted every single page and copy back. Publishing any of the information would compromise them enormously and they would know how to prevent this.

Redman discussed neither the content of the files nor how the CIA would be compromised.

Lena gradually calmed down.

They really do seem to be groping in the dark.

Aaron, who had so far been passive, placed two sheets of paper in front of her. His eyes flashed dangerously while he spitefully eyed Lena. She read names familiar to her: Manx and four different first names. The next page also contained her mother's name.

Aaron was threatening her without even raising his voice by a fraction. His aggressive air of confidence increased the pressure. His appearance didn't help either. The acne-scarred, gaunt face without eyebrows and the greasy black hair. Pretty much the look of a particularly ruthless agent.

She instantly understood. How mean and nasty to involve their loved ones. *What complete and utter scum!* Lena thought furiously. There was no way they could escape from the clutches of the CIA. The realization did nothing to alleviate her tension.

Now it was all up to her. She recollected herself, gathered all her energy and pushed her luck. This once chance was all she had.

"The files you're looking for are safely stored in a program!"

Lena, too, didn't mention the documents' content.

Only use short, concise sentences, she reminded herself. Every word could make her position even worse.

"Handing them over is out of the question."

The documents are my life insurance.

"If we don't input a certain key every week, the program will release the files to all the major media."

"Forget your little games, Ms. Eck. The program we can't crack doesn't exist," Redman remarked, visibly impatient.

A ringing telephone interrupted the onset of his anger fit. He hadn't the slightest intention of answering it.

Is this just more psycho terrors to make me sweat?

Aaron finally walked over to the phone in the corner and picked up the receiver. After several seconds of listening he hung up, his expression giving nothing away.

He went over to Redman and whispered in his ear: "The ambassador wants to talk to you. Now!"

Redman got up, Aaron gathered the sheets of paper and both left the room.

Lena's brain was working overtime.

What was all that about… What could be important enough to interrupt this meeting? Did they get wind of Markus' arrest? Am I trapped?

She wondered if the door was locked from the inside, but didn't dare to check.

Some minutes later the door burst open and Aaron stormed into the room, his scarred face as devoid of expression as usual. Just behind him Peter Redman, grinning sardonically.

Aaron sat down and silently studied Lena for several seconds with apparent relish. She could virtually smell his conceit.

"We've got your boyfriend!"

He paused to let the words sink in. His triumph was obvious.

"Your Minister for Special Affairs has just informed our Ambassador of his arrest."

Aaron leaned forward so that his face nearly touched Lena's.

"Your game's up! We want all the documents. And we want them right now," he hissed menacingly.

She smelled his disgusting smoker's breath. His bad mouth odor caused by excessive tobacco consumption indicated advanced tooth decay.

Nauseated, Lena stared at him in disbelief. Her worst fears had just come true. Her rising panic stopped her from thinking straight. How could she save herself and Markus?

But she stoically stuck to her strategy.

"We are not handing over the documents," she repeated and tried to disguise how shaken she was. "Without the key being entered on a weekly basis, the files will be released to the media." She intuitively added: "Midnight today is this week's deadline!"

As soon as she had said it, she doubted if that had been a wise move. If the CIA kept her until midnight and nothing happened, her bluff would be exposed and she'd be done for. But was the agency prepared to gamble on that risk?

Neither Redman nor Aaron reacted to her statement.

Aaron started scribbling numbers in front of the names on his lists. Redman calmly watched her and evidently enjoyed his advantage.

Lena had to act. The silence was deafening. She forced herself to look right at Redman and asked as if incidentally:

"When did you actually visit your CIA homepage last?"

"Very funny. What's that got to do with anything?" Redman flared up, clearly irritated.

Lena tried to concentrate.

HP: CIA – click: Eye of the Eagle, Boris had written.

"Did you ever click on the eye of the eagle on the CIA seal?"

Despite her desperate situation, she was gripped by enormous curiosity. What would happen now? She had no choice but blindly trust Boris.

Redman looked at Aaron. Was this broad trying to bullshit him even in the face of the massive threat to her? He contemplated compromising himself and calling up the homepage.

Lena watched him without a word.

Redman nodded at Aaron who got up and took the wireless keyboard from the conference table. A click and a high resolution image was projected onto the white wall.

He quickly typed some characters and the CIA page appeared: the logo with the wording *CENTRAL INTELLIGENCE AGENCY* and *UNITED STATES OF AMERICA* on a blue background surrounding the crest with the compass rose with the American eagle above it.

Everything looked the same as it always did.

"So?" Redman asked.

Eye of the Eagle...

"Just click on the eye of the eagle," Lena needled him.

Aaron was visibly annoyed at this stage. A click on the eye enlarged the crest and moved it onto the middle of the site. Then everyone gasped when the eagle turned its head. If it had looked to the left before, it was now looking to the right. Simultaneously the compass rose gradually folded away and revealed an input field.

Phew! Boris and his buddies have surpassed themselves!

Redman glanced at Aaron, then back at the image.

Lena registered their surprise.

"And? What now?" Redman asked abrasively. Aaron got up and left the room, clutching his phone to his ear before he'd even reached the door.

Two minutes later, at half past seven local US time, the decryption department at the Langley research center started to panic. The IT specialists on duty had to quickly explain how what had just happened could be possible.

Aaron came back and briefly nodded at Redman.

"And?" Redman asked Lena once more, but now in a more urgent voice. "Nice little gimmick. Was that all?"

"Just enter the password. Try *Intelligence*, but lower case for every second letter," Lena explained, sensing that her position had slightly improved.

Aaron entered the password and the CIA crest returned to its original shape and position. There was just one small, hardly noticeable difference. Instead of

UNITED STATES OF AMERICA

it now read

VIGILIA PRETIUM LIBERTATIS

in Cyrillic letters.

Aaron didn't understand the writing or its significance. But Redman spoke fluent Russian. He had also been top of his class in American history.

"What does it say?" Aaron asked gruffly.

"Vigilance is the price of liberty, Thomas Jefferson, third President of the United States of America," Redman promptly told him. He was still incredulously staring at the image. Reentering the password revealed the original crest again.

The grin on the men's faces had been replaced by a mask of perplexity.

Lena's strategy was starting to pay off.

Aaron left the room again. His angry: "Fucking hell!" echoed through the corridors.

When he came back, he whispered something to Redman. *Bad news*, Lena interpreted his expression. And she was right. The CIA's decryption department suspected the high-tech encoding of the program was of Russian origin. They couldn't tell how long it would take to remove it from the homepage. The type of coding was unknown.

Redman didn't comment, but his eyes were ablaze with fury.

Lena got the impression they were finally taking her seriously.

Everything happened very fast then. Redman had regained his composure and calmly and firmly summoned up the CIA's position.

Don't make any mistakes now, Lena thought. *Let no-*

body look like a loser. Make it a win-win situation!

She made it very clear that she took the CIA's threat very serious. Neither she nor Markus, she assured them, would publish anything. As long as nothing happened to them, the documents would be kept hidden. A smart move which made Redman save face and scored him a point at least.

Although Redman didn't like the conditions, he grudgingly agreed to the deal.

Aaron went to a corner of the room and, facing the wall, quietly talked into his phone.

"The arrest warrant has been overturned," he said as he said down at the table again.

That ended the discussions. Their leave-taking was as cold and brief as their initial introductions had been.

Lena felt as light as a feather when she stepped into the elevator taking her upstairs. Only a few more feet separated her from freedom. A whole new freedom. She swiftly left the embassy, no longer finding the weather too windy and damp, but rather friendly. Even a little like spring.

… Markus! Lena quickly phoned him. Before enquiring what had happened, he rapidly told her that the Federal Police had put him on the train just minutes ago.

"Everything's fine, Markus," Lena assured him. She'd fill him in properly an hour from now.

Lena hurried and managed to catch the next Inter City Express to Hamburg. She let herself fall into the first available seat and sent a text message to St. Petersburg:

Spasibo – Thank you, Boris!

*

The Inter City Express had left Berlin and was swiftly rolling towards its destination. Lena gazed out the window at Mecklenburg's flat countryside: neatly plowed fields interspersed with small redbrick villages. Magnificent horses on extensive pastures. Deer grazing as twilight settled in. Everything seemed so calm and peaceful now. The day's tension gradually faded away.

That was a damn close shave, Lena, she thought.

She looked around the compartment. Two young women animatedly chatting about the weekend in Berlin. An elderly man on the phone. A mother reading a story to her child. A steward pushing his snack cart through the aisles.

Nothing felt menacing anymore. It was hard to believe this was the same world she had encountered earlier.

She motioned to the steward and bought a cup of coffee. Nobody took any notice of her. She enjoyed the feeling and was looking forward to a normal life with Markus.

As the Inter City Express reached Hamburg Altona, he was already standing on the platform. Markus could hardly wait to hold Lena again. He wondered how her meeting had gone. She had sounded quite positive over the phone.

At last the train came in. Just like in the movies, he spotted Lena standing in the carriage door. He waved and walked the last few feet beside her until the train came to a stop. She jumped right into his arms.

"Are you going to squeeze me to death now that we're finally out of danger?" she quipped. "I never met a man who missed me so much after just a few hours apart."

"I'll never let you go again," he said, caressing her hair. Then he kissed her cheek. It was finally obvious that her mission had been successful.

"I am starving," Markus told her. "If we can use our credit cards again, we could go to a good restaurant to celebrate. What's the story?"

Over dinner she told him everything in detail.

"Are we actually going to write that program?"

"No," Lena replied. "We delete all the incriminating data. We're safe as long as they believe the program exists."

Monday

Frankfurt, Central Bank Headquarters, 1000 Hours.
The Central Bank had issued a short press release:

FEDERAL AUDIT OFFICE INSPECTION COMPLETE
ACTING ON BEHALF OF THE GOVERNMENT AND WITH THE CENTRAL BANK'S PERMISSION, THE FEDEERAL AUDIT OFFICE EXAMINED RANDOM SAMPLES OF THE GOLD RESERVES HELD IN FRANKFURT. THE INSPECTION ESSENTIALLY DIDN'T REVEAL ANY COMPLAINTS.
IN ONE INSTANCE THE PUBLIC PROSECUTOR'S OFFICE IS INVESTIGATING A CENTRAL BANK EMPLOYEE'S PERSONAL MISCONDUCT.

Thus the audit was quietly filed away.

*

Frankfurt, Main Train Station, 1400 Hours. Lena had wanted to spend their last night in Hamburg at the Hotel Atlantic. She'd always dreamed of booking into the place where so many celebrities had stayed over the years. Markus had agreed, even though the price of the room had seriously affected his bank balance.

On Monday morning his first call was to the pawnbroker's. As soon as it opened he redeemed his watch for a hefty fee including interest.

"You should have seen that cutthroat's face," Markus grinned afterwards. "He would have much rather sold the Rolex for its real market value once the deadline had expired."

They took the 10:24 train to Frankfurt. It had been a mad week.

"We've actually been pretty lucky," Lena observed as they left the terminal. "We met exactly a week ago," she said with a provocative look.

Markus laughed.

"What is it?" Lena prompted him.

"I love you," he said. "Let's start over somewhere else."

"New Zealand! Lena suggested playfully and kissed him.

"Why not," Markus concurred, teasing her back.

"Right now?" she asked pertly.

"Let's have a coffee before we leave," he suggested. At Café Wacker, of course."

"Honduras Marcala, naturally. Or can I invite you for some espresso at my place?" With a meaningful smile, she took his hand.

*

Frankfurt, Airport, 1440 Hours. The American Airlines plane to Washington D.C. had departed on time and was now crossing the Atlantic. The stewardesses were doing their usual rounds with the drinks trolley.

"Would you like some tea or coffee, Sir?"

"Tea, please!" answered the passenger on seat 32 D.

The stewardess poured some tea into a cardboard cup and handed it to him with a paper napkin.

"Sugar, milk or lemon?"

"No, thanks."

"Mineral water?"

"No, thank you."

The stewardess pushed her trolley towards the next row of seats and put on the foot brake to stop it from rolling away. Behind her she distinctly heard a creaking noise like someone unblocking their neck vertebrae.

"Are you alright, Sir?" she asked.

The man just nodded. On the vacant seat beside him was a *Frankfurter Allgemeine Zeitung*, the front page framed by a black border. The editorial paid tribute to the second last President of the German Federal Republic. His death the night before had come as a surprise to many, but had not been totally unexpected considering his medical history. His funeral, with full military honors, would take place on Friday in Berlin. Besides the heads of the German Government and numerous European leaders, the US Ambassador would also be present.

One has to make sacrifices to achieve greatness, Aaron cynically reflected, knowing only too well that his own country's representative may not survive this engagement.

He was proud that he could serve his country. And he did it very successfully. Hadn't he played his part in ensuring that Poland and France were on their way to becoming reliable American allies again? In a few days Germany, too, would be shocked. The plan was perfect. Aaron was certain that they'd soon get the Germans in line.

He leaned back and enjoyed his tea. For the first time today a smile flitted across his scarred face. Nothing would stop operation *Snow White* now…

*

Berlin, Chancellery Building, 1920 Hours. Sven Stahl had already worked for thirteen hours straight and there was still no end in sight. The previous evening he had been informed about the former Federal President's death and had arranged the state funeral for the coming Friday in Berlin. Stahl was sure that by the end of the week much would have changed in the right direction. And he would be among those who would profit the most.

But there had also been some depressing news. News regarding Dr. Jürgen Wieder, the Central Bank's President and his press officer Rose de Jong. Right after her arrest, Stahl had hired one of the best law firms. Its high profile lawyers had got the by now suspended media spokesperson out of custody that morning. Wieder had to explain the situation to her. The evidence was overwhelming, he had told her. There would be no way to avoid a prison sentence. But after her release in two or three years they would handsomely provide for her if she cooperated.

Two hours later they had found Wieder shot dead in his car. On the passenger seat beside him another corpse. Investigations showed it to be that of Rose de Jong who had evidently carried out her own justice. Bernd Brandner, the bearer of the sad news, didn't envisage any risk to himself, Stahl or the rest of those in the know. Even if the police would find a suicide note on Rose de Jong and subsequently searched Wieder's house, there would be no indication of fraud. In the worst case Wieder would turn out to be Rose de Jong's accomplice. But as they were both dead, it made no difference.

The conversation between Brandner and Stahl hadn't taken long.

Now Stahl had to decide who would fill Wieder's shoes. At least he now had a legitimate excuse for not attending the former Federal President's funeral on Friday. Everyone would understand that he was under pressure to find Wieder's replacement. He would surely be called by the Chancellor within the next hour to discuss suitable candidates to become the next Central Bank's president.

Stahl opened his briefcase and extracted his personal notebook which stored dossiers about various politicians and industrialists. He had to pick one of them. Someone he could manipulate and who would seamlessly fit into their team.

Once the notebook had booted up, it demanded a password. The Minister for Special Affairs entered it extremely carefully. After three failed attempts all the data would instantly be destroyed.

He hesitated. Then he entered the password:

S-n-o-w-w-h-i-t-E

Epilog

Frankfurt, Head Office of the German Federal Police, seven years later. Nils Schuhmacher, Chief of the Federal Police, closed his office door behind him and opened the parcel his Serbian colleagues had sent him.

Schuhmacher, with his slightly graying temples, now occupied the large corner office since his predecessor Hans-Joachim Hartmann had retired five years earlier. Schumacher could look back on a successful career. So far he had nearly solved all the cases he had been involved in.

On the desk before him were the opened package and a letter from the Serbian police written in English. Beside it a large gold bar. Schuhmacher took it in both hands and eyed it with interest. The engraved writing was easily legible: Heraeus - 997.4 - 13023.7 - 20863.

He read the letter. According to the Serbian Police it was a forgery which had been sold as a doorstopper on a flea market in Belgrade.

Lost in thought, Schuhmacher closely inspected the gold bar. He remembered the spectacular gold heist seven years before. The murder of the driver of one of the transport vehicles. All the details were firmly etched in his mind.

It was one of the few cases that had never been cracked. Since the counterfeits turned up in Luxembourg, no more had been found. Neither had the genuine bars stolen from the Luxembourg vaults. The perps had never been apprehended. The whole affair had been cursed.

Nils Schuhmacher put the bar back into the package. He marked the parcel:

ARCHIVES

For him the case was closed.

Also read Part II of Over & Out!

Exklusive Extract:

Available in the fall of 2017

Operation Snow White

The USA are facing three powerful enemies simultaneously and need European allies. But right now they are more a hindrance than a help. If Europe keeps being so unprepared, America can't win its wars. Something has to give. And fast.

Operation *Snow White* is intended to trigger the necessary turnaround in Germany. A perfidious attack on the Federal Government. Clinically planned and executed.

Markus Manx, a reporter from Frankfurt, investigates. But nobody heeds his warnings. The catastrophe takes its course…

The day before...

Sunday, Berlin-Dahlem, 1955 Hours. Dr. Klaus Schulz received the phone call at five to eight in the evening. Schulz was in the prime of his life. His career and private life were highly satisfactory, his medical practice was flourishing and even his colleagues acknowledged his success and envied his marriage. Andrea, his wife, twenty years younger than him, had given him two wonderful children who now attended grade school in Dahlem.

A cloudless evening in the fall. The easterly wind was already quite biting, not unusual for this time of year in Berlin. Dr. Schulz was jogging through the pitch dark Grunewald forest. His LED headlamp illuminated the path ahead so he could avoid obstacles in time. He had nearly reached the river Havel.

A quick glance at his fitness tracker showed: basic endurance, pulse rate 160, distance covered 3.8 miles. Exercising was starting to pay off. He was well on the way to beating his personal best marathon time of 3:54 hours.

His cell phone rang. He slowed down and then stopped, facing the dark river. *Unknown Caller*, the display read. Although he wasn't on call, he answered without hesitation.

"Yes?"

*

The villa at the outskirts of Dahlem was brightly lit. The large lounge afforded stunning views over the lake. Inside a tiled stove radiated comforting warmth. Matthias Röhler, 78 years old, former President of the German Federal Republic, enjoyed his retirement.

Röhler was sipping a glass of Chianti; he felt great. His wife and he were still mentally fit, which didn't just show when they were playing chess. He smiled to himself. Occasionally his two grandchildren tried to take him on together. They didn't stand a chance. But he sometimes let them win so he wouldn't spoil their pleasure.

Röhler and his wife still loved each other as much as they had done when they'd first met. A wonderful record after fifty years together. He lovingly glanced at her. She and their daughter in law were relaxing on the heated bench in front of the stove.

Bettina Röhler briefly looked up and smiled back at him before continuing her conversation.

What a wonderful woman, he thought, *and still so beautiful*. Yesterday's checkup had confirmed that he was in excellent health. His blood pressure was perfect, Dr. Schulz had congratulated him.

He enjoyed his retirement. Ten years ago, towards the end of his second term, it had been a very different story. The stress of all the travel, his busy schedule, representing his country at so many functions had taken its toll. Even a Federal President isn't superhuman. Two major heart attacks inside two years had nearly killed him. But yesterday Dr. Schulz had confidently assured him that he'd live to be ninety. At least! Dr. Schulz had been his personal physician for years. He trusted him blindly.

The Röhler's housekeeper had set the table for dinner in the small salon. Today, in keeping with the season, they would have pork with apples, onions and potatoes. Cooked in the cast-iron roasting pan, of course. Her culinary skills were legendary.

As she was slicing the roast in the kitchen, her cell phone vibrated. She quickly wiped her hands and answered it to hear the caller utter the agreed code word.

It was twenty five minutes to nine when she went to the medicine cabinet. Back in the kitchen she ground the tablet in a Carrara marble mortar the Röhlers had brought back from Italy a long time ago.

*

Dr. Schulz received the housekeeper's emergency call at ten to nine. Mr. Röhler had suddenly fainted and presumably suffered another heart attack, she informed him. At that stage Schulz had already been waiting for the call two blocks away in his car, freshly showered and his bag beside him. Two minutes later he reached the villa.

The private bodyguard immediately escorted him inside. The former President of the German Federal Republic was lying on the floor in the middle of the small salon surrounded by his anxious family and domestic staff. The leftovers of the pork roast were still on the dining table.

Schulz knelt down and opened his medical bag. The ambulance would arrive in five minutes. He sent everyone out of the room. Alone with his patient, he carefully inserted his index finger under Röhler's eyeball and prised it slightly out of its socket, revealing the empty cavity. The ocular muscles and the optic nerve were clearly visible.

Time was of the essence. Schulz knew that the harmless pill would stop working soon and Röhler would wake up. While he gingerly held the eyeball in his left hand, his right took an already prepared syringe out of his bag. Any minute now a member of the family could walk back into the room.

Without hesitating for a second, Schulz did what he had already imagined dozens of times. The sharp needle penetrated deep into the optic nerve, the area between the eye socket and the cerebrum. The syringe's deadly content shot right into Röhler's brain.

Schulz could already hear the paramedics running

across the hall, the sound of the wheeled stretcher, the clattering of the foldable aluminum frame and the rattle of the rubber rolls on the terracotta tiles in the foyer. He withdrew the needle and quickly reinserted the eyeball. Not a drop of blood.

The emergency doctor and two paramedics had now joined him in the room. Schulz quickly filled them in: suspected cardiac arrest. They carefully lifted the patient onto the stretcher and secured the fasteners.

The former Federal President was breathing steadily. A tear started to form in his right eye. Schulz wiped it away with the corner of his scrubs before the emergency doctor positioned the oxygen mask. On the way to the hospital, Schulz would regrettably diagnose Röhler's death.

*

On the ten o'clock news all the channels broadcast this lead story: Matthias Röhler, former President of the Federal German Republic, died today at his home in Berlin Dahlem. His death was unexpected.

*

Operation *Snow White* had started!

About the Author: John Kellermann

The pseudonym John Kellermann is used by the co-writers Dr. Georg Friedrich Doll und Stefan Loipfinger.

Dr. Doll studied business economics and is the author of several non-fiction books. He was employed in the industrial and banking sectors for many years. For the last decade he's been a consultant. He lives and works in Hamburg.

Stefan Loipfinger is a freelance economics journalist and a funds and investments specialist. The recipient of the Helmut Schmidt Journalism Award and the author of numerous non-fiction books, he has also been distinguished for consumer-friendly reporting. He lives and works in Bavaria.

Thank You!

This thriller has been close to our hearts for a long time. We wanted to write an entertaining novel for everyone and not yet another textbook for experts. We hope the result is a gripping and entertaining story.

It needs many friends to turn a good idea into a thrilling novel, much inspiration and, not forgetting, critical feedback. Now that the book has been printed, we would like to thank our families and friends. Without your help, it couldn't have been produced in its present form.

The most difficult part fell to those who read through unfinished and not fully developed parts of the manuscript very early on. The earlier, the harder it was. The story's plausibility grew over time.

Dear Wera, Moritz, Hendrik, Wolfgang, Judith, Anna, Hildegard, Manfred, Jakob, Eberhard and Uta: Thank you for your help, your ideas, your patience and corrections.

John Kellermann

For more information visit: www.John-Kellermann.de